EL RENO

Kevin L. Evans

ISBN: 1548274682
ISBN 13: 9781548274689

Dedicated to
My wife and muse Linda
With her love, these words are possible,
Our sons Matthew and Luke
and to the tree of Jesse and Alice

TABLE OF CONTENTS

Do not be afraid to walk the path that you must go just because you cannot see the end. The path becomes clearer as you continue...

St. John of the Cross

The journey is difficult, immense. We will travel as far as we can, but we cannot in our lifetime see all that we would like to see or learn all that we hunger to know.

Loren Eiseley

CHAPTER 1

THE PORTAL

I was young and full of a young man's confidence and arrogance. My wife, our two sons, and my career bound my world, but this world of expectations well met was forever changed, a long time ago, by a man I thought I knew.

I always liked the window seat when I was a child so I could see where I was going. On Braniff's old DC-3s and Convairs, the highways were a good landmark, and around Texas, could be counted on as a direction finder. The clouds were to be flown through or around, not over. Now on longer flights with jets flying seven miles high, the ground had lost its markings. Only a wide meandering river and the larger towns gave a sense of where I was, so my gaze turned toward the clouds. The plane had caught up with a cold front and was above the cloud base, leaving two towering thunderclouds on either side of the plane, like giant pylons guarding an Egyptian temple. These sentinels of tumult reflected the last rays of the sun so that the western walls were in exquisite detail while the eastern walls were in shadow with little form. The grey floor below seemed to suspend the plane between the formless palette of the clouds and the darkening blue of the clear sky above.

I recalled stories told by my mother and grandmother of great black clouds bringing not rain or hail, but choking dust, death, and despair to Oklahoma in the Thirties. It was a time and a world removed, but those stories told by my old relatives seemed ever present to those who had lived them. These stories, told to me as a young boy, flowed together and mixed with people and events so long ago, leaving me with only a clouded sense of those distant times. I knew my Grandfather Jesse and Grandmother Alice had a rough time during the Depression and that Jesse drank, and drank a lot sometimes. Alice had left him just before the war, but as a child these stories fell on my disinterested ears and now as an adult, I just wanted to see my grandfather. He was old and sick and dying.

The plane, buffeted by the wind and rain, made a turbulent descent through the clouds, but the pilot brought the plane to a smooth landing and taxied to the terminal at Will Rogers Airport in Oklahoma City. I cleared the jetway and scanned the waiting crowd for my grandfather, but didn't see him. Doubts had surfaced when I'd called him last night to remind him of my visit, and I was greeted by an enthusiastic but confused voice. Now a phone call confirmed my suspicions. After twelve or more rings, an obviously drunk Jesse answered the phone.

"Granddad, this is Kevin."

After a long pause, "Cavin? Oh, Cavin." He spoke with a rough growl as if he had just awakened angry from a dream. He always called me Cavin. For years, my mother, Iris Jeanne, had said her father thought I'd been named after some country preacher, Reverend Cavin. The unlikely chance of some old preacher being my namesake apparently never seemed to matter to Jesse. He just remembered old Cavin, the preacher. More than once, my mother had explained that her oldest son's name was Kevin, not Cavin, but Jesse just never heard the difference. For Jesse it was always Cavin.

"Granddad, I'm at the airport. Remember I called last night to give you the flight information?"

"Cavin, where are you?" he said in a grumbled and confused voice.

It was obvious that this conversation was pointless. "I'll rent a car and see you in a couple of hours."

Such a short phone call said so much and confirmed the stories of Jesse's binges. He would be on the wagon for months, then some precipitating event, mild or moderate or serious or nonexistent, would trigger a binge. Sometimes he'd end up in the El Reno hospital and a friend would call Iris Jeanne or his son, Kendall. Usually, Iris Jeanne and her mother Alice, widowed after her second husband George Oberndoerfer had died, would drive up from Dallas and tend Jesse back to health and temporary sobriety so that he could go back to work, driving trucks for Canadian County. Alice never complained. She was no longer a part of Jesse's destructive behavior.

I stood at the phone, deciding my next move. Instead of finding the car rental counter, I dug my cousin Jim's phone number out of my wallet. I hadn't seen Jim in several years but he called me regularly. He had always looked up to me as his older cousin and this affection was returned so, as young adults, we had maintained a phone relationship. The last time we had spoken, Jim had invited my family and me to move south and escape Colorado because the glaciers were coming. Jim actually believed that so his offer, funny as it was, had a sweetness about it. While the unprepared residents of Colorado were being buried by the racing glaciers, my family and I would have safe haven on the plains of Oklahoma. All these images were cycling through my memory as Jim answered the phone.

"Jim, this is Kevin. I'm at the airport."

"I'll pick you up in thirty minutes," interrupted Jim with glee.

"Hold on now. I'm here to see my grandfather and I need to get to El Reno."

"I'll take you to El Reno. Be there in thirty."

The conversation was set and over. I had immediate misgivings. Years ago I had driven with Jim and my clarifying recollection was one of trepidation, trepidation born true because in thirty minutes plus two, I quickly told Jim to stop the car and offered, ordered actually, that I would drive.

Jim was in good spirits and very talkative. "So Jim, tell me what you've been up to," I asked.

"I'm taking an astronomy course at the community college. I got to take astronomy if I'm going to be an astronaut."

Jim had always wanted to be an astronaut or an airline pilot for Braniff, like my father. Fixed and limited at birth, Jim's intellect and emotional maturity were of a twelve-year-old. As a child, Jim Bob as he was called then, was prone to sudden and extreme swings of emotion and anger. I confess that I triggered a few. His outbursts could be quite comical. Jim Bob was big for his age, never violent, but some of his classmates were frightened by these outbursts and friends were hard to keep. He grew up with the taunts of his schoolmates and suffered the hurt deeply. He was always mainstreamed through school, culminating in a charitably awarded high school diploma. The army took him during the Vietnam War and his mental disability was compounded with developing paranoid schizophrenia, further aggravated by the death of his sister during childbirth. The VA's medicine and his parents' money kept him afloat. I liked Jim, and he knew it.

"Still want to be an astronaut, Jim?"

"Yeah, or a pilot."

"How have you been feeling? The VA taking good care of you?"

"Yeah, I just got to remember to take my pills and so forth like that. I'm taking care of my granddad here in Oklahoma City."

"That's your mom's dad, Angerman, right?"

"Yeah, we have lunch on Sundays and so forth like that."

Jim's "and so forth like that" punctuated many of his responses. It was obvious to me that the "taking care of" was the other way around.

"I met him once in Longview when we were visiting you and your family. He seemed like a very nice man," I said.

"Yeah, Granddad and I have lunch on Sundays and so forth like that."

"Well, I'm going to spend a couple of days in El Reno with my grandfather, Jesse Sheets, my mother's dad. You've met him before at holidays with us in Dallas or on the farm outside of McKinney."

"Yeah, I remember him," he said with an air of uncertainty.

We headed west on I-40, parallel to the old Route 66, leaving the globe of city light. The rain had stopped and the low clouds were breaking up, allowing an occasional glimpse of the dark sky and its jeweled starry lights. When we passed under a bank of low clouds, the remnant light from the city reflected back, illuminating our way. As we approached the El Reno exit under a clearing sky, the tires splashed through puddles and the heavy wet air held the evidence of the earlier rain. It was after ten when I found the old downtown and a pay phone near a late-night diner. Many rings later the same grizzled voice answered.

"Hello."

"Granddad, this is Kevin. I'm downtown," I said slowly.

A moment later the same confused voice, "Cavin? Where are you?"

"In town. I need directions."

"Nineteen an'a half South Reno Street," he answered.

"Yes, I know the address Granddad. How do I get there from downtown?" I asked, becoming a bit frustrated. After a long pause that spoke plenty, I knew I'd have to wing it. "I'll see you in a few minutes."

I realized I should have stopped out by the freeway to ask directions, but then wondered if the young clerks in the all night gas stations would even know their way around the old part of town. The diner looked like it had been there forever, and above the doorway I could just make out the faded letters, "McClennan's". It had a long counter with round bar stools and a row of booths along the opposing wall. The diner's light passed through the paned windows, illuminating the sidewalk in sharp angles of light and shadow, appearing to me as an Edward Hopper painting. In front of the large glass front was a counter with the same round stools. Everything was either dull chrome or old green cracked vinyl. Seated at the window counter were two El Reno policemen on break. I was amused to see them having a donut but swore to not state the obvious. Jesse's second and third wife, Buena, had a son who had been, or maybe still was, an El Reno cop, but I couldn't remember his name so I missed an opportunity to connect with the locals. The two men were happy to give directions, and again we were off.

The little house was located behind and to the side of the main house. I had never visited this residence before and was taken aback by its rundown appearance. I drove the car around to the back where light was coming out the open kitchen door and the crunch of the gravel was enough to bring Jesse to the screen door. Jesse came bounding, yes with a bounce to his step, and warmly embraced me.

"Cavin, it's so good to see you. It's great that you came all this way to see me," he roared with a hint of the old Jesse, and more than a hint that his binge was still on.

"I've been wanting to come for a long time. Thanks for having me. You remember my cousin Jim Graham, my father's nephew?"

I saw a quizzical look cross Jesse's face. He had met Jim a number of times at holiday gatherings, but no one would expect him to remember now. Jim wasn't sure who Jesse was either. He was my granddad, but the details just weren't important.

After I brought my suitcase in, we sat down in the main room. It was then that I noticed Jim's tremor. As soon as Jim became still, his right hand began an uncontrollable roll. The rhythmic roll was no doubt induced by the pharmacopoeia of drugs he was taking. It reminded me of Humphrey Bogart in *The Cain Mutiny*, but Jim had no ball bearings in his palm.

"So, Mr. Sheets, how you doing?" Jim began an easy conversation.

Jesse looked quizzically at Jim, so I tried to help him sort through the relationship. "Granddad, you've met Jim at our house. Remember his dad and my dad are half-brothers. That's why he's a Graham, not an Evans."

"Sure, I guess I remember your good friend here. Friends is worth havin', Cavin. I'm real glad you brought Jim here to see me." Jesse's welcome seemed to show more confusion than clarity.

Jim took the conversation over. "Do you know my granddad, Angerman, from Oklahoma City?"

"Sure, I knew an Anderson. Ran the truck stop east of town. Bald as an egg and had a mean streak."

"No. Angerman, my granddad in Oklahoma City and so forth like that."

Jesse's confusion was furthered by Jim's "and so forth like that."

"Once, ol' Anderson kicked a boy takin' a quart of oil. Kicked him hard. I told Anderson that the boy would have paid for it, but Anderson said he deserved the kickin'. I knew that boy. He was no thief."

"No Sir, that wasn't my granddad and so forth like that."

"Good, cause I didn't much like ol' Anderson."

Jesse and Jim settled into a moment of silence and Jesse took the opportunity to empty his glass of whiskey. I took the break and turned my attention to the little house. It was three rooms:

kitchen, living room, and bedroom with a small bath. It was fairly clean except the kitchen, where the counter was stacked high with dirty dishes, empty beer cans and a half empty fifth of Hiram Walker. The room was quiet for another minute, then Jim was up and moving towards the door.

"Call me when you want to go back to the airport, or if you could stay with me for a night I'd sure like that," Jim said.

A quick hug and he was out the door. The Buick's engine rumbled to life and Jim was headed down the drive, protected by the Angel of Tender Mercy.

Jesse made up the sofa sleeper and handed me a faded yellow quilt as cover.

"My ma made this when I was a boy. Still use it."

"Thanks Granddad. I'll see you in the morning."

Jesse nodded, walked to the bedroom, and closed the door. I looked at the old quilt. It was a log cabin design using cotton calico in different yellow fabrics. Some of the stitches had pulled loose and the cotton stuffing was out in a few places. It had a musky smell but I found it comforting. It cradled me to sleep.

CHAPTER 2

JACKSON'S TWENTY

I was awake by seven and lay quietly wondering how my grandfather could function today. Perhaps I should call my mother in Texas and suggest that she drive up and care for him as she had done numerous times before. Should I even be here, and what could possibly come of the day? I figured I would deal with these questions after a shower. I opened Granddad's bedroom door hoping the noise might rouse him, then made my way the few steps to the bathroom, making as much noise as I could, but it was drowned out by Jesse's thunderous snoring. Jesse was well known in the family for his snoring. At Christmas gatherings on our farm, Jesse would sleep in the large mud and utility room off the kitchen, isolating his roar from the rest of the family. I thought for a moment that maybe that was why Alice had left him. Dismissing that with a laugh, I made even more noise. I shaved and showered and kept the door open, but no luck. The same thunderous rumble greeted me as I exited the bathroom. Direct action was needed now, so gently at first, and then with purpose, I began to shake Jesse's shoulder.

"Granddad, it's time to get up. Granddad, come on now, big day today." I kept the shaking up, and my voice lost its polite tone. "Time to get your lazy ass out of bed!" I think I was kidding.

Finally, a rudimentary awakening, and Jesse opened his confused eyes. His brain, dulled by his binge, was slowly starting to respond, and his body began to shake. He spoke no words, but his eyes passed through quick and successive quizzical gazes, ending with his recognition of me.

"Good morning, Granddad," I said more softly.

"Mornin'. I'm gettin' up."

The day began and Jesse shuffled off to the bathroom. There were no newspapers or magazines, so my attention was guided naturally to the sounds emanating from the bathroom. A cacophony of moans, grunts, and deep cigarette induced coughing flowed in rapid succession. There would be a moment of calm, then again the sounds. Then another moment of calm, and then more noise. I wondered how the day would unfold and how could Jesse be up for any visitor. My intention was simply to spend a little time with my grandfather, have a few meals, and perhaps drive around town. My expectations were low and I wondered if even that bar could be met.

The bedroom door opened and Jesse stood slumped with his head tipped so far forward he looked ready to fall. He raised his head and looked around the room trying to locate me. He was in dark slacks, still holding their pleats, ending in a slight wrinkle on his polished brown shoes. He wore a clean white long sleeve shirt with a tee shirt showing below his pale and wrinkled neck. He was wearing a belt instead of his usual suspenders.

Jesse's earlier confused look was replaced by one of determination. "I need a beer."

"A beer?" I asked in a perturbed tone.

"I'm outta beer. I just need a beer and then we can start."

I was pleased that he wanted to start something, but after thinking about that for a moment, I wasn't so sure what he wanted to start. "Let's go get some breakfast first."

"I need a beer," Jesse stated coldly and very matter-of-factly. "If you won't go get me some, then I'll go myself."

"I'm not buying you any beer and you're not driving either," I said with a defiance that surprised me. "Besides, Kendall wouldn't buy you a beer and neither will I."

Jesse was pissed. "Goddamn it! If Kendall was here, he'd buy some beer and drink it with me!" he roared, genuinely mad at me and frustrated by my defiance.

I was pissed too. "Well here's the phone. Let's call Kendall right now," I countered with my lower lip jutting out. I'd never dealt with an angry drunk and really had no absolute sense of the proper action. Invoking Kendall's name and the threat to call him just seemed like a tactic to try in the face of such anger. It worked. Jesse stared deeply into my eyes for a few seconds, first angry then confused. He lowered his head, turned away and said nothing.

"Come on Granddad, let's go have a nice breakfast. I don't see much food around here. We could both use a good meal."

"I really need a beer Cavin, and then I'll be fine." His tone was soft and almost apologetic. "Otherwise, I'll just start on the whiskey I got left."

Faced with the choice of the present, which was bad, and the future, which might be worse, I chose to acquiesce and trust my grandfather. After all, he had no doubt faced many mornings like this before. Just maybe he knew what worked.

"Give me your keys."

He gave me a ten-dollar bill and directions to a hole-in-the-wall liquor store three blocks away. Jesse's car was a twenty-year-old Chrysler Imperial Crown in a rich alabaster color with a tan interior. It had been his brother George's, who had died several years earlier of cancer. The car had an elegance of an earlier time with its huge V-8, soft ride, shiny chrome, and a push button transmission. After a few cranks of the starter, the engine came to life, then settled down into a low idle. Soon, I was cruising old El Reno looking for Jesse's booze.

I returned in a few minutes and set the six-pack and change on the kitchen counter. Jesse said thanks and quickly popped the first tab. He chugged the first one in a few swallows, then sat on an old wooden chair, one arm leaning on the table, and wiped his mouth with his free left hand. He took a second can and finished it a bit more calmly.

I sat on the sofa and witnessed the proceedings with interest and pity. I had only slight reference to Jesse's past and the strains he had placed on his wife, family, and friends. The flash of anger and his resolute stubbornness gave me pause and I knew there was no easy or obvious action I could take that might help him. I knew that today Granddad would be calling the shots.

"Well Granddad, how about that breakfast?" I said as I stood and positioned myself between Jesse and the four remaining beers.

"I'm not hungry. I've been eatin' fine. Just had some cheese before you came last night."

Sure enough, there was cheese in the refrigerator, but that was about the only food present. I examined the cheese. Cheese should be aged before it's sold, not after, and the mottled color indicated the aging had been done in the refrigerator.

"Let's go eat. I'm hungry," I said again.

Jesse stood, straightened his back, gathered his wool hat and started for the door. I smiled and for the first time since I'd arrived, allowed a little optimism to show.

It was midmorning as I drove the old Chrysler down the drive into the mixed neighborhood of small, neatly kept frame homes. Interspersed with these smaller homes were several larger brick homes. Most were well cared for and had big mature trees full of summer's verdant growth, now starting to lighten with fall's arrival. The Chrysler's tires thumped over the asphalt repairs in the concrete street giving rhythm to the mostly silent ride.

Jesse lived in a mature neighborhood, but not the oldest. Downtown El Reno was near the intersection of Highway 81 and Highway 40, the old Route 66, and along the rail line. Here the houses were aging dames with big elms and sycamores shadowing their now rundown appearance. They still maintained a dignity and their memory of the past. The Chrysler passed slowly along these shaded streets.

"That's where I was livin' when you came huntin' with me," Jesse said unexpectedly, pointing to a narrow fronted, but very deep and large, two-story house. "That was Buena's."

I remembered the old house where my family would stay when we visited. Buena was a solid and kind woman who had run a cafe by the old Kerfoot Hotel. Jesse and Buena were married the first time, around 1950. Even as a child, I had seen no romance, but a polite space sharing agreement, Buena on the first floor and Jesse on the second.

I was pleased that my grandfather remembered the fall after I had turned twelve. My big gift that Christmas was a single shot 20-gauge shotgun. My mother walked with me to the gate at Love Field and advised the flight crew, whom she knew, that her son's gun, wrapped in its flannel cover, was not loaded. They laughed and treated me like a royal visitor. It was a great adventure to fly by myself on a big Braniff DC-6, and hunt quail for two days with my grandfather. Jesse was strong then, pushing sixty. He had a rounded belly but was straight backed and could walk all day over the broken fields. He knew every farmer and all the places the coveys of quail would be. Along with his English Setter, Sport, we wandered and talked and hunted the rolling land along the North Canadian River. It was a child's delight and an experience one shared only with a grandfather. It remained a great memory, and

I always felt my grandfather and I shared these memories, unique and just between us.

Jesse directed me south past newer and larger brick homes, and then we crossed I-40 towards the new hotel and restaurant. Jesse exited the big car with ease and walked alongside me. Inside, a woman looking about fifty, greeted us. Her nametag said Loni.

"Jesse, is that you? Where have you been?"

"How ya doin', Loni?" he asked in return, ignoring her question. "This is my grandson Cavin here, from Colorado."

"Hi Cavin. Welcome to El Reno." She said, pronouncing my name as she heard it. I didn't correct her.

"Nice to meet you, Loni."

She showed us to a booth, grabbing the coffee pot on the way. She poured each of us a cup and after thank yous, we took a welcome first sip.

"What can I get you boys?"

"Just some toast," said Jesse.

"Whoa, Granddad. Let's get something more. How about two nice omelets with extra cheese and some orange juice?" I remembered Granddad's fondness for cheese and felt augmenting the omelets with extra cheese might make him feel better.

"Be right back, boys," Loni said with a bit more perkiness than the situation seemed to call for.

Jesse garnered strength as he consumed his coffee. He'd always taken pride in his appearance, and this morning was no exception. As hung over as he was, his shirt was pressed and he was clean-shaven. And he had the omnipresent Old Spice. It was like the clock swallowed by the crocodile in *Peter Pan.* You knew Jesse was coming and you knew where he'd been. The Old Spice tapped a deep olfactory memory and I could, for a moment, see my grandfather when he was younger. But now, just less than 5'10", he was the man you would pass on the street and not notice, with his belly rounded and protruding over his belt. His hair was very thin, and only a few carefully combed strands kept him from being bald on top. His arms and shoulders were loose and rounded but still strong, built up over a life of farming, hauling freight, lifting milk cans, and other manual work. His complexion was fair, with deep wrinkles along his mouth and neck. I noticed the fingers of his right hand as he lifted his coffee cup. They were stained yellow and the fingernails had a gold, almost topaz color. Three packs a day had taken their toll. His eyes, once crayon blue, were veiled with grey and instead of inviting a deep gaze, as they once did, now only reflected back from their surface. I knew the blue eyes would never return. Jesse was dying.

"Here you go boys. Enjoy," said Loni, as she set the steaming omelets on the table.

"Thanks," we both said.

Then suddenly Loni exclaimed, "Hey Stanley, look who's here!"

A nice looking man in his fifties, dressed in a suit and tie, walked quickly to the booth.

"Jesse, it's been too long. How have you been?" asked the newcomer.

"I guess okay, Stanley. I want you to meet my grandson, Iris Jeanne's son, Cavin Evans, from Colorado. He's a dentist." Granddad seemed proud.

"It's a pleasure to meet you, Doctor."

"Just Kevin, please. Nice to meet a friend of Granddad's."

"Jesse and his family are always welcome."

"Stanley here is Mike Leonard's son. Mike used to own the old Kerfoot Hotel," explained Jesse.

"My dad, Mike, hired Jesse to manage the Kerfoot. When was it Jesse? Around 1950, wasn't it? I think that's right."

"I remember the Kerfoot," I said. "It had heavy dark oak furniture in the lobby with red upholstery, didn't it?"

"Yes, that's right. Sorry to see the old place torn down. If it had lasted another few years, it might have qualified for some sort of historical preservation. Didn't happen though."

"Sit down and have some coffee," directed Jesse. Stanley took Jesse's invitation, grabbed a clean cup, and poured it full of black coffee. "Stanley owns this restaurant," explained Jesse.

"After my father, Mike, sold the Kerfoot and retired, I went into the restaurant business. Owned a few, but now just this one and one east of here in Yukon. El Reno'll always be home though. Right Jesse? I see you've got some good cheese with your omelet there," he added as an afterthought. The mystic of cheese grew.

As Jesse picked at his food in silence, he allowed the conversation to flow to Stanley.

"So you're from Colorado, home of the Golden Buffaloes. I'm a Sooner myself. Majored in history, but my father told me take some business too. Good idea."

"Well, except for some high school in California, my schooling, college, and grad school was in Texas. I moved to Colorado right after I graduated. It was my plan all along to live in the high mountains." I figured that was enough background on me. "So you've known my Grandfather a long time?"

"Most of my life. Jesse here has friends all over Canadian County. Good friends. What do you two have planned for the day?"

Jesse spoke up. "I'm going to show him the old homesteads where his ma's folks lived, where Alice and I came from."

This was the first I'd heard of his plans and I was very pleased. Stanley interrupted my thought.

"Jesse, your family goes back to '89 doesn't it?"

"Yeah."

"Boomer Sooners!" exclaimed Stanley.

"My folks was no Sooners. They was legal," Jesse replied in a serious matter-of-fact tone."

"Kevin, your grandfather here is talking about one of our Oklahoma creation stories, the Land Runs."

"Sure, everybody's heard of the Runs, but you said 'one' of Oklahoma's creation stories. I'd like to hear more."

"The Runs were the White Man's story. The Trail of Tears is the Indians'. It wasn't grand or romantic. It was a terrible time and to this day, it resonates. Do you know there are still Indians that won't carry a twenty-dollar bill because of Andrew Jackson's portrait?"

"I didn't know."

Stanley continued, willing to share his knowledge. "These creation stories are full of great events, great people and powerful myth. Pretty much anytime people gather together and form a clan or a village or anything larger, they create the story of their beginnings. Many are alive to this day. Just put your ear to the ground, Kevin, the stories can still be heard."

"Myth?" I asked.

"I'm talking about myth, not fairy tales. Great myth has great truth. Never discount the power of myth."

The table was quiet for a moment and I saw Stanley shift his gaze to Jesse. It was a kindly look, and I knew Jesse remained a link to Stanley's youth and to his father, long ago.

Jesse had finished half of his omelet, some toast, and two cups of coffee. He set his fork down with purpose. I wasn't sure if Jesse had been listening and I doubted he had paid much attention.

"Granddad, have you had enough?"

"Yeah, that's all I can eat. You ready to see some things?" He was certainly more alert and seemed remarkably lucid and energetic. He stood and reached for his wallet.

"This is on me, Granddad."

Farewells were exchanged with Stanley and Loni. The Chrysler's big V-8 roared again.

CHAPTER 3

THE HAIL BELT

Hope now rested in the new day. I reasoned that my grandfather knew how to rebound on relatively short notice. This certainly wasn't his first morning after a binge. I observed his new energy and figured that just maybe, the timing of this trip might not have been so bad. We crossed the freeway, drove west a short distance then turned north on a gravel road.

"Pull over here," Jesse directed.

I pulled over on the side of the road, across from a row of sweet gum trees marking the north-south property line. We remained in the car.

"This's where I was born," Jesse said coolly. He pointed to the flat wheat field on the other side of the sweet gums. Fifty yards farther north was a white barn with a metal roof. There were no other outbuildings. The land had been under cultivation for eighty years and had long ago lost its character of folds and shadows. The winter wheat, recently drilled, was just beginning to sprout, giving faint green lines of color to the dark red earth. It was flat. Before the plow, this would have been long grass prairie with scattered shrubs and trees.

"You knew my ma and pa homesteaded this quarter section, didn't you?" he asked.

I had just heard stories, snippets here and there, with no cohesion. I rarely knew which relative was being discussed and showed little interest through adolescence. I cared more about Jesse, simply as my grandfather. I never really considered the generations before him.

"My ma did the Great Run of '89 with her folks. Pa'd met Ma back in Kansas before the Run. Pa told us kids later that he was in love and was gonna follow that Stafford girl to the Indian Territory. That's jus' what he done. The Staffords wasn't farmers, so they took a lot in Kingfisher and started a laundry and café. They was hard workin', saved a little money. Everyone back then wanted land. Land was the measure. People would come into the café and talk about ol' so and so's quarter, and he sold it or bought another or had a good year or a bad year and so on. The old man Stafford gave Pa the go ahead on to court Ma, and they was married. After Ma and Pa married, they signed for the Kiowa-Comanche-Apache lands Lottery of '01."

I was almost startled by this rapid retelling. It seemed to flow so easily. "What do you mean by a lottery?"

"The Great Run of '89 was a God-awful mess. People was cheated, land was stole, some good folks killed. You know all about that don't you, Doc?" he asked as he patted my shoulder firmly. I could tell he was enjoying himself and using the out of the blue "Doc" put a big grin on his face.

"Well just a bit," I said, not wanting to interrupt the rhythm of the story.

"The government decided a lottery would work just as well, so people signed up for the draw. Ma and Pa got this quarter section. Decided he'd be a farmer too. Our house was just beyond that barn. Our barn was where the new one is. Nothin' left now. Me and Grace was born here but I don't much remember this place."

"Why did your folks move?"

"This was the hail belt. Two years of wheat ruined by the hail."

"What do you mean by the hail belt?"

"Just what it says. This belt of land got the hail when our neighbors didn't. Don't know why. What else would you call it? Pa sold this quarter and never owned land again. Kept the money and rented a quarter section north of town. He'd farm a bit. Just never did as good as some. Made a livin' by haulin' freight with his wagons and teams."

"So how old were you when you left this farm and moved north of town?"

"Around six I reckon. That's where we're headed now." He pointed to the northeast and held his arm straight for a moment. Only after I turned my head and looked in that same direction, did he lower his arm.

The sky was clearing as the sun continued to climb. Scattered white clouds tried to build, but ran out of heat and moisture and lost their gathering force. The atmosphere seemed worn out from yesterday's storm. Some of the rain had pooled in the parallel ditch alongside the road, but the packed gravel road had no muddy holes, and the ride was smooth and dust free. The glimpse of fall seen that morning in town was visible here too, and the leaves, backlit by the bright sun, were beginning to give up their earned summer's green. A mild breeze shook them gently but they were not ready to fall.

The road back to town passed the site of old Fort Reno. Granddad told me to stop. I pulled over and pushed the big "P" button, but kept the car idling. "My brother, George, fought in the first war, but I was too young for that war, too old for the second. I'd quit school by the time of the first war and was making money for the family. Nowadays people can't understand why a boy would quit, but back then most of the neighbor boys did just that. You and your brother and sisters, all got college done, and that's good, but times was real different then.

"Worked here during the second war. General Sheridan named this place Fort Reno after a West Point friend of his, killed in Maryland back in the Civil War."

We'd stopped along a large field of cut and raked hay. It would be baled in a few days after it dried, but now the curved rows traced a broken labyrinth on this long abandoned parade and assembly ground.

"I knew stock real good back then. Still do, Cavin. The army hired me to tend some of the horses and mules kept here. This old fort had the last horse commission in the whole army. Closed it after the second war when they stopped using horses. I tended stock and drove German prisoners out to farms that paid for their labor. That was a good job. Got to talk to those boys. Really just boys, most of em. Never had a problem. Think by then they'd figured out that Hitler was an asshole."

Hearing Granddad talk about stock reminded me of a Christmas when I was fourteen. "Do you remember branding those heifers that Christmas on our farm?"

"Course I do. Your farm was the 4-K. Your daddy said he thought I could show him how to brand his new heifers. Kendall and your little brother Kent was there too. Don't think your daddy could've done it by himself. He made a better pilot than rancher."

"Remember we only had the loading ramp, not a squeeze chute, to hold those angry heifers? One jumped it right towards me and I had to dive away to keep from getting trampled. I heard some mighty colorful language that day from you and Kendall."

"Colorful? Wasn't the first time you'd heard them words was it?"

"No. Seemed appropriate."

Jesse shook with laughter and the whole car seemed to rock. He showed a little of the entertainer he could be. "Do you recall the next morning, Christmas Day it was? Alice thought she saw a dead heifer belly up in the pond below your house? She shrieked so loud it woke up the whole house."

"I'll never forget it," I said. "Kendall ran into the living room and saw it was only the reflection of a heifer standing on the dam above the water. I don't know how long we all laughed. Then Kendall jumped bareback on our mare, Punky, and rode the pasture till he had a full eighteen count. They all survived your branding, Granddad."

"You could ride that mare, too. I watched you. Those was good times on your farm when Kendall and his family would come down from Illinois, and Alice would drive up from Dallas."

A big smile was still on my face as I pulled the car back onto the gravel road. After entering El Reno, Granddad directed me to intersect Highway 81, the north-south artery. Turning north, we soon came to a long gentle rise leading to the bridge over the North Canadian River. In the northeast corner of New Mexico, the easternmost uplift of the Rocky Mountains ends in low broad mountains and small isolated mesas. The snowmelt and rain runoff from these uplifts form little gullies and washes that come together as the headwaters of the North Canadian River. As it meanders east and the gradient slows, it picks up more feeder creeks, and at some point, depending on the year's rainfall, carries water year round. In the flat panhandle of Oklahoma, the North Canadian River begins to look like a real river with oxbows, floodplains, and water chasing cottonwoods.

This is the river we crossed, four hundred fifty river miles from its beginning. The long bridge and its earthen approaches over the flood plain and river channel stretched over a half-mile. On the other side, the trees of the river bank gave way to neatly tilled fields of the red Oklahoma clay and intermittent fallow fields grown over with grass and low shrubs. Other sections were feral, as trees and patches of thick brush had reclaimed some of the old farms. I wondered if this was the area I had hunted with my grandfather twenty years past. Just then I noticed a roadside sign, "Darlington Indian Agency Site -- 1 mile". Past the simple sign, Jesse directed me to slow down.

"Take that section road," he directed.

The sign said Hefner Road. The pavement was left behind and the tires began noisily throwing chunks of mud underneath the Chrysler. We drove east. Where the lay of the land allowed, the Indian lands had been divided into square mile sections with a section road tracing the square. Each quarter section, one hundred sixty acres, would have two sides along a section road and two sides abutting neighbors. Inside this square, four families were bound. A century later the old farms were gone or hardly recognizable. New houses with satellite dishes, even a small holding pen with a white llama being harassed by two ostriches, could be seen as the new rural.

But through these modern dressings, Jesse was able to see the images of the past. "That rusted fence there is the Shaw's line." I knew the Shaw name because Jesse's little sister Grace had married a Shaw. Jesse pointed to a line of cedars. "Them cedars there was a windbreak for the Estep's barn and house."

And where scattered cedars and a hackberry grew, he saw the site of another house now gone. There were two worlds overlapping here, and through his clouded eyes, I believe Jesse could see both clearly. It was at such a place that he asked me to pull over. I stopped far to the right, just past a T intersection and turned off the engine.

"This is where your mother was born," Jesse announced. "After your grandma and me was married, we lived with my folks on these leased forty acres. She taught a year at the Elm Glen School and the next summer, Iris Jeanne was born."

"That was 1925, Granddad," I added.

Jesse was bringing a pulse to his story. "Must be so, Cavin."

"So this is where you lived after your folks sold their quarter section west of town?"

"No, that farm's just east of here a bit. We'll go there next. That's where I was mostly raised and where I mostly grew up, but this place here is where we lived when I was courtin' Alice, and where Alice and me lived with my ma and pa right after we was married. Being a schoolteacher was a pretty good job back then, respected. She'd walk or I'd drive her to the school 'bout a mile back west. We passed the site but there's nothin' to see now. It was a one-room wood frame school. Eight grades. All us kids went there. I think Alice's mother's folks gave that corner for the Elm Glen School long before Alice was born. Their name was Myers. Those big farm families would have three, four, or even five kids at the school at the same time. Those eight grades might only have a few last names. The Sheets, Jennings, Shaws, Esteps, and a dozen other families, we all grew up together and was more like cousins than neighbors. Most girls would finish the eighth grade and go on to the high school, and if they didn't marry, might finish their school. More'n us boys would stop schoolin' and take work. That's what I done, Cavin."

Jesse opened the car door and waved for me to follow. We walked slowly up the dirt drive to a site shaded by cedars and scrub oak. Just off the drive were concrete steps, all that remained of the house. The site was on a high point and the land dropped sharply to the east. An old outbuilding with hogwire pens attached leaned steeply with the prevailing wind. No stock were visible and the fences were down. The place had been abandoned for many years. Down the hill past the hog wire pens, the land smoothed and a large group of cedars formed an irregular circle with green grass in the center. Jesse stood very still and directed his grey eyes towards the old cedar flat.

I watched Jesse closely for several long breaths. I felt my Grandfather wanted me to be here. He had things he had to say. I was the only grandchild to have made a special trip to El Reno, and I had the sense that if Jesse would talk to anyone, it would be to me. Jesse stood motionless for a few minutes. I didn't want to say anything to break his thoughts, but I was beginning to wonder if he was okay. Then Jesse simply turned his gaze away from the old cedar flat and walked to the car. He was silent. I knew this spot held a memory.

The day was beautiful. A few cumulus clouds had formed but showed no sign of coalescing into a threat. Their shadows danced across the land, yielding to sun every few minutes. The air was moist and cool. The old Chrysler started easily, and we drove slowly east for only a mile where Jesse directed me to turn right on another section road. A short distance later, we stopped at a rutted dirt road that turned back east. There was a metal gate blocking the drive.

"Damn! I was hoping we could drive on up. This is where I was raised. Moved here after the quarter section in the hail belt was sold. Most all of my early recollections come from here."

The house, a hundred yards away, faced south. It was in terrible shape and leaned heavily. The paint was gone and the view through a dense line of cedars revealed a two-story traditional rural house. It seemed to me that a good wind would knock it over, and then I saw that it was being used to store hay and figured the bulky hay inside was all that was keeping it up. All the outbuildings were gone and I could see no trace of where they once stood.

"The fella that owned this quarter, he done the '89 Run, built this nice house, but his wife died havin' their first baby. He just gave up the place and moved to town. Never wanted to sell the quarter, so he leased it out to us Sheets. My ma and pa made some good money on the sale of the lottery quarter section and bought a nice wagon and four-horse team. Never owned land again. With this one sixty and his haulin' business, he done good by the family. But Ma never let Pa forget that we didn't own land anymore."

Jesse stopped for a moment and looked at me. "Sure you want to hear all this, Cavin?"

"Your folks died long before I was born. Yeah, I'd like to hear it all."

Jesse nodded his head up and down, then turned back to the old house. "Ma used to tell all us kids about land. About how the peasants in Europe could never own land. That's what made so many leave and come to America. It was the land that brought 'em. If a person owned land, then they was somebody. Had somethin' that set 'em aside from others.

"Now my Pa didn't see things that way. He always figured what mattered was money in his pocket and takin' care of his family. He didn't see the need to have perfect straight rows of wheat or corn, when he could have a good business with his neighbors and the town folk. He was real good with meetin' folks and he had a good reputation. Always had work and always had the crops, except one year when the weeds took over the wheat.

"My Pa was a fine dresser. Loved his silk ties and spats. Ma wasn't one to be swayed so don't know who else liked his fine clothes. Never knew Pa to get red angry. He was a quiet man. Would walk away from an argument if he could. I always felt there was a space between my ma and pa. At least when I was growing up. Ma was the rule maker in the house. She wouldn't get loud angry, just made you know when you'd let her down. She was the hardest on Pa and Edwin, my oldest brother. That was what she did. Too much maybe. Kept the house perfect and tried to get all us kids to go to church, play the piano, and stay in school.

"George and Floyd were my best pals growin' up. Taught me lots of things. Us brothers knew everybody in this part of the county. People said we was good kids, but you had to keep an eye on us. Couldn't see stayin' in school when I could make money helpin'

Pa. Ma lost her temper when I told her, and Pa wouldn't stand behind her. Said she was sorry the next day. I shoulda listened. After that, Ma seemed to accept this new way of things. Think she was tired of the space she'd made between Pa and my brothers. Guess I was the last son to disappoint her and she was happy there wasn't no more. She and Pa got along pretty good after all that. Pa told me once that girls with an accent was hard to ignore. Ma's ma was German. She still spoke of land but didn't much give the needle to Pa about it. Stayed good to her church, but only my little sister, Grace, would go with her, 'cept on Easter we'd all go.

"You know, Cavin, I think Ma felt a tender spot for me. One maybe she didn't have for my brothers. Probly just cause I was the youngest boy. Yeah, that's prob'ly it. She was real good with me.

"I'm getting warm here in the car, Cavin. Let's start her up and head back west. I gotta show you the Jennings' place."

I turned west on the section road and retraced our route past the forty-acre place where my mother was born. It was another mile down a low hill past the site of the Elm Glen School and a second mile to a north-south section road. I repeated the succession of the three places Jesse had lived to myself and tried to commit it all to memory. We had passed this intersection earlier but Jesse had made no mention.

"Turn left here. This corner starts the Jennings' quarter. Take that dirt road there."

Jesse was pointing to a rutted dirt road that led irregularly to the right. I slowed down and negotiated the ruts. He pointed to a large tree. I parked the car and Jesse was out of the car before I had closed my door.

"This hackberry wasn't here when the house was, but it's a good shade giver now. Let's go sit on those steps."

Below the tree and in solid shade, was a block of three concrete steps, maybe four feet wide. It was the only remnant of the house. Thirty feet past the steps, the metal tower of a rusted windmill still stood tall. The trailing vane and its two remaining blades hung motionless but straight. It's shadow, cast on the thick grass, appeared intact and I wondered if it had been the same for ninety years.

"I'm gonna take a rest on these steps, Cal. It's nice shade here." Jesse made a few grunts and settled on the second step. He looked up at the windmill. "Your grandma was born here and this is where I met her. Guess it was where I met her. Not sure about that but must've been close by."

"So Grandmother's parents, the Jennings, made the Great Run of '89 and claimed this quarter?"

"No. Weren't that simple. It's a big story that started long before '89. Think I remember most of it. My mind's still good, Cavin. I can tell you a lot about my family and me, and your grandma and her folks. Knew some things then. But now, I know more. All them people are gone now, either dead or moved away. I'm the one that's still here. I never left. I knew them all and I still know their stories, the Indians and their Trail. All their stories. People say I talk a good story, but Cavin, I listen too. I listened to my folks, to Alice and her pa, Robert Jennings, all those people here along the river, even an old German cowboy, Kurt. Heard 'em all. For me, it was all yesterday. I still see Alice with a daisy in her hair, sayin' she'd marry me. Got no one left now, Cavin. If you're willin', I can tell you things. It'll take a while though."

I found a soft spot of grass a few feet beyond the steps and settled into the green cushion. This is their story.

CHAPTER 4
KURT

Oklahoma, in 1914, was a growing and prosperous state with electricity, paved roads, and good prices for wheat and corn. The new war in Europe was little more than a headline. In Canadian County, work was plentiful and twelve-year-old Jesse was as free as any man. Most of his young friends were still in school, but Jesse had slowly removed himself from his formal education. Some days he would walk along the road with friends on their way to school. He would play around with them outside, but when the bell sounded, he would give his good-byes and continue on his way.

On an October morning, Jesse waved to his friends entering the Elm Glen School, and started walking west. No freeze had hit, but the grasses along the road were turning brown and their seeded tops were bent as the moisture in their stalks was beginning to dry. The wheat and corn had been harvested and were only stalks and stubble. A small but brilliant orange stripe of a pumpkin patch contrasted with the earthy browns of its surroundings. The air was still cool from the night, but held promise of warming as the sun climbed a cloudless sky.

To the east, where he had begun his day, Jesse could make out a small herd of cattle, maybe twenty head. They were slowly headed his way as they grazed the right of way between the fences. A rider on a very large horse was slowly driving the cattle, giving them time to grab mouthfuls of Johnson and Bermuda grass. Jesse studied the herd. The odd mix had several mature cows and a few young steers purchased from dairy farmers as soon as they'd been weaned. They were a colorful collection of breeds and mixed breeds and no two looked the same. Jesse could make out a combination of Hereford, two all black old cows, Jersey steers, some Shorthorn and even one with a lot of Longhorn. They were healthy, except for one old cow whose shoulder bones looked like they would poke through her hide.

The rider and his mount drew closer, and Jesse suddenly realized who had just appeared. He'd heard stories of Kurt for years, but had never met or seen the man. Boys told of a weathered old German who drove his collected herd each fall to sell to the Darlington Indian Agency. The boys spoke in tones of awe, filling in the gaps of their knowledge with created tales, so that Jesse knew little of the real Kurt.

As the rider approached, Jesse confirmed as fact the most persistent story. Kurt rode a bull, not a horse. It was a great blue-grey animal with a soft hump on its neck. Its long drooping ears gave it a sad donkey face. Jesse looked up at this exotic and new animal. At the shoulders, it was as taller than his family's tallest horse. It had a narrow head and a long sinewy neck sweeping to narrow shoulders. Beyond the shoulders, the huge body was the largest he had ever seen. There was a dangling flap of skin beginning at the throat and tracing the long neck down, growing larger and finally hanging loosely between the front legs. His horns curled upwards, ending three feet apart and between them, Kurt had wrapped a faded blue cloth in a repeated figure eight. It gave the great bull a festive appearance, as if it were leading an ancient parade.

Some strange mixture of wild cattle, water buffalo, or beast unknown had created this towering bull. Jesse's eyes fixed on the figure astride those tall shoulders. Riding high on a saddle of layered dark wool blankets was its master, holding a simple rope rein attached to a nose clamp.

"Hey Mister," Jesse said.

"Hello to you, Son," the rider responded.

"Name's Jesse. I know who you are. You're Kurt. I heard about you. I never seen a bull like that," said Jesse quickly with no hint of shyness.

"It's a Brahma. They're from India."

"I never seen a man ride a bull before, exceptin' at a rodeo."

Kurt looked ahead at his small herd. Most had stopped walking and two had flopped down on their bellies, centering over their folded legs. He pulled his right leg over the bull's neck and slid down, landing firmly on his feet facing Jesse.

"Well this is a good spot for lunch," announced Kurt.

Across the bull's back and sides were four large wool panniers, cinched below the bull's belly. He opened the top of one and pulled out a partial loaf of dark bread and some dried meat. With his canteen of water, he headed for shade. Jesse followed.

"I knew who you was right off. I heard about you, but when they said bull, I figured a regular bull, not like this one. And you really do, you really ride him. I seen it, so it must be true, huh?"

Jesse was pleased that he could now confirm and add to the local tales, and he became even more talkative as Kurt settled down for his meal.

"Where're you going? Where're you from?" continued Jesse, giving no time for Kurt to answer. Jesse had heard accents before, but Kurt's was different. Instead of signaling a possible divide with the man, Jesse found the accent and Kurt's voice welcoming, and he felt encouraged to continue his questions.

"You're not from Oklahoma are you, Mr. Kurt?" asked Jesse.

Kurt motioned for Jesse to sit down, broke the bread, and offered his young friend a piece. Jesse thanked him and they ate in silence for a few minutes. This man was different in so many ways. A bit under six feet, his face was deeply wrinkled and darkened by years in the sun. His hat once removed, revealed a large head covered with long thin grey hair that fell loosely over his ears and collar. A brown woolen shirt and pants ending inside laced-up leather boots were his constant attire. He had a little belly now, and his shoulders were no longer tall and square. He had a rather long neck, almost too long, like his head needed a little balancing to keep it centered. His eyebrows were very bushy and protected dark brown eyes. He had no beard, but stubble of several days masked some of his wrinkles. Jesse thought he must be from a faraway place.

"So where you goin'?" asked Jesse again.

"Tonight I'll stay at the Jennings' place. Let the herd rest for a few days. Clean them up, then take them to Darlington and sell all but the bull. I keep the bull to ride and put to stud along the way. Some ranchers like the great size of this bull, and its narrow shoulders promise an easy dropping of the calf. Overwinter west of the agency. Got a wife there. Head back east in the spring. I'm just a simple cowboy, Jesse."

When Jesse heard Kurt describe himself as a cowboy, he first thought of the big ranches down in Texas, but then realized Kurt was a different kind.

"So Mr. Kurt, how'd you get to be cowboy like this. I mean most cowboys work on ranches. Don't they?"

"My ranch is the grass between the fences. It's as much mine as any man's, and my ranch stretches from here to back east two hundred miles. That's a pretty good spread now wouldn't you say, Son?"

In these few words Kurt gave a synopsis of his life these past many years. He was independent, worked for no man, beholden to none. He was a cowboy, simple and true. Come spring he would buy, barter, or trade for stock and assemble a new herd as he headed back west, following the north bank of the North Canadian River. He would rely on the kindness of the farmers along the way if he needed to purchase any supplies, but mostly he grazed the rights of way and slept under the stars. His sinuous ranch was a thin green line.

What do think of my bull, Jesse?"

"I never seen anything like it. Where'd you get it?"

"This old bull's only got a few more years left in him. When he's gone there will not be another. People have been asking for years how I come by this animal and I never say. Wouldn't be right for you to be the one to know, now would it? I just say no man can own such an animal. We're just together here for now?"

Jesse was a bit confused by this evasive answer but not deterred from finding out more about this man.

"So, Mr. Kurt, tell me where you come from. How'd you come to be here?" Jesse would always wonder why this stranger told him so much. He mimicked Kurt's position, leaning his back against the same tree and just listened.

"I was born in Hamburg, Germany. It's a big city along the Elbe River in Northern Germany. My father was the grounds keeper of our little church and school, and my mother helped the nuns teach piano and violin. My folks weren't highly schooled, but they made sure me and my two older brothers were. We had a pretty good life. I liked school and I liked to read. You read much, Jesse?"

"Not too much."

"Well, at night our mother would read to us or have us read out loud from Goethe and Shakespeare, and the classics from Homer, Augustine, Aquinas, Dante, Milton, and others. But I liked stories of your American West. They were hard to come by in German so I picked up a little English. I read of your great county and its aborigines. You know what an aborigine is, Jesse?"

"Can't say I do. Mr. Kurt. What is it?"

"The American Indian, your lands' first inhabitants. You ever think about them, Jesse?"

"Sure, they're all over the county. Know some at Darlington."

"That's good to hear."

"After school and chores, I'd sit on the big Elbe levee and read about your West and watch those ships come in from all around the world. Decided I would come to America.

"I was only fourteen when my parents died. Typhus. Took the few marks they left me and talked my way aboard a three-masted steamer bound for New Orleans. Can you imagine? For cleaning floors and toilets for three weeks, I got passage to New Orleans. I was shined upon, Jesse. You know what I mean?"

"You was lucky?"

"Well, maybe that too. We sailed through the Florida Straights and I had my first sighting of America. A few days later we found the mouth of the Mississippi and steamed upriver. They call it the Crescent City, Jesse, because it's on a big bend of the river. After unloading our cargo, I just walked away. Germany is so uniform and predicable. New Orleans is a controlled riot. Just walking down the docks I heard French, Spanish, English, and tongues I thought must Caribbean. Spotted a very well dressed gentleman having trouble loading some leaded glass onto the back of his wagon. I gave him a hand and he said, '*Merci*'. I knew some French so I answered back, '*de rein*'. He stopped, looked me over, and saw the ship I'd just sailed on with its German flag, and had me sized up. He asked if I had a place to stay. I said no, and with no hesitation he offered the seat next to him. That's how I got to know Christoval Morel.

"He was a fair man. His family had come to New Orleans during Napoleon's time and still spoke of old ties to the emperor's family. You've heard of Napoleon haven't you, Jesse?"

"I think so, Mr. Kurt."

"Well the Morels were well known in New Orleans. Christoval was an attorney and had a trading business with his in-laws. DeArmas was their name. They were Spanish from Galicia and the Canary Islands. Called themselves *Los Islenos.* These two families were in business together, and I began to work for Monsieur Morel. First as simple help around his house, then later because I was good at math and spoke English, French, Spanish, and of course German, I began to help in their warehouse. Odd that over in Europe, those countries might be at war, but there in New Orleans, those two families were a powerful enterprise. Monsieur Morel's father-in-law, Felix DeArmas, was a notary and he was the one that exposed Jim Bowie's land fraud. If Bowie hadn't fled Louisiana with the law on his tail and been martyred on a Mexican lance, you'd never have heard of him. Anyway this was a proud family with Old World tradition and New World spirit. Monsieur Morel tried to keep the old traditions alive and taught a lot of the old family sons fencing. You know what fencing is, Jesse?"

"Sorry, Mr. Kurt. Guess I don't."

"Swords. It's sword fighting and duels. I heard stories that Monsieur Morel had killed two men in duels when he was younger. Not sure if it was true or not. Good story though, huh?

"They lived in a nice house along the Bayou St. John, in the Creole part of town. In time, they'd have me for their Sunday meal and treated me like family. Jesse, I'll tell you, I loved the Morels and the DeArmases, and I loved New Orleans. Loved everything about it. After Mass, I'd wander the streets and hear music that danced in your ears. The Africans had the old brass instruments the Union army had left, and they mixed their rhythms and created something new. Never heard anything like it since. There was this café that you could get hot chicory root coffee with thick cream and a French pastry with powdered sugar for a nickel. For five years, I was an adopted son of New Orleans. Could have stayed and had a good business on my own. The Morel and DeArmas sons would inherit their business, but I knew enough to start my own."

Kurt stopped talking. He finished his meat and bread and took a long drink of water. Jesse said nothing as he watched him wipe his face and glance over to his resting herd. All seemed in order.

"I had a yearning Jesse, that I didn't speak of. I still had to see the West. I kept reading and that yearning just swelled up and finally I had to act. Had to meet your American Aborigines. I had this vision of a great warrior on a painted pony following the buffalo. The great noble Red Man. That's what I believed. That's what those silly dime novels told me. Back then, couldn't tell what was true. Found out on my own. After a Sunday meal, I told Monsieur Morel my plans. He gave me his blessing and the whole family toasted me with a special wine just arrived from France.

"I'd saved most of my wages and bought a four-year-old, twelve hand chestnut gelding. He was no prancer or wagon puller. No sir, he was a cow horse. Monsieur Morel gave me a fine Spanish saddle as a farewell gift. In a few days, I'd booked passage and was steaming upriver to the Arkansas. My plan was simple. Go north then head west into the Indian Territory and from there? I'd just have to see what lay ahead. I met people on the steamer, but I was careful not to speak of my plans. Thinking back, I told myself that I didn't want to be followed on my journey to the Territory. No one would have cared. I disembarked at the Arkansas River and I rode my fine mount west to Fort Smith. It was no town of the West. It was settled, with shops and hotels and two brick paved streets. There was an encampment of Cherokees on the edge of town, and they were not welcoming when I set a canvas tarp and camped nearby for the next four weeks. After a few days, they would say a few words and I'd try to say them back. Always had a good ear for language and, soon enough, I'd picked up enough to talk with them. I spent time with the Cherokee. The Trail of Tears was still hard on their memory and they spoke of it in sad and melancholic tones. I'd never given much thought to your President Jackson, but those Cherokee told me how wrong it all was. In Fort Smith, I finally began to realize there was no such thing as the American Indian. They were as diverse as the Europeans I had left. Figured I'd be lucky just to know a few tribes. The Cherokee were my first Indians, but I still wanted to see the Indians of the Plains.

"I introduced myself to the commanding officer of Fort Smith, Captain Montgomery Bryant, a spit and polish officer who'd received a Brevet promotion to Colonel in the Civil War. He was unhappy to be only a captain in the regular army and thought Fort Smith was a backwater. He must have thought I was crazy. I liked him anyway, and he was kind enough to give me a letter of introduction to John Miles, the agent in charge of Darlington, the agency for the Cheyenne and Arapahoe. Rode west the next day. Followed the Arkansas and crossed it at Webbers Falls, then traced the Canadian and the North Canadian to Darlington. John Miles sized me up. I told him I wanted to run a small herd each year and bring it to the agency in the fall. We had a deal. Signed a paper.

"Finally at Darlington, I'd met the Indians of the Plains. This is where I saw the truth. It is different from what I'd thought in Hamburg, but it's mine and it's clear and I see things now I couldn't see before. It's only a shadow, but a man can tell a lot from a shadow."

Jesse looked up at Kurt and saw his eyes were wet. "Are you sad, Mr. Kurt? You're sad. I can tell."

Kurt kept his gaze on his herd, and continued. "Early each spring, no matter the ice storms or early tornados, I say my goodbyes, and I reverse the circle, following the Cimarron, the Arkansas, and the two Canadians. After my second horse died, I came upon this great bull and kept the circle going. An old German, riding a bull, it was only natural that stories would start. Most not true, but I like them. I knew the Indians would never welcome me as a brother, never could I share their vision. I just wanted to glimpse it for one golden moment. Maybe I did once, frozen between two worlds. I was the last European explorer, planting neither flag nor cross."

Jesse's attention had never wavered. "I hear lots of stories about you. You're right about that. Some say you know things we others don't know. Why's that Mr. Kurt?"

"Today's a school day. Why aren't you there, Jesse?"

"Don't go much anymore. Just don't."

"Well that's why I've told you these things today."

Jesse wasn't sure what this kind cowboy meant by that, but he knew he would always remember the day a stranger had told him a story, good and true.

CHAPTER 5
RUNAWAY

A few weeks after Jesse had met Kurt, the first hard freeze hit, pushing fall towards its colorful climax. The daytime was very comfortable in the sixties, but by sunset a coat or sweater would be needed. The previous day, Saturday, Jesse had worked hard. He had helped his father haul fifty bales of hay a neighbor had sold to another farmer six miles away. Loading the wagon was tough enough, but at their destination they had to lift the bales into a loft twenty feet up. It was hard work and even with the cooler days, hay dust would get under clothes and mix with sweat, making any man hot and uncomfortable. Charles gave his son three quarters for his help and Jesse was grateful for it. That evening, after supper, Jesse's mother helped him heat water for a full bath so he could wash the scratchy dust away. She set a heavy wool shirt on his bed for the next morning.

Sunday was church. By this time, all the men in the Sheets family had sided with their father and decided against any regular attendance. Only Grace, the youngest child, would remain her mother's Sunday companion. It was a complete victory for Jesse, but he still had to listen to his mother's criticism of his decision to stop attending the Elm Glen School and now church.

"Jesse," she would say, "come a time you'd wished you'd listened to your mother. You want to haul freight all your life long?"

Charles heard every word and harbored the hurt inside. He didn't want his sons to see how a woman could hurt a man. Jesse knew this and more.

The men's defiance became resolute. Charles, in his hurt, was only too willing to welcome his youngest son as an ally. Charles and the two middle sons, George and Floyd, taught Jesse the physical world and things mechanical, but neglected those things of which they had no knowledge. What they didn't know they could not share.

Jesse's education was frozen. So was his theology. He would equate religion with his mother's evening prayers and little else. It's not that he didn't believe, he just didn't care. If God was indeed merciful, then God would grant Jesse mercy and in the meanwhile, the physical world of the Sheets' men was the object he could grasp with his worldly senses.

This first Sunday in November, Jesse had a nice breakfast with his family and then walked his mother and sister to the section road, where the Shaws would pick them up for the short buggy ride to the Oak Chapel Church and Reverend Cavin. The rest of the day was free. He returned home and gathered cheese and biscuits from breakfast, filled a metal canteen with water, tossed it all in a canvas shoulder bag, and headed west. As he reached the section road he looked back east where he had first seen Kurt and wondered what he was up to these days. Jesse's plan was to walk the three miles to the road between El Reno and Kingfisher and try to hitch a ride in an automobile. He would go either north or south but preferred the longer ride north. He figured if he got a ride going either direction, it would be just as easy getting a hitch for the return. If he really turned his charm on, he figured he might even get to steer for a while.

The sun climbed higher and the day grew warm. A rapid clicking noise reached his ears before he saw the small grasshopper land on his left sleeve. Fleeing some unknown threat, it had warmed just enough in the morning sun and expended the stored energy to make the short flight. Jesse picked it up softly with his fingers and brought it close to his eyes for study. It was a smooth brown with glistening green outlining the junction of its wings to its body. Its large back legs were coiled in a double bend but it remained calm. Its small jaw moved rapidly from side to side for some reason Jesse couldn't figure. Jesse loosened his fingers expecting the hopper to fly off, but it remained motionless in his palm. Jesse took a breath and blew it softly away. It was in free fall for a moment then Jesse heard the clicking and saw the hopper take control of its freedom. Jesse thought it would have made good bait for a catfish.

He began to regret taking his mother's advice about his heavy shirt. Jesse had started out with just a cotton t-shirt but Anna had insisted he wear the heavy woolen shirt she had set on his bed the night before. After he stopped walking, he cooled down and didn't think of it again. He thought about catching that ride, but after two hours with no luck, he began to question the use of such a fine day. On the section road coming slowly from the east, Jesse noticed a slow-moving wagon surrounded by a cloud of dust. The still air kept the dust at its point of origin, so the wagon, its one horse, and its driver were all blurred. It took a while for Jesse to see who was coming.

"Afternoon, Young Mr. Sheets," hailed the driver. It was Newt Jennings, the oldest Jennings' son.

"Hey Newt," answered Jesse, pleased with his new moniker. He liked the sound of "Young Mr. Sheets".

"You just standing around or you got something in mind?" asked Newt, with a smile on his face.

Jesse was seven years younger than Newt, but had always thought Newt good for a friendly word. "I been waitin' to hitch a ride in an automobile, but haven't had any obligers."

"Well I'll give you a ride in this old-fashioned horse thing if you want. Where you headed?"

Jesse had no intention of hitching a ride on a wagon, but he didn't want to hurt Newt's feelings. Besides, he could just ride a bit and talk with Newt. He climbed up next to him.

"Your way's fine, thanks. Whatcha haulin'?"

"Just a few of my old things from the place. You knew Pa married the widow Mary Hawkins a while back. Well, she's got four kids of her own and they needed all the room they could get."

"Makes sense."

"Did you know I married Vi? Got a little place in town, but I'm thinking about doing some farming if I can find some land."

"Heard you got married. Vi's a Pickard ain't she?"

"Yeah. Your folks sent a butter mold when they heard. Nice thing to do. You know, now that we're family we do those sorts of things."

"Yea, we're family now. You see Edwin and Ina much?" Jesse asked.

"They don't live far, but we don't see 'em much." He paused, looked at Jesse and seemed to size him up. "They're not what I would call the life of the party, if you know what I mean?" Newt laughed heartily and gave Jesse a firm elbow to his ribs.

Jesse broke out in instant laughter and continued long after Newt had stopped. He looked up at Newt and continued nodding his head. Edwin, Jesse's oldest brother, was just dull. Newt put both feet on the front rest of the wagon, took a deep breath and leaned back with his two hands behind his neck. The horse kept a slow walking gait.

Jesse thought Newt would have made a good brother and knew the two agreed on Ina and Edwin. Newt's big sister Ina was the most beautiful of the Jennings' girls, but stern beyond normal. She was hard to know and protected her feelings from everyone. Her new husband, Edwin, was hard working and responsible and never let a laugh interfere with either. Newt and Jesse were the two most likable of the Jennings' and Sheets' boys, and just about everyone they met would agree.

"Marriage is a funny thing, Young Mr. Sheets. I swear it's hard to figure these things out," said Newt after a pause. He was looking straight ahead, not at Jesse.

This seemed an adult topic to Jesse and he found himself interested. Newt had an entertaining style and didn't talk to Jesse like he was a little boy.

"If there were ever two more stiffed legged serious souls in the county, I swear they were meant to be married," said Newt.

"They was meant," parroted Jesse.

"If I tell a good joke," Newt continued, "everybody in the room laughs and then a second later Edwin starts his laugh, after he's glanced at Ina and gotten the okay. Not the way I see things. Now Vi and me, we laugh whenever something worth laughing at happens."

"Why'd you leave home a while back?" Jesse asked abruptly. The direct question seemed to catch Newt by surprise. He turned his head toward Jesse and studied the young boy's face for a long moment. Jesse apparently passed the test.

"How'd you know about that? Was my business."

"Us boys hear lots a things. Sorry, Newt, I don't mean nothin'. I'd just heard things."

Newt turned his head back to the road and looked straight ahead, never at Jesse.

"I was only two years older than you are now. Being Pa's oldest son, he was always hardest on me, and I tell you, I didn't like it," he began with his voice rising, belying a still present conflict. "Hell, he'd run off from Missouri to chase cows in Texas. Same difference. Met this girl, Bertha, on a Saturday in town. Don't know why, but she just started talking to me. She was tall and dark haired and she looked at me different. When she was talking I couldn't hardly move."

Jesse's attention was rapt. He had been looking at girls in a new way. His brothers, Jack and Floyd, had filled him in on the basics of how things worked, but now here was a married man telling about an actual time with a girl. Jesse tilted his head just a bit so no words would pass him by and waited anxiously for Newt to continue.

"Shawnee. She was from Shawnee. I bet we didn't talk more'n ten minutes. Seemed like a whole afternoon, but I swear it was only a few minutes. She gave me her address and said write. I did and she wrote back. Hell, I was in love. Decided right then no need to stay here in El Reno and no sense asking Pa. I just left."

Jesse's eyes opened wide and his brow furrowed, as he tried to understand how a fella could meet a girl, fall in love, and take off for another county. All told in a few words. "You was fourteen then?"

"Bertha was two years older. Didn't care. Stayed in her barn for two days. Didn't tell her folks. I hired out to a neighbor one day. I could make money as easy in Shawnee as in El Reno. Nighttime, Bertha'd come down and bring me food. She'd stay till her ma called. Not sure her ma knew or not. Her pa never did, until my pa showed up on the third day. Used the buggy whip. My pa whipped me bad. Still carry the scars on my back. Whipped me right in front of Bertha and her folks. Whipped me so bad, Bertha's pa didn't have to. Last I saw her, her pa was pushing her through the front door." Newt stopped and sighed.

Jesse was afraid the story was over, but he wanted to hear more. "You ever see her since?" he finally asked.

"Haven't seen her ever."

The quiet between the two was welcome. Jesse could see the emotion in Newt's face. The story was still on the table, but Jesse felt he should let it settle. After a few moments, Newt shifted his weight to the other hip and looked up at the sky. It was blue with no hint of a cloud. The high sky had no ceiling, no beginning and no end.

Finally Jesse's curiosity powered the next question. "What'd you two do in the barn?"

Newt's quick laughter released him from the spell. He couldn't fault Jesse for wanting to know more of the physical.

"I'll tell you this. I can still smell her."

Jesse sensed that Newt was enjoying these sweet remembrances.

Newt kept talking. "People think remembering is just thinking about what's passed. Maybe, but the nose remembers best of all. Sometimes one little breath makes it all real again. One time Vi brought home a bottle of perfume. It was the same one Bertha wore. Don't remember the name. I threw it away. Told Vi I'd knocked it over it by mistake. Bought her a new one. A different one."

The story was over. The wagon was approaching the river. Jesse grabbed his pack and began to roll out of his seat before Newt could bring his horse to a full stop. By the time the wagon had stopped, Jesse was standing, waiting for the dust to clear.

"I thought you were going into town?"

"Not today. I'll head home by followin' the trail alongside the river. Thanks for the ride, Newt."

"Watch yourself now, Young Mr. Sheets." Newt shook the reins and headed south over the bridge.

Jesse stood and watched the wagon until it had crossed the middle of the bridge and pondered this meeting with Newt. He also pondered what went on in the barn between Newt and Bertha.

CHAPTER 6

THREE VISITORS

The day had not followed Jesse's original plan. He decided he liked Newt as a great storyteller and because he'd treated him kindly. He would always regard Newt as a friend. He had not given much thought to the Jennings in the past. Maybe each family was more complicated than he had imagined.

The food and water Jesse had brought with him were gone. He knew of a spring along the limestone cliff below the Jennings' place. The day had grown warmer and Jesse knew he would have to take off his wool shirt if he did much heavy hiking. A cool drink sounded good. The trail along the North Canadian had always been there. It was as constant as the river. Marked first by large mammals and their predators, the trail welcomed the Plains Indians' footprints thousands of years ago. Jesse followed the ageless path. It was easy to see and even fallen tree limbs could not conceal the way. Jesse always kept a watchful eye for deer. Their numbers had dropped, but the white tails were hardy and on occasion, Jesse was given an encounter.

By fall, the current of the river had slowed. A twig tossed in the main channel would appear still, then almost imperceptibly begin to move, its progress noted by its relation to a fixed limb on the far shore. Where the channel would narrow, a small riffle on the surface could be noted, then as the water widened and the riffle disappeared, a deep pool would form. Here, life would gather. A turtle stared at Jesse from near the shore but its head was so dark its eyes could not be seen. Snakes were plentiful, but not often seen. Most were harmless, but occasionally the deadly cottonmouth moccasin would enter the pool from a low hanging branch. The few Jesse had seen had created a shiver of root fear, so deep he would have nightmares for weeks.

It was in these pools that the North Canadian held its treasure. Along with suckers, shiners, and chad, swam the catfish. Jesse had once seen the skeleton of a thirty-pounder caught by the old man Shaw. He had never caught one over five pounds, but even a five pounder was a feast and one that allowed Jesse to feed his family a supper's worth of meat. He would take a simple single hook and a twelve-foot length of line, and tie the line to a fresh green limb broken from a willow or a cottonwood. That was the only tackle he needed. Insects or a small frog were his bait. He would allow the line, weighted with a small rock, to settle in these deep pools and then wait. He could usually land one or two, but it could take all day. His mother would always give him a big kiss and brag to Jesse's delight how her little boy put meat on the table.

Jesse knew these pools and the life inside them. He knew they could disappear, move downstream, merge with others or for some unknown reason, not hold these prized fish. Fishing was not on his mind as Jesse approached the spring. A bank of limestone rose twelve feet above a flat grassy patch. An oxbow of the river had long ago shaped the stone, then the channel shifted, leaving this stonewall of ashlars standing above the river. The river mud of the cut-off oxbow had slowly been reclaimed with sedges and horsetails and tall prairie grass. At the base of the stonewall, a spring ran cool and clean. It gathered in a clear pebble lined pool drained by a small rivulet, which, after a few yards, was consumed by the grassy patch, which did not allow it to enter the river as a whole. Jesse took deep drinks satisfying his dusty thirst, then washed his face and arms past his elbows. Refreshed, he slowly raised his eyes to the trees, giving him shade.

Above the limestone wall, the deeply grooved trunks of the cottonwoods accentuated their tall columnar shape. These mature and beautiful trees reached sixty feet, and their highest branches stretched to meet a like row of trees lining the near bank of the river across this grassy patch. High above, the leaves from the two rows of trees almost touched, giving a high ceiling of flickering leaves. The fall colors, long hidden in the leaves, now shown as yellows and golds, and their gentle movement filtered the blue light from above, darkening to a deep lapis as the sun began to hide below the earth.

The shorter days would allow the temperature to drop quickly and Jesse countered by buttoning his wool shirt and thinking perhaps his mother had been right. Jesse brought his gaze down from the ceiling of this gold and blue apse and was surprised to see a camp along the far wall of trees.

A table and three wooden folding chairs surrounded a fire pit, the source of a faint thin thread of smoke curling upward like incense. He walked forward with no hesitation and saw a car in the darker shadows of the trees. The car had followed a path from outside the grassy clearing and was able to enter by carefully snaking between the trees. Jesse recognized the car as a new Packard touring car. It had four doors, a fabric top, and a big spare tire mounted on the left side enclosed in black metal to match the high gloss black of this impressive automobile. The oversized fenders flowed into large running boards, and on these were strapped matching black metal storage trunks. A small two-wheeled trailer was still attached. It had a wooden frame also in glossy black and was crossed by two shiny brass straps. Jesse thought it looked like a coffin.

He walked to the Packard and ran his hand along the smooth steel of the curved fenders and smelled the rich leather interior. He then turned and walked back to the center of the camp and, on a long foldable table, saw why this car was parked along the banks of the North Canadian. Lying on an oiled tarp was the largest catfish Jesse had ever seen. He figured it at forty to fifty pounds and a full four feet long. It was very fresh. No insects were present, and its grey sides and white belly were still moist. Its eyes were open and the great fish looked as if it only needed legs to return to the river. Along its right side, sharp cuts had been made and the best filets removed.

The fire ring below the table held hot glowing embers roofed by an iron grate. To the side of the grate, away from the hottest part of the fire, a round cast iron pan held a large filet. Popping bubbles of hot oil told Jesse it was cooked and ready. The filet had a thin breading covering the white meat. The wonderful scent and Jesse's hunger enticed him to come closer, and he was rewarded with a unique and lasting pleasure. He reached and quickly broke free a large piece of flesh and tossed it whole into his mouth. From that point on, all fish would be compared to that one bite. The unusual flavor and the setting in the cottonwood apse, all helped focus his senses forever on this delightful and pleasurable moment. It was seared into his memory and into his palate. It was only after he had swallowed that Jesse felt the pain. At first he thought it was the spices, but then he realized the roof of his mouth had been burned. The hot oil had raised a painful blister. Jesse yelled a few words appropriate for a twelve-year-old then a very distinct, "Goddamn!" as he tried to find water.

"Hey there, you all right?" rang a voice from somewhere.

Jesse could not see the speaker but reacted apologetically speaking to no direction. "I didn't hurt nothin'. I was just tastin' your fish. Honest, I didn't hurt nothin'." Slowly, he focused on two figures emerging from the trees.

The same voice in a calming tone spoke again. "Did you burn yourself? Here take some water." The man handed Jesse a canteen, and Jesse quickly soothed his burned palate with the cool spring water.

"Obliged," said a calmer Jesse as he handed the canteen back.

The two tall men were dressed in dark woolen pants tucked inside high-laced leather boots. Suspenders creased their woolen shirts, one a solid blue, the other a faded yellow. The man who had spoken had a mustache, the other was clean-shaven. The man in blue with the mustache stepped toward the table with the great fish and with a sweeping hand ending towards Jesse spoke.

"Welcome to our camp."

"I'm awful sorry to barge in like this and take a piece of your fish. Honest, I didn't hurt nothin'." Jesse was still nervous and wouldn't have been surprised if the men had been angry.

The man in yellow now spoke and his voice was also calm and assuring.

"We're glad you had some, young man. We'd had our fill. You came at a perfect moment. Did you like it?" he asked, and seemed curious what a twelve-year-old boy thought.

"I'll tell you mister. It's the best I ever ate."

"Here, have another piece," the man offered.

Jesse's one taste would have to last forever. Jesse could never duplicate the flavor and he was never able to explain a taste so wonderful. "No thanks, Sir. My mouth still burns, but I'd take another drink of water."

The man in blue handed him the canteen.

"What's your name, Son?"

"Jesse."

"J-e-s-s?" he spelled.

"No Sir, J-e-s-s-e," Jesse spelled his name.

"Not Jess-ee?" said the man in blue, carefully enunciating the two syllables.

"No Sir, not Jess-ee, just Jess," he answered, perplexed with the interest in his name.

"Well, Jesse, I'm Mike and this here is Gabe."

Jesse didn't care how they spelled or said their names. "Nice to meet you and thanks again for the fish and water. Where you from?"

"St. Louis," Mike answered.

Jesse had of course heard of the place, but it might as well have been New York City. It was beyond his sphere of familiarity and blended into other exotic sites east.

Gabe spoke now, "We're here because we'd heard of your river and its great fish. Mike and I and our other friend have a love of the West, so we take a trip each year. Landing a big cat and bagging a few quail were this year's goals."

"But what do you do?" Jesse was trying to comprehend this new idea of leisure and was not quite sure how it figured in with work.

"Oh, we're in sales. Travel all over. Work for the Bell Telephone Company. We were in Oklahoma City last year and heard stories of a great river close by. Decided to come here and see for ourselves."

Jesse appreciated the straightforward telling of their background. On the same day, three adults had treated him as a young man. He was pleased, took a long breath, and nodded his head a little. Gabe and Mike moved to the canvas chairs near the fire ring and sat down stretching their long legs toward the warmth of the coals. Gabe motioned for Jesse to take the third chair. He obliged and stretched his legs in a like manner.

He turned his attention to the two men now staring straight ahead toward the darkness of the trees. They could have been brothers, Jesse thought. Both had angular faces with long prominent, though pleasing noses. Mike's face was weathered, but Gabe's was noticeably smooth and evenly tanned. Jesse was relaxed and he initiated conversation.

"So you take a trip like this every year?"

After a short pause, Mike decided to answer for both. "Yes, for twelve years now we've headed west. We three get together, and one of us talks the other two into a trip he's been thinking about. This year, Gabe and I wanted to head to the former Indian Territory and see if the big catfish stories were true. Talked our buddy-" as he spoke his friend's name, a murder of crows, high in the cottonwoods, started a loud chorus of caws, drowning out Mike's voice.

"But he wanted to see Sioux Country and the Dakota Badlands," added Gabe.

"What do you think of Oklahoma?" asked Jesse.

"Well, look about you, Son. At this place and time, how could we not love Oklahoma?"

The sun had set and the earth's shadow had gathered all the individual shadows of trees and people together into one. The twilight had lit the lapis sky above the trees with a darkening golden hue.

"Yes," added Mike. "This is one of our finest resting spots. Not sure how we happened here though. We seem to be guided to beautiful places."

"Where else you been?"

Mike began. "Well, we've been all over the Rockies and clear to the Sierras. Been to West Texas and the Red River country, then out to Santa Fe. Saw the old churches and pueblos. Liked it so much, the next year just kept going west to the Navaho and Hopi lands. Saw a place called Walpi. I swear it's been there forever. Saw part of a sacred dance till an old man told us to leave. From there to the Grand Canyon and we just kept finding more places that called out to us. Saw the Holy Cross Mountain in Colorado three years ago, then two years past stumbled on a grizzly sow. We were fishing the Lamar River in the Yellowstone Park and came around a bend. She wasn't thirty feet away standing on her hind legs, sheltering her cub. She looked ten feet tall. We were motionless for a moment, didn't know what to do. Since she didn't do anything, we decided on the same course and for a minute we just took each other in with our eyes. Her snout shifted side to side and tipped up and down, but she was upwind and couldn't get a good scent. Finally she backed away, pushing her cub with her snout. I'll tell you what, Jesse, I was sure afraid, but at the same time I never felt so alive. Every breath I took went clear into my finger and toes."

Here Mike paused. He had been talking to himself as much as to Jesse. He called up the memory. "She remains the most beautiful animal I have ever seen."

Jesse's rapt attention was unbroken as he tried to imagine the great bear. He'd heard of a few black bears long ago in Oklahoma but these were a far cry from Mike and Gabe's mighty she-grizzly. "So you always head west?"

"Well, one year we went south to New Orleans," answered Gabe.

"Wonder whose idea that was?" laughed Mike with a loud rumble as he elbowed Gabe. They both laughed and shook their heads.

Jesse remembered Kurt's city of New Orleans and didn't understand the joke, but laughed anyway with his new friends. The three sat quietly for a moment, shifting their gaze from the glowing embers to the golden twilight above. Jesse stole a glance at Mike and Gabe. He felt great admiration, mixed with awe. He decided he too would have a life full of great beasts, exotic places, and fine smelling women. He imagined hunting the high Rockies for those great large deer, elk they are, and catching trout in fast moving streams. He would always drive a new automobile, and gather friends along his way. He would dress in leather and wool and steal the heart of some cowgirl at a Montana square dance. Yeah, Montana or maybe Colorado, or even this place here along the North Canadian. Maybe he could just go with Gabe and Mike. He could be their pal. Hell, he was only twelve, but he knew how to shoot and clean game. He could even drive with just a bit more practice, and he knew this country. Been all over four counties hauling freight with his pa. St. Louis might be far away, but it couldn't be all that far. He'd tell his folks. They'd be proud. Not like Newt. No, they wouldn't whip him and take him home. He was leaving for some place good, where a man could make it on his own. Where he would live story-to-story and his great adventures would grow in number and danger. That's what made the grizzly story so powerful for Jesse, the danger. Hell, that bear could have killed his friends, but it didn't. He thought of Newt getting whipped and maybe Bertha was a she-bear too. Never mind. Don't matter. It's all adventure and smells and it's all to come.

Jesse sat still and for a moment teetering between his Oklahoma reality and this new vision of penetrating beauty given to him by these visitors from a world beyond. The crisp snap of a breaking twig on the path by the Packard broke the contemplative quiet.

A second later an unsettling, "Goddamn quail!" reverberated through the camp. A huge shadow of a man came through the trees. His face caught light as he moved closer to the fire.

"Five hours and I got one goddamn bird."

"Welcome back," said Mike calmly. "We had some luck. Cut yourself a filet and toss it in the pan. It's as fine as you'll ever taste."

The man threw the bird towards the table and stood tall above the fire. With a little breeze, the coals had been fanned into flames and were licking the sides of the cast iron skillet causing the oil to start popping. Jesse could see the man now. He was very large and was wearing similar wool pants and leather boots. He wore no suspenders, and his red shirt had been pulled out of his pants and hung low to his crotch. It gave the appearance of a torso too large for the legs. His face was deeply wrinkled and his long dark hair was oily and hung loosely over his collar and ears. There was a white streak of hair behind the left ear. He had not shaved in several days and Jesse imagined if he got close enough, he would smell like the woods. He set a magnificent double barrel shogun against the cooler rocks of the fire pit. Jesse had never seen a finer gun.

"You went huntin' quail without a dog?" Jesse saw the problem immediately and was straightforward with his question. You just don't just walk around trying to scare up a covey without a dog to smell them out then go to point. Any fool knows that, he thought.

"You see a dog?" growled the man as he approached Jesse. He assumed a menacing posture. "Outta my chair, boy!" he barked.

Jesse was standing before the last word stopped resonating. "Sorry," he mumbled as he moved to inspect the gun.

The stock was carved from perfect walnut with subtle curves to fit large hands. The wood was dark but not dark enough to hide the lovely grain that gave it depth and contour. The metal of the receiver had an intricate etching of what looked to be something like an alligator, maybe a dragon, on its tail. Jesse couldn't quite figure it out, but it seemed out of place on such a gun. The polished twin barrels had a pewter glow and raised slightly between the two barrels was a flat piece of metal attached below by ribbing so that most of the space above the barrels was open.

"What's this on the barrels?" asked Jesse, intimidated, but not enough to stay quiet before the gun's secrets.

There was silence from the man.

"Hey Les, our friend Jesse asked you a question," interceded Mike. Jesse now knew the big man's name, but Les kept silent as he sliced a filet from the fish's side, dipped it in breading, and tossed it into the sizzling oil.

Mike answered for his big friend. "That's a ribbed barrel. Keeps the heat waves from the hot barrels from rising and distorting your aim. Also gives a better sight line, flat between the barrels. Ol' Les there is the best shot in Missouri. I promise you if he brought one bird back, he only fired that gun once."

Jesse turned to make eye contact with Les. He met Jesse's eyes and nodded. "Want me to clean your quail, Sir?" Jesse asked meekly.

"My bird. I'll tend it."

That ended any thought of leaving with Mike and Gabe. His initial fear of the big man had not passed and was now paired with an intense dislike of him. Jesse thought him capable of great harm and wondered why Mike and Gabe traveled with him. Jesse walked to Mike then to Gabe and shook their hands.

"Where you headed?" asked Gabe.

"Home now."

"Careful as you go," said Gabe as he gently patted Jesse on the shoulder.

"Thanks, you too." Jesse left the shelter of the trees and headed east above the river. He could easily follow the trail for a mile and, at a small draw, turn north toward home.

As Jesse entered the kitchen through the open screen door, his mother said, "You missed supper." She turned her head from the sink and the just cleared remnants of the supper table and gave him a welcoming smile.

"I ate already." As he walked past his mother she touched his head softly.

Jesse told Floyd about meeting Newt but before he told of the three men, Floyd walked away, thinking that was the end of the day's recap. Jesse started to call him back to hear the rest, then thought, just as well. He retold the story to himself before falling asleep.

CHAPTER 7
CURVES OF INA

In 1915, Jesse had heard his parents and others talk about the war in Europe, but he had no idea of the slaughter occurring across the Atlantic. He had plenty on his mind. He was in the middle of a big growth spurt and was well over five feet with a muscular chest tapering to a small waist. He had no fat or softness in his youthful body, and his arms showed their developing strength with curves defining the hardening muscles. He had a very light growth of facial hair, but had not begun shaving. A gaze at Jesse always began and ended at his crisp blue eyes. Girls looked at him and whispered approvingly as he passed.

Jesse would do his share of chores and help his father try to farm the quarter section, but his farming interests and talents were less than his father's. The Sheets' reputation as mediocre farmers was well earned. Why work that hard on a fragile young plant when freeze, hail, or a flooding rain could wipe out all your labor in one stormy day. Even as a thirteen-year-old, Jesse understood that his parents lived on the rented farm simply because they wanted to remain tied to their, or at least his mother's, romanticized view of how a person should live, free and on the land. The fact that they actually had to earn a living and provide for their five children from this land presented a problem. A problem solved long ago by hauling freight.

His mother's earlier admonitions to stay in school, go to church, and farm the land, had lost out to his father's joyful embrace of earthly delights. Jesse remembered one evening when his proud father wore his new spats till bedtime, showing Anna and his children his fine new style. His mother just shook her head. Jesse's little sister, Grace, was left to choose her own path, and Jesse could see his mother was losing that battle also. Jesse's oldest brother Edwin, seemed willing to work for some long-term goal, and his mother was very proud of his choices. But everyone, even his mother, could see that Edwin was lacking in joy. He expressed little happiness. If there was ever any doubt about staying on this humorless path, his new wife, Ina, made sure the road was followed.

Edwin, Ina, and their baby Helen were to have noon dinner with the Sheets before heading to the Jennings' for a large supper gathering with a few North Canadians, an informal group of ten or twelve families that farmed the north side of the North Canadian River. Summer's Sundays were usually composed of some combination of family or friends, and the whole Sheets family was excited to host Edwin and his new family. The midday meal was the largest of the day and Anna was preparing a feast. Jesse asked why they were eating earlier than usual and his mother told him that Edwin and Ina were attending an evening meal with the Jennings. He thought he sensed a hurt in her answer and figured it was because they had not been invited.

Jesse heard the Model T chugging up the narrow lane before he saw it. Edwin was working in El Reno at an automobile service and gasoline station. Talked of buying it. Buying a two-year-old Model T seemed only natural, and this Sunday visit was to show his new daughter and the automobile to his family.

Jesse was the first out the door and held the car door for Edwin as he proudly stepped out of the automobile. Jesse jumped behind the wheel and took in the interior. Ina was still seated, holding their new baby as she gathered her things. Ina looked at Jesse and extended a warm greeting.

"Good morning, Jesse."

"Mornin' Ina. Helen's sure a cute one." Jesse was easy to talk to and always had a quick friendly word.

"Well thank you. God has blessed us with a perfect little girl."

"You're sure lucky, you and Edwin."

"We're not lucky, we're blessed."

Jesse didn't hear the difference.

Anna had prepared a lavish meal of pot roast and plenty of fixings. She had purchased the meat in town the previous day and it had been slow cooking all morning. Jesse knew his mother would prepare a delicious meal. She always changed her offerings by adding a few unusual flavors. Today's special ingredient was lemon and its citrus sharpness mixed wonderfully with the deep earthy aroma of the roast. Anna had just removed the roast from its heavy iron pot and placed the steaming tender meat at the table's center.

The old six-legged oak table with eight straight back oak chairs had been Anna's hosting center for years and was showing its age, but she lovingly kept her dining room the cleanest and most welcoming area of her home. Parallel to the long table, along the solid wall, was an oak buffet holding her prized china. Jesse was surprised to see these treasured possessions being used today. They were rarely offered for any but the most special guests. In the corner, near the door from the kitchen, were two simple ash chairs and along the far wall was Anna's upright piano, cut from beautiful quarter-sawn oak. It reflected Anna's love of the arts and her failed attempts to teach them to her children. There were better pianists in the county, but Anna's face took on a serious countenance when she played her favorite hymns. Jesse took his piano lessons even less seriously than his schooling, but somehow picked up the harmonica and could accompany himself as he skipped around the parlor in his original choreography. Charles loved it. Anna did too and had to admit that Jesse could be quite the entertainer.

It had become infrequent for the entire family to gather for a meal, so today Anna played the role of grand hostess. Surrounded at the table by her five children, husband, and now a beautiful daughter-in-law and granddaughter, she wanted to enjoy this day and the memory it would imprint. Jesse sat straight backed on his chair and appeared slightly taller than he was. The table was quiet at first.

All were admiring the creamed corn, beets, green beans, fresh bread, butter, cherry jam and two large pitchers of sweet tea. After Anna offered grace, the calm was broken.

"Pa, tell me how the farm's doing. Did you sell that new litter of pigs yet?" asked Edwin.

"Farm's doing good, Son. Looks like I'll put as much in wheat as I can. People say the price is going up cause there's no end in sight to the war," said Charles.

"I don't want my boys going to fight someone else's war. We'll sell 'em wheat and corn and can our beef for 'em, but they can't have my boys." Anna was never shy.

"May come a time we'll have to rethink that Anna, but for now, let's just pray we don't get pulled in," added Ina. The men nodded in agreement, and in that, welcomed Anna and Ina into such a serious discussion.

Jesse was not included in this talk, so his mind and gaze drifted across the table towards Ina. Jesse thought she was quite beautiful. She was tall and graceful and oval faced. Her smooth skin and shiny dark hair accentuated what Jesse deemed the perfect face. Her back was always erect and her shoulders kept straight or pulled back, further accentuating her breasts. His eyes fixed for a moment on her breasts. They were large and firm and round and a hint of cleavage appeared above the top button of her blouse. Jesse shifted his gaze quickly back to his brother so he wouldn't get caught staring.

Edwin was taller than average, but Jesse and everybody else knew he was not handsome. His mouth turned down at the corners and he never stood or sat up straight. This gave him a rather dull appearance, and coupled with his mumbley way of talking, well he was Jesse's big brother, but still, he just wasn't a girl's first pick. What a mystery Jesse had uncovered. He was sure he wasn't the first to ask, but why would a woman like Ina end up with someone like Edwin?

As the meal progressed, Jesse kept his gaze on Ina as much as he could without being obvious. He was relieved when she began to take over the conversation and he didn't have to steal a glance.

"Edwin and I are thinking about buying the shop. The owner, Abrams, says there's just too much to keep up on. Edwin now, he reads and knows all there is to know about automobiles. Think he'd do just fine."

"Nothing much changes out here, Ina, but change happens so fast in town, hard to follow," Charles said with some sadness in his tone.

"Edwin can manage all that real fine now, can't you Edwin?" said Ina.

After a short pause, Edwin agreed, "Sure can."

Charles and Anna addressed their questions to Ina, not Edwin. Jesse noticed. Edwin accepted it. Jesse was pleased because now he could look at Ina while she was talking and no one would know what he was thinking. He looked at Ina and tried to imagine the shape of her body under her clothes, and wondered what a woman's breast really looked like.

Usually, after the dinner meal, the family would simply leave the table with little lingering, but today, after the dessert of sweet bread pudding, no one left for a while. The men pushed their chairs back from the table. Jesse did the same.

"So Edwin, you think I could drive your new automobile?" asked Jesse, now fully engaged in the conversation.

"Don't see why not, Brother. Are your legs long enough?"

"You know they're long enough. And I already know plenty 'bout automobiles," Jesse answered.

While Jesse and his brother kept up the friendly banter, their father was silent. He could talk about horses and wagons, but not the new automobile. Charles would never leave the farm and his children would never stay.

After a brief lull in the conversation, Ina announced their imminent departure for the Jennings' farm. The Sunday supper at his in-laws would be full of young neighbors and fun, so Edwin asked if Jesse if he would like to accompany them to the Jennings' half of the day. Jesse accepted immediately and looked forward to the raucous play of the Jennings and Hawkins and whoever else might show up. He might play with the boys his own age or maybe follow his big brother around. There were things to discover.

Anna and Charles extended warm goodbyes. Ina did not hug. She shook hands and dipped her head in thanks.

"Come along Edwin."

CHAPTER 8
THE JENNINGS' FIEFDOM

Jesse glided to the middle of the front seat before Ina could direct him to the back. He feigned interest in the starting sequence, a process he already knew, and awaited the contact of Ina's hips. Ina read Jesse's intentions and gave him an exaggerated bump with her hip, giving herself adequate room on her side of the front seat. She knew thirteen-year-old boys, and she knew Jesse would enjoy the ride.

Edwin drove the Model T west on the old section road. The late summer afternoon gave no indication of relinquishing its warmth. The bright sun hung high in a concave apse and its outstretched rays gave a grace filled light to the fertile land. Edwin drove slowly past two section roads, then turned south on the third. The drive to the Jennings' place was just a short way down this section road, and Edwin's Model T joined six other automobiles parked on the grass south of the house.

Edwin and Jesse exited on Edwin's side, but Ina remained seated and quiet. Her eyes and the memories behind them were enjoying this beautiful farm, her birthplace. The Jennings had been on this land for twenty-six years. Robert Jennings had recently purchased a second quarter section, including an old ox-bow of the

North Canadian, bordering his land on the south, and now owned three hundred and twenty acres. Come spring, these bottomlands would flood and coat the land with thick and rich red mud. The lower acres near the river were good for alfalfa and grazing but could not reliably support a cash crop of cotton, wheat, or corn because the flooded land would not dry out in time for planting. That suited Robert just fine. He liked this open land leading to the river just the way it was.

So did the nearby Arapahoes from Darlington. For many years they had returned to these bottomlands to set up a summer camp near the old ox-bow. The elders would camp here with their sons and try to return to a time past. The men would instruct their sons with bow and arrow and snares, trying to keep these fading skills alive. They would use canvas stretched over tree limbs as their summer shelter. Robert left them alone and they returned the privacy. All the Arapahoe knew Kurt, and knew the two men were friends, but they did not extend their hand to Robert. Robert let them know they were free to borrow any tools they needed, and they were always returned to his shed. His friend, Ed Shaw, thought Robert was daft to allow them on his land.

The slope of the land increased steadily as it stretched north. There was a large tree-filled draw separating the land into west and east halves. This crease in the land was not a solid woods, and in two spots the trees gave way to long grass so that the two halves were easily accessed. At the north end, the big draw flattened into solid grass stretching to the north property line, the old section road, now a county connecting road. This north section of forty acres was usually planted in winter wheat, allowing the stock to graze after the grass browned in the fall. Every few years Robert would rotate the wheat with corn or cotton.

Only a few generations earlier, this landscape was Pleistocene. It was untouched prairie with wolves, black bears, and an occasional plains grizzly living with the aboriginal people and competing as apex predators. Dark moving herds of bison followed the grass and its woods were full of deer and turkey. Flocks of migrating birds created flowing shadows on the grass, and above these huge flocks, hawks and eagles circled in great arcs. The big predators and the bison were gone now, but bobcats and coyotes still frequented the draws. Robert maintained these dark woods as a holdout for the predators. Maybe even a lone wolf, searching for a mate, would wander through some day. Ed Shaw thought he was just odd about those things.

Robert and his wife, Ida Emma, dead now six years, had settled their little corner of prairie, and as with each of their neighbors, they infused and animated their land in their own unique way. It retained its shape and texture, and for a time, most of its native grass cover. Their homestead presented as an ordered and self-sufficient village.

The two-story house, facing south, was white frame with dark green trim. Below the windows of the second floor, a broad sloping roof covered a deep porch that guests would enter before knocking on the green kitchen door. This large porch was the center of male interaction, paired with its female consort kitchen beyond the door. It had two comfortable rockers, painted the same green as the house trim, and men could bring additional chairs from the kitchen, find a box, sit on the floor with their legs dangling to the grass or find a spot on the concrete steps.

The large kitchen had gravity fed water to the big porcelain sink. Robert had made cabinets, pantries, and counters out of four different woods and these took up two sides of the room. Ida Emma had laid out the cabinet and counter design, utilizing the different shades of the woods as accents. They were lovely. Along another side were two stoves, one wood fired and one fed by carbide gas.

Robert had electrified the house the previous year, but kept the carbide tank and line to the kitchen. The old wood stove, rarely used anymore, usually held prepared food or even cut flowers. The comfortable living room was neatly furnished with padded chairs, a high back sofa, and a simple low table to hold a few books and the drinks of friends. A new Victrola sat proudly on a simple library table. A coal fired stove along a kitchen wall heated the entire house. The parlor on the east side had a rarely used door to the outside and housed two dark Eastlake chairs with a high table between them. Along the longest wall, was a simple upright piano, a house-raising gift from Ida Emma's parents, Newton and Carrie Myers. There was no second story above the parlor, giving the house an irregular and appealing roofline.

Mary Hawkins, Robert's second wife, had been widowed the same year Ida Emma died, and two years later she and Robert were married. Their bedroom was on the main floor, along the north side. Stairs left the kitchen to the two rooms above, one for girls and one for boys. They were heated by the coal stove's pipe that went through the girls' room and exited the roof above. The boys' room was always cooler. The children's rooms were furnished simply with beds, nightstands, a chest of drawers, and one armoire in each.

The grounds surrounding the house were ordered and neat. A few steps from the porch, the steel latticed windmill and nearby elevated water tank provided water for the house and the animal areas down the gentle hill. With a breeze, the turning blades sounded a soft comforting rhythm. If a strong wind arrived from a winter norther or a summer thunderstorm brought a gale, woe to the son who didn't lock the blades tight. A broken shaft was a major repair and if it was compounded by an omission of a Jennings' son, the darkness of Robert's anger would surface. The smoke house was a few steps beyond the windmill. There was a large expanse of grass that stretched two hundred feet farther south, towards an arrangement of five outbuildings. The largest was a hay barn and garage for the Jennings' automobile, tractor, and implements. A second large barn had seven horse stalls along one side with a center run separating the other half for feed, tack and a small shop with Robert's tools. There was an adjacent holding pen and shed, and across this pen was the small milking barn. South of the horse barn was an open sided building that sheltered excess hay or additional implements. The function of each structure gave the layout symmetry. Robert thought it was just the way it should be. No matter the weather, this was where Robert was to be found.

Just off the porch, the green grass outlined the white concrete domed storm cellar. It looked like a partially excavated sarcophagus, except for its slanted wooden door. The family would retreat here during the earth-shaking thunderstorms. Along the shelves were canned goods and candles and two decks of cards. Robert would always be the last one in, after quickly checking to make sure the windmill was locked tight. Beyond the north side of the house was the garden and just beside that, the hen house. It was called the hen house, but it had a collection of chickens, guinea fowl, geese, and turkeys. Most days, they would roam the grounds and Robert's dogs knew to leave them be.

The garden was the same dimension as the house. Mary and the girls grew a smorgasbord of corn, beans, peas, carrots, tomatoes, three or four types of melons, okra, radishes, lettuce, cucumber, and multiple annual surprises. Mary would study the seed catalogues by the winter stove and find an unusual plant. She delighted in trying eggplant, hot peppers, asparagus and once, some inedible gourds, just because she liked the way they looked. Fruit trees, three apple and three peach, formed the northern boundary of her garden. The one-hole outhouse was beyond this ring of produce and was moved every year to a new spot.

The farm could produce most necessities, and what it could not produce could be obtained by trade. Cash was raised by the crop grown on the north forty and by Robert's constant dealing. He was well known in Canadian County as the horse and cattleman. Most farmers had stock, but Robert brought his reputation from his days as a Texas cowboy and often fed this with an altered telling of a tale. He was known to buy and sell with significant profit. If a man didn't know the value of his stock and Robert did, well, "Knowin' not used is knowin' wasted."

A strong bond had developed between Robert and Kurt. The fall visit of Kurt riding his great Brahma bull, then an old mare after the bull died, and leading his small herd was one of Robert's favorite times. The fact that Kurt never had more than a couple of dozen head did not diminish his standing as an expert on cattle. Robert knew and valued Kurt's intellect like no other man in Oklahoma and treated him as a royal guest, even if he did sleep in the barn. Evenings after supper, the two would talk on the porch, long into the night, exchanging sacred knowledge.

These Jennings had their story woven with the land and its cycles. When Ida Emma died and was laid under its grass, and the weeping slowed then stopped, new stories began and the cycle continued. This was the Jennings' place, that Sunday afternoon in 1915.

Jesse had been standing quietly by Ina's open door and when she was ready to rise, she handed a bag of Helen's diapers and extra clothes to him. She rose tall and proud and cradled Helen in her arms. Jesse escorted her up the steps onto the porch and they entered the kitchen beyond. Her stepmother, Mary, their neighbors the Esteps and Shaws, and her sisters were helping to prepare the lavish meal. The youngest, Alice, had entered just before Ina and Jesse, and emptied her apron of fresh tomatoes on the broad wooden counter. Ina had helped raise Alice and the youngest child, Buck, after their mother, Ida Emma, had died. Alice and Buck remembered little of their mother, perhaps only a smell or a touch at night.

Jesse said a quick, "Hey," to Edna and Alice, set Helen's bag down, and backed out the kitchen door, to join the men who had gathered in the barn. Alice watched him run down the hill as he caught up with Edwin.

CHAPTER 9
GOURNAMAND

Edwin and Jesse entered the barn and as their eyes were adjusting to the light, they heard a sharp neigh. Yesterday, Robert's favorite gelding, excited by a clap of Autumn thunder, had run head down into a barbed wire fence. In the close confines of a stall, Robert was able to clean and dab some iodine on the forearm's open gash. The horse's audible displeasure continued until Robert was convinced the wound was clean and the muscle not torn. Stitches would have been placed but Robert had no way to hold the young gelding still. It would heal with a scar.

Robert stood tall and as he stretched his back he noticed Edwin standing behind the other men. "The new father has arrived, no gelding there."

The men gave a hearty laugh and the congratulations followed. Edwin lowered his head and mumbled, "Thanks."

Besides family, the guests included Ed Shaw and Bert Estep and their children. On another Sunday the gathering might be at their farms or at another North Canadian neighbor. They knew each other and their stories and some secrets. Their common story was the taming of the prairie and building a life on their land. Their houses, all wood frame and simple, held their wives and children and lives. Many of their children would marry neighbors, growing the prairie weft stronger.

Jesse stood with Edwin towards the back of the horse barn. He knew everyone present and all knew him. Jesse made eye contact with Newt and they gave each other a simple nod of recognition. Jesse was free to wander or find a mate and play or explore. He decided to look the place over and headed the short distance west to the upper draw. It was a wild place of a few acres, and Jesse was sure bobcats and coyotes used these woods as a regular hunting ground. He scrambled over a fence.

This pasture and the larger pasture to the south had never been plowed and still had a little native fescue and grama tall grass. The county agents were touting the farmers on the non-native Bermuda grass and had convinced Robert of its superiority for his stock. The Bermuda could be grazed short repeatedly and still grow back fast. The native tall grasses, once grazed, would take much longer to grow back. If a rancher overgrazed the native grass, it would never come back. Robert agreed, and three springs ago had a hundred acres drilled with Bermuda seed. The new invaders had taken hold and in a few more years the last of the tall grass would be gone. Jesse raked his hand along the tall seed stalks as he walked. Stopping with a hand full of seeds, he blew his hands clean and watched the ripe seeds fall to their new earth. Where the undergrowth began, he stopped and sat down.

The draw drained south toward the old oxbow of the river, not far from the place Jesse had met the three men from St. Louis. Jesse was contemplating a hike down the game trail, leading through the undergrowth in front of him, when he heard his name called. Edna was standing at the fence Jesse had just climbed, and was motioning him to come her way. Jesse arose with curiosity and retraced his steps.

Edna was the second youngest daughter, the smartest and the most delicate. She was four years older than Jesse but because of her slight frame, they looked about the same age. She was still in school, as were the other school age Jennings' children. Edna was the child her mother, Ida Emma would say, "Took after no one." Robert and Ida Emma recognized their child as wonderfully unique. Her imagination was uncontained and the only way to express her discoveries was to herself. She wrote. She wrote journals, stories, plays, dialogues of famous people, filling her life with a complexity her siblings and parents could not imagine.

Fortunately, her parents, even her brothers and sisters, allowed her to express herself, and after evening meals, Mary would sometimes ask Edna to read a page from her story journal. The family would pull their chairs back, pour another glass of sweet tea and indulge this wonderful child. Of course poetry and fiction were favorites of the girl, and trips to the Carnegie Library in El Reno gave her the opportunity to read Dickenson, Alcott, Teasdale, and Yeats. Some nights she imagined herself as Lord Byron's bride of Abydos. The library was a haven for Edna, and she could read books like *The Scarlet Letter* there, so she wouldn't have to answer awkward questions at home. She also indulged in romantic novels and their predecessors, tales of Middle Age chivalry. She was well versed in Arthurian legends and the history of England and Europe.

Jesse placed one hand on a wooden fence post, and then easily swung his body over the top wire, a little show for Edna. She greeted him warmly. Her wispy brown hair flecked with red almost begged accompanying freckles, and she and her little sister, Alice, had plenty.

"You're just the man I'm looking for," she said as she took his hand and started walking briskly towards the house. Jesse liked the feel of her hand and kept up the pace. She continued, "I've written a short play and I need a leading man. You shall be he."

Jesse's knowledge of this thing called a play was limited to church and school pageants. He didn't much care to be a Wise

Man or a pioneer in a silly hat and fake beard, and slowed his pace but kept hold of Edna's hand. "I don't think I'm the right one for your play."

"Nonsense, you're just perfect," she countered. "I need a dashing knight to rescue a fair lady from the evil sorcerer."

Jesse had no idea what a sorcerer was, but figured it wasn't good. Then again, if he got to rescue Edna, perhaps he could give it a try.

"You see, the maiden has been captured and locked in a tower. The sorcerer guards the tower while the maiden's unicorn circles, crying for her maiden to be set free."

Jesse knew of unicorns and figured the magical beast could talk if it wanted to. "Okay, I guess I'll be your knight."

Edna began. "Alice will play the unicorn, Amis. I've made a costume for her." It was an old hat that Edna had sewn a tubular white fabric looking more like a bleached carrot than a single horn. Imagination was required. As they approached the smoke house tower, Alice waited anxiously, shifting her weight from one hip to the other. She was very excited to have such an important part in her sister's play. Her hat costume covered all of her forehead.

Although separated by seven years the two sisters looked very alike. Alice had Edna's features, but in a more robust version. She was not the quiet, introspective child like her sister, but an engaging, active little girl. Her father and Mary had given her confidence at a very young age, and she spoke with a vocabulary and directness beyond her years. She idolized Edna, and Edna treated Alice as a kindred spirit. Between these two freckled sisters, there would be no secrets.

The fourth actor in the play was Maud, the third oldest sister, four years Edna's senior and no longer interested in childhood fantasy. Edna had to use her best persuasive skills to convince Maud to play the role of Blanche. She was smitten by John Hawkins, the oldest of Mary's children, and didn't want her budding courtship interrupted by Edna's play.

Jesse's initial inclination to flee had passed when he realized he would be alone with these three girls, acting the dashing young knight. Edna passed out handwritten scripts, only two pages each, to her little group of thespians. When she gave Jesse his script, she added an odd afterthought. "Jesse, if you'd like to make any changes, just go ahead and say what you feel."

Jesse looked the script over quickly. His reading skills and a few strange words made him nervous. Edna began arranging the actors. Maud, the damsel Blanche, would remain in the smoke house. Edna opened the door, but kept Maud in the shadows. Edna had tied a pink ribbon in her hair, the ends trailing to her waist. Alice, Amis the unicorn, began to circle the smoke house nervously, scanning the horizon for the Savior Knight to appear. Edna cast herself as Gournamand, the imprisoner of Blanche.

The scene opens with Amis running to the unnamed knight.

"Oh Sir Knight, Milady is imprisoned against her will in yon tower. You, Noble Sir, must rescue her."

The knight replies stiffly, "Lead me to your lady, magical beast."

Quickly, Alice hands Jesse a stick and whispers, "Here's your sword."

Jesse takes the sword, raises it over his head and walks resolutely towards the tower. "Evil captor!" he cries. "Ready ahead. Release fair maiden or prepare to die!"

At the open door of the smoke house, a bored Maud tries to feign distress. "Oh release me from these tower walls and allow me to enter the world."

Gournamand walks confidently towards the knight, unarmed with palms open. "Why, Sir Knight, do you threaten this kingdom?"

"I challenge any man who holds such fair maiden against her wishes."

Taking another step toward the knight, Gournamand outstretches his hands and raises them, further accentuating his vulnerability. "I will release Blanche to a worthy knight, a knight with courage, strength, and wisdom. Are you such a man?"

Jesse looked deeply into Edna's eyes and wanted to ad lib, "I'm him. I will prove myself worthy." He took a breath, but the words never came. He looked down at the script. "Prepare to die!"

Gournamand slowly begins to circle the knight. "Well, Brave Knight, I see you have courage and you appear most strong, but where is your wisdom?"

"I shall find wisdom, once fair Blanche is free from yon tower."

Gournamand takes another step towards Knight Jesse. He reflexively takes a matching step back.

"Brave Knight, you are the one hundredth knight summoned to this tower by Amis." Alice smiled. "All showed courage and strength, but none has shown wisdom. Brave Knight, Blanche is not my captive, she is my daughter and she remains here waiting for the Wise Knight.

"The Wise Knight must ask, 'Why is fair maiden in this tower?' Wisdom, Brave Knight, must precede courage and strength. Return here again to win her hand when Brave Knight has found wisdom."

Jesse looked at his script. The play was over. His lines ended. He wanted to tell Gournamand he was ready but lacked the courage to say his own lines. Lines that would tell Gournamand and Blanche and the silly Amis that he knew more than all the neighborhood knights. His courage would protect the kingdom and wisdom would be his guide. But he didn't. He dropped his sword, turned and walked away.

Jesse's retreat carried him quickly down to the barn. The men were standing near the large door talking and paid him no mind as he joined the gathering. Behind him, walked Ina. She stopped at the fence enclosing the barn area and announced supper was ready. Not waiting for a reply, she turned and walked back to the house. The men knew to come when called, so they wasted no time and started for the house. Robert walked in tandem with his three neighbors, Ed Shaw, Bert Estep, and John Turner and their adult sons. Edwin walked with Robert's two oldest sons, Newt and Jack.

The men entered the spacious kitchen and took seats preordained from previous suppers, but there remained one untaken chair. Jesse took a bold move and quickly sat down. No one seemed to notice. He was seated with the men. They were fed first, attended by wives and daughters. Because of the mixed audience, the topics shifted to crops, weather, and general news of the country. All these could be discussed within earshot of the women and sometimes the women would join the conversation. Mary would add a "Yes, Dear," or an "Oh my". Often she would smile if Robert cracked a joke.

Ina was always quick to comment, and on multiple occasions would freely disagree or criticize the prevailing table views. She was the first daughter of a North Canadian to graduate High School and her confidence continued to swell. She could handle her new husband and no man would silence her.

Edna, still too young to breach the men's table talk, would whisper her comments, humorous or perhaps sarcastic, into the receptive ears of her sisters. Their responding giggles often caught the attention of the men. Most may have thought, "Silly girl."

Normally the noon dinner was the largest meal, but since this was a festive gathering, celebrating Helen's birth, it had been skipped and all the efforts of these three families went into the preparation of a feast. The fast was broken. Pitchers of sweet tea were at the table's ends and loaves of fresh baked and sliced bread were placed on two large platters. Alongside each loaf was a pat of butter, churned by the daughters the day before. Each was pressed in a wooden butter mold with a pineapple design. The table was crowded with bowls of carrot slices, sweet and dill pickles, beets, pickled okra, and tomato wedges. Chilled on ice, you could hear their freshness as the men bit into these bounties. Green beans, creamed corn, and Mary's favorite eggplant were placed in smooth white ceramic bowls, but the center of the table was reserved for large plates stacked high with fried chicken and ham.

Each wife had a variation on these common meats, rarely written down. Mary's chicken had a finely ground red pepper in the meal and she made sure the lard was bubbling hot before dropping the pieces into the pan. Splatter was the rule but by keeping the lard hot, it didn't penetrate so quickly, leaving the breading crisp and the meat moist and sweet. The ham, cured where the damsel Blanche had been imprisoned, was a lightly salted, thick piece of meat enjoyed best with molasses gravy.

The kitchen was silent as Robert said a short blessing, "Lord, bless this bounty and bless our family and our friends gathered here today. Amen."

The men were hungry. They served themselves generous proportions, and began eating as soon as the food touched their plates. Their manners were decent and rural, and they offered multiple compliments to the women. They all tucked their napkins at their chins, all except Edwin. Ina had advised him that the city men kept their napkins on their lap. When the men had finished, there was no lingering. They were ushered out of the house, coffee to be served later. Now a cascade of children circled the table. Some cleaned the dirty dishes while others restocked the bread, vegetables, and meat. Extra chairs were squeezed in and if need be, two smaller children would share a chair. Manners were in flux dependent upon ages. The older girls sometimes took a motherly role and gave instruction to the younger children. They were grudgingly accepted or completely ignored.

When the children had finished, they were herded outside for a treat. Robert and Newt had just added rock salt to the wooden drum and asked for volunteers to churn the soon-to-be ice cream. All the youngsters willingly took their turns. As the cream hardened, the boys tried to show their muscle. Mary brought three fruit pies, two apple and a peach already cut into eighths, and set them on the back concrete steps with spoons and plates. The men and children would have to fend for themselves. It was the ladies' time at the meal table. The three older women along with their three married daughters took their places around the reset and resupplied table. Laughter outside drifted in and became a background of contentment for the ladies. Ina opened her blouse and nursed Helen. The conversation was mother's milk and all things domestic.

These three families were prospering. The war in Europe, now in its second year, had driven up prices for their cash crops and the ladies, always good money managers, had extra to spend and save. A piano at the Esteps, a new chandelier at the Shaws, and numerous cash stuffed coffee cans at all the households were this year's bounty. All the families had accounts at the bank in town but these were for holding just enough money for payments on equipment or automobiles if needed. All daily transactions were handled in cash and each of these practical women knew the meaning of a rainy-day fund.

Robert and Mary had over two thousand dollars hidden in coffee cans and books. Robert held title to three hundred twenty acres, and had three rental houses in town. The largest was the Jennings' boarding house for their children who had graduated from the eighth grade at the Elm Glen School and were enrolled at El Reno High. Depending on the weather they would be driven to town early Monday mornings and return to the farm Friday nights.

The Jennings, the Esteps, and the Shaws were recognized as successful, along with most of the North Canadians, but there was never any hint of exaggerated pride or hubris. The Sheets, though well liked, lived month to month with little to show and little to save. They were not invited to these smaller more intimate feasts, but at larger gatherings and school events, were greeted warmly and treated like the friends they were. The Shaws were the bridge between the North Canadians and the Sheets, and remained close friends with the Sheets. Even the marriage of their oldest children would not bring the Sheets and Jennings closer.

The women sat around the table long after the meal was finished and reveled in these moments of friendship. Outside, the children were anxiously circling the ice cream drum when Newt pronounced it ready. Edna passed out the pie, and Maud doled out the magnificently cold ice cream. Soon all were served, and soon there was no trace of the pies or of the cold treat. The children drifted away leaving the four older men, their oldest sons, and a curious Jesse.

The four men were seated in chairs while their sons sat on wooden boxes or on the floor with their legs dangling to the grass below. Jesse picked a spot near Newt, to the side of Robert. He liked and wanted to know Newt better, but Robert intimidated him and he didn't want to be in his direct line of sight. Jesse looked at Robert's profile. He was forty-seven and carried his tall muscular form in a way that people took notice. Jesse didn't think much about a man being handsome or not, but there was something about Robert that Jesse respected. Maybe it was the way his bushy brows protected his eyes and the intensity within.

The afternoon warmth had peaked and the sun was beginning to dip below the tall trees of the draw west of the house. Five miles due south across the river, the huge concrete grain elevators of El Reno were catching the last of the sun's light and reflecting a hot white glow. The men brought out their pipes and Bert Estep offered each a plug of new tobacco he had just purchased in Oklahoma City. The group was silent until the pipes took fire.

"Prices look good for wheat this fall," Robert stated factually.

"Pickard sold his crop on the come this spring for thirty percent less than it's worth sitting in his field today. Poor fool," Estep added.

"We'd be the fools if prices had gone south. Pickard got a good price and he'll do fine, but we'll do better," Robert said with a smile. "Only thing to stop us now is hail. If it don't hail, we'll have our best year. Pray it don't hail."

All nodded in agreement. Bert Estep said an amen.

"Bet you wish you'd put part of your new one sixty in wheat," Ed Shaw said to Robert. "I'd be worth a pretty penny."

"Thought about it. But even if it didn't get flooded out, I need the pasture. You know I like ranchin' better than farmin', and the new quarter give me more grass and alfalfa. Plan to mix some cattle up and see if I can improve my yearling steer weight." Robert's keen eye had shown him the characteristics to breed for, and the most important to a cattleman is the first year's growth. An extra ten to twenty pounds is gravy.

Ed Shaw kept the topic going. "You know you can make more dollars per acre farming, Robert. Why keep the grass and the risk of disease or rustling or whatever else can take an animal?"

Robert looked at his neighbor with kindness and agreement. He took a slow draw from his pipe. At the foot of the steps, Jesse was drawn into this dialogue between these thoughtful men. They were discussing how to make a living by using their own initiative, an acquired understanding of agriculture, economics, and what Robert called, "passing the trait." Jesse heard these words of accomplishment, even excitement, and wished he could be part of it.

Robert added a new dimension. "I didn't break the sod because I wanted the grass. You know it'd been farmed for ten years after the Run of '89, but since then, the old grass come back, and it looks like it did thirty years ago. You walk down a row of cotton or corn and you can pull up the whole plant with your hands. Try that with grass. Can't do it. Won't come out. Those roots, so deep in the sod. Kurt tells me of the old Arapahoes huntin' the buffalo in Colorado long before the Civil War. The elders told him of huge herds takin' days to pass. They'd eat the grass and churn up the earth with their hooves and crap, and three months later the grass was growd back and greener than before. Only thing that kills the grass is our own cattle. Don't that seem odd? I know I could pull more dollars with wheat, but I need the grass."

"Robert still thinks he's riding Station." The words were spoken by Kirk John Turner, Ida Emma's uncle. John, or Uncle John as he was sometimes called, and his older sister Carrie Myers, Ida Emma's mother, ran the farm northeast diagonally across from the Jennings. After the death of her beloved daughter, Ida Emma, then of her husband, Newton, Carrie had retreated into unhappy solitude with her two adopted children. She had become bitter and unpleasant to be around and had stopped coming to the Jennings for regular visits. Robert treated her with respect but after multiple invitations were refused or unanswered, he honored her quiet. Her brother John remained a close friend of Robert and the two shared much.

John continued, "Just like it was in '84. Robert, some of your guests don't know about you and Station."

"We all got stories, John. Me and Station's just another."

"I'd like to hear about this horse. I think it musta been what give your eyes the edge," Bert asked sincerely.

Robert gazed south across the river. He took a slow draw of his pipe, turned, and looked at each of his friends and his sons. It had been a long time since he'd last told his story and there were new faces around the porch. Robert began slowly.

CHAPTER 10
STATION

Southern Missouri was never a prosperous place and in the years after the Civil War, not much seemed to change. The Jennings' farm outside Lebanon was better than subsistence, but not by much. Robert's parents, John and Martha, were resourceful and kept their family of seven well cared for and fed. Education was never stressed, and the three boys and two girls learned most at their mother's side or in the fields with their father. School was dutifully attended for a few years then faded from their routine. The county was stagnating and seemed to affect its residents in a like manner. The settling of Missouri had occurred generations ago, and there was little chance of land for the many sons reaching adulthood.

The Jennings' forty acres was a mix of cash crops and a few stocks of beef and dairy cattle along with the usual pigs and chickens. Most of the forty was planted in cotton, but every four years, John would grow corn. Robert hated the cotton. He hated everything about it from the planting to the weeding, but most of all, he hated the picking. Come fall, he would pull a canvas bag over his shoulder and down the long rows he would stumble, picking each tuft by hand. Every fiber grown was hand-picked, leaving the poor sucker who was forced to do this goddamn job with sore hands, a sore back, and a sour disposition. He hated the goddamn cotton.

Robert was the oldest son and the quiet one. His father did fatherly things and his mother did motherly things. One fatherly thing Robert caught was whipping. There was little thought given to the seriousness of the infraction. You messed up; you got whipped. A leather harness left out in the rain or a calf dropped during a rainstorm and dying in the mud; he got whipped. It didn't much matter if Robert had anything to do with the cause. His father's self-imposed rules were simple: no face, not much blood, no bones broke. Just an ass whipping. His father's rage would dictate how many strokes and how hard. This was all well within the norm of the times and, as a young boy, Robert took it, as did all of his neighbors and friends and brothers. Robert hated two things in his young life: picking cotton and getting whipped. He was no different from any other boy. He just decided to do something about it.

His mother had an open heart and a loving counsel. She consoled and comforted and made him feel loved. She would tell him he was too sensitive, that he should toughen up. But with no pause in her counsel, she also told Robert it was okay to see things differently. One evening, after Robert had been whipped by his father for spilling a bucket of grain, his mother took him aside.

"Robert, you're not obliged to stay in any one man's shadow. These old Missouri hills can still sprout a good man. Be that good man, Robert." That was a tender moment for Robert, and it would always remain in his memory.

In 1884, sixteen-year-old Robert was finishing a growth spurt and beginning to shave. He was already over six feet and had developed a firm body, not rippled muscles but a leanness holding great strength in each taut muscle. He struck a determined pose and held himself erect. His chestnut hair was unkempt, but he tried to keep it combed back to cover his ears. Ears that he thought stuck out too far so he usually wore a western hat. Better than a farmer's small brimmed hat, it became part of his silhouette. His smooth forehead led to thick eyebrows overhanging intense blue eyes. His face was set hard with his jaw line visible its entire length under tight skin. The girls thought him a nice look, but he was not the type to set them in a twitter. As he would pass a young lady, he would usually lower his head and mumble a greeting. Some thought he might be slow in the head, but he was just shy.

In quiet moments, Robert would try to figure out just how he folded into his Southern Missouri world. What was he going to do, and where would he be in a few years? His time devoted to such weighty thoughts proved fruitless, and Robert became heavy with despair. He felt that his friends' jovial spirits and easy laughs would perish into doom if they knew the truth. They had no land, no money, no schooling, and worst of all, no future. He saw these things so clearly. Why was he the only one to have these thoughts? He was carrying the dark secret himself and not one of his neighbor friends understood he was carrying this darkness for them too. He felt he was helping his friends by remaining silent and carrying their unrealized hopelessness, and in this resolve, he grew even more distant from friends and family.

The winter of 1884 was a bad one. No one starved, but a wave of flu swept through the county. It wasn't as virulent as previous strains, but took some elderly and a young neighbor. Robert's family was spared, but the three funerals the family attended further weakened his spirit. After the funeral of a six-year-old neighbor girl, Robert spent the following day in bed. He feigned a stomachache but his mother suspected the truth. A wet spring kept the planting delayed for three weeks, setting his father on the worry path. The worry was accompanied by anxiety and the anxiety by anger and the anger by whippings.

One cool crisp Saturday morning in late April, John told Robert to hitch up the team. They were headed to town for a few supplies.

Robert always enjoyed a ride either in the saddle or on the wagon, and he quickly complied. The Jennings' two horses were general-purpose animals. The old mare, Sally, was past her age to foal but she was a good worker and her calm demeanor was a good trait, even though she had developed an irritating barn sour habit. She was small at ten hands, but had given seven healthy foals. Storm was the best, now a ten-year-old gelding, a fine bay, and Robert's great companion. He was twelve hands and a good plow horse, but more importantly, he was the partner for Robert and his quiet rides after supper. Storm responded well to Robert and his commands, and it was this horse that Robert would talk to, not his friends. Robert and his father were attending Sally when she dropped the bay foal during a heavy rainstorm. His name was only natural.

The ride north to Lebanon was quiet. That was usual, but this time Robert ventured a question. "Pa, how old was you when you met Ma?"

His father seemed a bit taken back by what he must have thought a foolish question. "Fourteen I think. Why?"

"I's just wonderin'."

Robert regretted starting the conversation. He wasn't ready to confide any deeply held thoughts with his father, but his father continued.

"I see those girls look at you. They'll a one catch your eye too." John seemed proud of such sage fatherly advice, so he sat up tall, shook the reins, and they picked up the pace on the rutted road.

The eight miles were covered in good time and before noon, the low wooden and brick buildings of Lebanon came into view. The rail line was on the north side so the road from the south entered through a more residential area, past the modest homes of Lebanon's working middle class. The road continued to the commercial center and at the north edge of these buildings was Brown's Tack and General Store. John found a shaded spot for the team about a block from the store and set the brake. As he was walking away, he told Robert to stay with the team. Robert expected this and obliged with a nod. He noticed the team on the other side of the road had just vacated a watering trough so Robert released the brake, deftly shook the reins, and directed the team across the road. After Sally and Storm had their fill, he aligned the wagon with the road. He tipped his head back and soaked in the sun's warmth and began to observe two old timers.

Seated on a backless bench beside solid double saloon doors, were two old men enjoying a competitive dialogue of silence. One would note something about someone and the other would simply nod. Each declarative statement was never really answered. It was a kind of check to see if the other was still breathing. In front of the team was an exquisite buckskin. It was a young gelding, seventeen hands. Robert figured he was only recently broken or else in a state of agitation from some unknown cause. He remained nervous, tossing his head from side to side and pawing the ground with his front legs. He had four black stockings and a long black flowing mane and tail to match. His glistening coat, still drying out from what must have been a hard ride, outlined his muscles. The saddle was gun leather and tooled with intricate designs. It had the look of a parade saddle but was weathered into the finest riding saddle Robert had ever seen, even counting those at the county fair. Robert knew the horse and saddle were worth untold hundreds or even thousands of dollars, and he wondered who owned such a horse. His question was soon answered as the saloon door slammed open, rousing the two old men.

A poorly dressed man in his twenties, wearing a torn hat, stumbled out. He was drunk. His unbalanced and haltering steps took him towards the horse, and after two tries, he grabbed the reins. Robert couldn't believe such a man owned the buckskin. He knew there was story behind it all. As the man was untying the reins, an older man and woman approached on foot from the south.

"Excuse me," the gentleman asked the man. "Could you direct us towards the train station?"

The young drunk bowed deeply and pointed straight ahead, in the direction they had just come from. Robert was amused and gently interrupted. "Sir, the station is behind us another six or eight blocks. Just keep goin' in the same direction you're headed and you'll come to it."

The drunk exploded in indignation. "Damn you kid! You don't know night from day. It's thataway like I said." Again he pointed south. His words were slurred and Robert wasn't sure he had even made eye contact. The couple by now had walked past Robert, sure of his directions and were almost out of ear shot as the drunk continued.

"I'll bet you a hundred dollars the station's that away. No snot nose kid gonna show me up."

"Ain't got a hundred, Mister."

"You got those horses, now, don't cha?"

Robert straightened his back, quickly analyzed what was going on, and immediately realized the opportunity. "You mean to say you'd bet your buckskin there against these two horses here that the station is that way?" His adrenalin was flowing.

"You got it right, kid," the drunk slurred with an almost comical delivery.

"Okay."

There are small things that affect one's life forever: a spoken word, a yes or a no, a kiss, one too many drinks, a train whistle. At that moment, the long draw of a train whistle pierced the space between two men. The drunk stood upright and for the first time met Robert's eyes. His quickly sobering gaze shifted to the two old men who were having their best laugh in years. The drunk's mouth opened in what would have been a futile protest when all four men saw a black column of coal smoke rise a few blocks away, exactly where Robert had pointed. As the drunken man stood gazing at the smoke, Robert moved with determination.

He sprang down from the wagon bench and in one swift movement pulled his suspenders off and with two quick cuts of his knife had it in three pieces. The smallest he tied just behind the horse's mouth. The other two were tied to each side, giving Robert two reins to exert neck pressure and control. The next fluid motion had the saddle and bridle on the ground. He steadied two hands on the horse's back, jumped and swung his right leg over.

"Tell my pa I'll see him home," he said to the two men. He gently put his heels to the horse's ribs and pulled on the left reign. The nervous horse responded with a full gallop, and moving as one, they thundered down the road.

A few minutes later, John returned to the wagon and found the drunk attempting to unhitch Sally and Storm. Before his rage elevated to a violent height he roared, "What in God's name are you doin'?" He saw the man was not armed. He pulled the man away from the horses and threw him to the ground. "Where's my boy?"

"Your boy? Your boy just stole my horse."

"That ain't how it happened," said the old man nearest the fray. "Your boy and this fella made a bet and this fella lost fair and square. Your boy said he'd see you home."

"Was it a bet or a trade?" John pointedly asked the man.

"A bet. He's drunk but he lost."

John took a breath. "What's your name?" he asked the now fully demoralized man, slowly rising from the dirt.

"Tom Porter."

John looked at the inside of the upturned saddle. The initials JML were clearly monogrammed. He stood for a moment, contemplating the situation. His son had bet two horses he didn't own against a drunk's horse that probably wasn't his to bet. John decided to end the encounter.

"Tom Porter, you lost your horse cause you're stupid when you drink. It ain't my job to protect you from yourself." And then to the men, "If Tom Porter here has a gripe to the law, I'd appreciate a fair telling. Name's Jennings, live south of town."

The talk was over and John wheeled the wagon back to the tack and general store, loaded his supplies, wheeled again down the street past the still dazed Tom Porter and headed back home.

Near the south edge of town, Robert gently coaxed the horse to slowdown. With much head tossing and snorting, the horse calmed and settled into a rocking lope. Robert also began to relax and sat more upright. He passed a few residents and politely nodded hello with a tip of his hat. The last houses were passed and they were soon in the broken fields and pastures of the country.

Riding a horse bareback requires a skill and a sense. The skill is having the perfect position, more forward than where your butt would be in a saddle. Your weight is cantered forward, and with knees bent, you apply gentle pressure all along your legs and thighs, no point contact but a smooth contact of rider and horse. The control comes simultaneously with a gentle pull on the rein, or suspender, and pressure on the same side leg. If the rider has done this all right up to this point, he starts to lean his body at the same time the horse does. It's called riding. It's hard to do and easy to get thrown, or more accurately, still going straight after the horse has turned. Robert had these skills and that extra something, sense. Mattering who's doing the talking, a horse is smart, dumb, or in between but anybody who knows horses will tell you they have sense, and sensing is what that horse was doing the moment Robert slid the saddle off and mounted him. A horse will accept human control but it has to be earned. No animal can reason in words so it senses the non-verbal. The tone, how excited, how calm, the touch, how and where, the authority of the new rider and then, how does the rider sit. Is the touch gentle, and is the rein loosened once a command has been followed? A horse can size up a rider in sixty seconds before mounting and sixty seconds after. In these two minutes, he will trust the rider or not.

Robert was riding a great horse. Within moments of Robert's presence, he sensed Robert's strength and confidence. Even without a bridle and metal bit in his mouth, this horse gave his trust to Robert and allowed the simple suspender halter to convey commands. Robert relaxed his left hand's clutch of mane. The horse was a unique color, a blend of dark tan and maybe blue, Robert thought. In bright sun, he appeared a classic dark tan, but in low sun his coat took on a blue tint that blended with his black stockings, nose, and mane. Long lashes shaded dark walnut eyes that were constantly moving from side to side. It was the finest horse Robert had ever seen.

When they were half way home, Robert stopped at a small stream crossing. He patted the horse along the neck and slid off. Keeping the suspenders around the horse's neck, he checked then retied the two splicing knots. The horse never took his eyes off Robert and kept turning his head to follow Robert. He led the horse to the stream and where there was a gravel-based pool, he lowered his head to drink. The great horse continued looking at Robert. Robert had never seen this before. Usually, a horse will look straight ahead and with its ever-present wildness, scan for danger while in this vulnerable position. Robert tucked his shirt in and ran water over his face and hair. He spoke softly to the horse. The words didn't matter, only the tone and touch. After they had parsed their thirst, Robert stood directly in front of the horse and their eyes locked. Robert thought of the train station bet and by some interaction of fate or luck or Providence, he had claimed this great horse.

In an echo of a Genesis ritual, Robert looked deeply into the horse's eyes and said, "Station, your name is Station." He repeated it slowly, "Station, Station, you're Station." Station snorted as

Robert leaped, swung his right leg over and gently squeezed his thighs. He touched his heels to Station's sides. "Giddup."

They walked the last four miles. Robert used the time and solitude to ponder his future. He was sixteen and before today, had few prospects. Missouri had offered nothing to Robert and his dreams of a ranch would only wither if he stayed. Before this afternoon in April, Robert might have sunk into depression, alcohol, or crossed the law. He sized up his assets. He knew how to hunt and live off the land. He had twelve dollars saved and now he had Station. He was better equipped to survive than most early settlers. His future was not set. He had learned a lot and figured there was a lot more to learn. He could do whatever the hell he wanted. Robert later would swear he heard the word spoken like a thundering revival preacher. Robert was prone to enhance a story in the telling, but he always held this to be true.

"Texas!" He would go to Texas. He would work a few years, learn the trade, and buy a ranch. He could have ridden to Persia.

CHAPTER 11
FOLLOW YOUR LIGHT

Near three o'clock, Robert took a shortcut across the back of the Jennings' farm and headed for the house. His mother was taking down the last sheet from the clothesline and folding it neatly before placing it in a large wicker basket. She didn't recognize the rider and was nervous as he headed straight for her. Then she saw the hat and recognized her son. She couldn't find words as he and the great horse came to a stop in front of her.

"Whoa." He slid off the horse's back gracefully, and pulled himself erect. "Ma, this is Station."

They stood a few feet apart. She saw the remnants of Robert's suspenders around the great horse's neck and was trying to find an explanation, but her mind couldn't piece one together inside the law. Her expression took on a mother's worried patina. Robert helped her out.

"Ma, I'll tell you all at supper. Pa'll be home in couple of hours and we'll talk." With a smile, he took his hat off and with outstretched hand made a low sweeping bow. "At supper, Ma."

"At supper, Son."

She watched her first-born lead the great horse to the barn. Her eyes were fixed on Robert, not the horse. She knew he would leave soon. Her husband was hard, and she saw the resentment growing in Robert. She had tried to moderate her husband's behavior, but the pattern was honed over generations. Any man breaking from a father's mold has to see another way, maybe that of a neighbor or an uncle. Robert had none, but he had his mother Martha. Freely given, a mother's love will not take the male away; rather it can make the man whole and able to slay the dragons of the world. The Eternal Feminine would ride with Robert.

Robert spent the next two hours preparing for his early morning departure. He began in the barn where he gave Station a hearty treat of oats and corn. He slipped a halter gently across Station's nose and cinched it under his chin. He tied two sturdy strips of leather to the ring below the chin and held these slack as Station ate and Robert gently brushed his drying coat. "You and me got an adventure in us," he cooed softly in Station's ear.

When he had finished the brushing, Robert led his horse to the large wooden water tank by the windmill. Station lowered his head and took a long drink, but again his eyes never left Robert. When Station's thirst was slaked, Robert led him back to the barn and to a small holding stall with a mounted rack that Robert filled with fresh hay. Station seemed at ease, and Robert was satisfied that he was safe. He would take no chances with the larger space outside the barn. He was concerned that he might spook in his new surroundings.

After he was satisfied with Station's comfort and safety, he pulled the varmint rifle off its pegs inside the main door. He figured it was his because no one else used it much. His father's larger .45 caliber rifle was kept in the house. He knew both guns well but had no claim on the big one. He realized he was assuming things he might not ought to, but he had to act. He found a large piece of oiled canvas and placed the .22 single shot bolt-action rifle on it. He cut a rectangular piece over twice as wide as the rifle and a foot longer. He quickly punched matching holes along the perimeter with an awl and angled them slightly wider towards where the stock would rest. He sewed the scabbard with rawhide. He was pleased with the tight result and the large flap at the top. The scabbard would keep dust and rain off the weapon and still allow rapid access. He cut a large rectangular piece of the canvas to serve as a raincoat and shelter. From the remaining canvas he fashioned two saddlebags that would balance each other just in front of Station's rump. They were connected by thick leather and sewn with the same precision as the scabbard. There was little else he could do in the barn before talking with his father.

He carried the new saddlebags back to the house. In the room he shared with his two brothers, he assembled his meager belongings. He packed most of what he had. A second wool shirt, extra sox and cotton underclothes mirrored what he would wear in the morning. The only warmth was to be provided by his hat and a thin wool jacket lined with an old faded red quilt his mother had cut up for insulation. It would add color to his travels and protect him from the rain and sleet he knew he would encounter. He had leather work gloves and a good rope in the barn. He would load the second saddlebag with food, a small fry pan, a knife, ammo, and matches. He went downstairs and found his mother in the kitchen with his two little sisters.

"Ma, do you think I could take a bit of flour and salted pork and maybe that old fry pan that you don't use much?" He purposely did not breach the obvious topic. He wanted to talk about it only once and with both parents present.

Martha sensed the same and nodded her head, "Take all you can fit in your saddlebag there." She looked the new bags over. "You did a nice job on those, Son."

"Had a good teacher," he said with a dimpled grin. After he had loaded the second saddlebag, Robert heard the wagon approaching and headed for the door with the saddlebags under his arms.

"Supper in twenty minutes," his mother said.

Robert's two brothers were running alongside the wagon ready to help unhitch the team and unload the supplies. Robert caught up with the team and his brothers. "Ma needs you inside. I'll help Pa."

The boys had been at neighbors and had not seen Robert ride in alone on the great horse. They seemed puzzled why Robert was not on the wagon but turned and reported to the house. Robert opened the double barn door and swung it wide, allowing his father to drive the wagon into the center isle of the barn. Robert deftly unhitched Sally and Storm and led them out the big door and into a pen with water and hay. He returned to the barn and closed the doors. Station had his head over the stall door, keeping his gaze on the new face. His father stood silent, admiring the great horse.

"A fine horse here, a fine horse."

"His name's Station. I named him Station," Robert stated firmly.

John slid his hand along Station's neck, then turned his back to the horse and leaned against the slated door. "There's a fair chance the horse weren't the drunk's to bet. He's got no brand. I seen initials on the saddle, JML. The drunk was Tom Porter. Don't match up."

Robert had figured the drunk might have been left of the law but hadn't put any particulars together. "Was a fair bet, Pa."

"Not so sure. You don't own Sally and Storm."

"Could have been his, Pa. Could've."

There was a very long pause. John knew Robert would leave the farm tomorrow. If the law showed up in few days, John could retell what happened and the two old men would back him up. If the horse was stolen, he and Robert had no knowing and he wouldn't have to admit he saw the contrary initials under the saddle. Tom Porter was the criminal, not Robert. That was their story.

"I got no saddle, Pa. I can pay you twelve dollars for yours, or not. Station rides good bareback and I can do fine." The saddle was an old simple one, unadorned out of worn dull leather, but it was a big one and would fit Station fine. John didn't use it much anymore since trips to town or to a neighbor were usually by wagon. Robert used the old saddle with Storm on their evening rides.

"And I need a gun, Pa. Don't need a bridle, but I need the twenty-two."

"Don't need a bridle?"

"Station does good with just a halter. If he don't need a bit, then I ain't gonna use one."

"Never seen a big horse without a bit, Son."

"Some Indians don't use 'em. Station don't need it."

John looked at his son and a countenance of peace crossed his weathered face. He knew Robert was prepared to leave. "Son, take the saddle and the twenty-two, and just the halter if that's what you and Station need. It's your ma's and mine to give you. Besides, it'll look damn good on that horse." He almost smiled.

It was the blessing Robert had hoped for and finally received. John's simple words gave Robert confidence and steeled his decision. "Thanks, Pa."

During supper, Robert said little at first and ate a lot. Finally Martha asked, "Where're you headed?"

"Texas. I'm going to Texas. Can hire on at a ranch, save my money and buy my own. Texas is where I'm headed."

Tales of the West, the great mythic land, were common, popular, and still believed. All the stories of Longhorns, and Indians, and outlaws, and space, plenty of space, must be true. Robert's sources were few, but every boy knew about Texas. Texas was more than a state; it was place of the mind's imagination. It was his future unknown.

John and Martha looked across the old oak table. Their eyes met and they both nodded in agreement. They were not sad.

After supper, Robert walked to the barn to see his great horse. His eyes were fixed on Robert as he entered the barn. He walked slowly towards the great horse and patted his neck. "Rest good, Station. Tomorrow. Tomorrow's our day."

Robert slept till four then rolled effortlessly out of bed. His mother was in the kitchen stoking the fire and the lard in the cast iron pan was beginning to sizzle and pop. A dozen eggs were in a bowl ready to be scrambled. Martha separated thick slabs of bacon and began to place them in the pan.

"Morning, Ma," he said and was out the door before she could turn.

He walked to the water pump on the side of the house by the garden. There he stripped and began to wash. He began with his head and worked his way down. He lathered each arm from his chest to his hands, then down to his legs and feet. Full buckets of clean well water rinsed the lather and dirt back to the earth. He brushed his hair back with his hands and stood erect. The moon was setting in the west and the first hint of light appeared in the east. The chill braced his skin and his muscles tightened. He stared west as the cool dry air wicked the moisture from his skin. He felt a power from an unknown source. Robert didn't always think in words. What he felt was no dime novel prattle.

He dressed in clean wool pants and shirt over his white cotton underclothes. He sat alone with his parents at the table eating a robust breakfast. His brothers and sisters came to the table after Robert had taken his last bite. Robert excused himself and walked quickly to the barn. When he opened the large double door, the sun's first rays entered the space and he began to prepare Station. The great horse was pawing the ground nervously, but Robert's words calmed him and Robert saddled him for the first time. He fastened the rifle scabbard below the right side of the saddle and the saddlebags behind. He rolled the piece of oiled canvas and tied it behind the saddle giving some cover to the saddlebags. He put on his gloves and looped the rope over the saddle horn. He checked the halter and then tied the ends of the double reins so the long loop would rest easily on Station's neck. He stroked Station's neck and led him out the barn and up to the house. John and Martha stood together, and his brothers and sisters reached up to touch Station's nose. Robert gave each boy a handshake and a rub on their head. The girls hugged him around the waist. John walked towards his son and gave him a two-handed shake. Martha came forward and wrapped an unbleached white wool scarf twice around his neck and tucked the two ends inside his coat, then pushed eight silver dollars into his pocket. She kissed him softly on his lips. He set his left foot in the stirrup, swung his right leg over the saddle and sat high above his family.

His mother bade him farewell, "It's getting light, Robert. Follow your light."

CHAPTER 12
DEE-DAY

Robert gently laid the reins on Station's neck. The great horse turned west and they left the farm in a gentle lope. Topping a low rise, Robert stopped for a moment, giving his parents an honest tale to tell the law. He was headed west the last time they saw him. Once over the rise, he turned south towards the Twin Bridges. The sun was on Robert's left shoulder. He avoided towns, having no way of knowing if JML had any pull or was even alive. A simple telegraph message to any law office in Missouri could mean his arrest. Besides, why go into town? He had no reason to cultivate conversation, and he had no need of product or people. He figured to ride into the Indian Territory where the U.S. Army was the law, and a Missouri horse was of no interest.

Fences were his obstacles. Most land was in crops and these regular rows were outlined by long stretches of wire fences. He found soon enough that drainages and creeks gave him unbroken pathways, but not necessarily the straightest. By dusk, Robert had traveled near thirty miles. He found a small creek with spring water flowing cold and grass for Station. He unloaded the pack-saddles and took the halter off Station. He used a simple neck rope, but took no chances and hobbled Station's front legs with his heavy work rope. He gently stroked the great horse's neck as he spoke softly. The words didn't matter. It was his tone and how it entered Station. It was of purpose and resolution and of confidence. Robert didn't know enough about the world and its evils to give his confidence caution. He only felt the muscles of his great horse and the smell of the black rich earth. He entered there a time of no words. He didn't have to be told how sweet the wisteria was or how the sun appeared differently when filtered by a tree's green leaves.

He was a new Adam that first morning by the creek, as if he had traveled with the sun underneath the earth, and risen with it, new. He opened his eyes that morning and saw Station's eyes returning his gaze. Breakfast was salted pork and his ma's last three biscuits. He didn't feel the need to travel hard and would take ample breaks for Station.

The spring day began cool and clear. He planned to follow Wilson's Creek southwest then traverse the border of Arkansas and the Indian Territory south to the Arkansas River. This route would keep him away from Springdale and Fayetteville, past an old Civil War battlefield, and through wild country. He could make his way and prosper in this wild land. He knew Fort Smith, near the Indian Territory, was on the south bank of the Arkansas River.

For two weeks he rode. He would let Station lead and for unknown time he would ride with his eyes closed, listening, smelling, allowing his skin to give him sense. Station would follow game trails and paths between trees. One silent stretch was near three days, three days with no spoken words, only soothing tones for Station. Robert discovered, in these long paths of silence, creation's first wordless language. He found his thoughts floating up and leaving his consciousness, so that for a time he was in wordless contemplation. If language crept into this time, it would be purged by the sound of a bird or of leaves rustling in a quiet wind. After these silent miles, Robert felt strong.

The great horse trusted Robert and would not break when Robert fired at squirrels or rabbits or turkeys. The country was mostly broken forest and low rounded mountains, and the new green of the forest sprouted overhead and under hoof. It gave strength and nourishment to the great horse, and game was plentiful. On a warm May morning, Robert came across a north-south road and turned south. In time, fellow travelers informed him that he was just north of the Arkansas River and Fort Smith. At a well-kept farm, he offered his labor for two days in return for fresh supplies of flour, matches, and a box of .22 ammunition. The old couple had him dig out a line of rotten fence posts and set new ones for a fence around the house and garden. The woman fed him heartily, and the old man put Robert and Station up in the barn and gave Station his fill of hay and oats. Once he commented on his fine horse but Robert initiated no explanation except a simple, "Thanks." On the third morning, the woman fed him well and gave him extra flapjacks to finish later. He tipped his hat and lowered his head, "Thanks to you."

He had the information he needed and headed due west. The green floodplain of the Arkansas was to his left as he confidently entered the Indian Territory. He approached the Arkansas River at Webbers Falls and paid fifty cents to be ferried to the south bank near the confluence of the Canadian River. He kept the Canadian on his left and continued into the Indian Territory. The river was swollen from the spring rains and Robert figured it was just another layer of separation between the law and him. He stayed clear of any significant towns, and the Indians he began to meet were neither friendly nor threatening. They just left each other alone. Robert would in time learn to initiate conversation, and he began to seek out small groups to talk with and perhaps trade. He had nothing that interested the Indians. These people did not need his modest rabbit pelts but on a few occasions, a family would trade a few pelts for a meal and Robert would be able to talk with these people and their children. They had no fear of a solo rider with only an aged .22. They rightly assumed he was staying clear of the law. They didn't care.

He became more comfortable as the summer grew warmer and he tried to keep track of the different tribes he came to see and know. He passed through the realm of the Cherokee, the Creek, the Choctaw, the Sac and Fox, the Iowa, the Kickapoos, and many others. He found they were tribes from the Southeast and other regions of the country, and many had a tradition of agriculture and long exposure to the White Man. These were not the Plains Indians of dime novels and little boys' imagination. They were farther west, where he was headed. He stayed with at least a dozen different groups and picked up a few words from each. He learned how to dry meat and could keep a few days of meat without having to make a new kill. He could dry a few rabbits and, with flour biscuits or hotcakes, a meal could be ready almost anytime. He developed a taste for roots and greens that seemed to be part of many Indian meals. He'd had a taste of good coffee with the old couple near Fort Smith and found his hosts on the prairie would share their meager coffee rations with him. He would always remember the smell of boiling coffee breaking the cool of morning.

His comfort in the new land grew to enjoyment and then began to evolve into a deep reverence for this land and its people. His new life had hard rules that he would not break: Kill what he could eat or trade, care for Station, enter a camp when welcomed and stay clear if not.

In mid-summer, Robert pushed farther west and came to the confluence of the North Canadian River and the larger Canadian River. Robert had taken on the look of a trapper from long ago and the Canadian trappers that had named these rivers would have welcomed Robert as one of their own. There was no ford or ferry so Robert did what any sensible trapper in a strange land would do. He followed the new river. He knew this river traversed the Indian Territory and roughly paralleled the larger river to its south. Its course would be his. Some days he would ride most of the daylight then for a few days, not ride at all. If a spot attracted him with its water or game or shelter or its beauty, he would stay. He continued his self-imposed discipline and kept his words corralled. He continued to ride for times with his eyes closed and allowed his senses and those of Station to guide him. What else could a sixteen-year-old want? His needs were met with his hunting skills and his great horse. The mix of forest and long grass were a manna that could provide all a person could need or want. He knew winter would be a test, but come fall, he would cross the Red River and find shelter and work. He had no need to store food or stockpile any items. Those he met took him for a man older than his years.

Midsummer in the Indian Territory is hot. The heavy moisture laden air clings to the skin and if there is a little breeze to wick the moisture, then the small pleasure is accepted. But this little breeze might be a harbinger of a coming thunderstorm, and Robert quickly learned how to prepare his great horse. He would sit below Station's neck with the oiled canvas over them both, as the sky would tremble. Station would toss his head and flare his nostrils, as electricity would fill the air and extend to the earth. Lightening would strike near and shake them both. If Robert hadn't held a firm grip, Station would have bolted. Robert grew to dread the gathering high cumulus clouds, not for himself, he was awed by the storm's great power, but because his great horse suffered. Station could not understand the storm. He felt the electricity and sensed the earth move. Only Robert could comfort him. After the storm would pass, Station seemed calmer than before, as if the passing tumult had taken away the turmoil from the great horse. Robert noticed this and spoke his reassuring tones until the sun returned and gave new energy to the great horse.

While the days were still long, Robert noticed the forest was yielding more to the long grass prairie. Large swaths of forests were plentiful, but there were also large areas of wind swept grasses that gave shimmering green flecks to distant rises. It appeared as an oasis as the light reflected off the fruiting tips of the grasses. Robert rode within a mile of the river. The water had receded to its channel, and in places he could see the riverbed for a few feet out from the bank until the silt-laden water clouded its depths.

Above a lazy ox-bow, an unnatural reflection in a copse of trees at the bottom of a draw caught Robert's eye and he turned north to investigate. As he rode closer, he saw it was a canvas shelter that had attracted his curiosity. A large square was stretched over thin cut logs, giving the "A" shaped structure its form. There was a small spiral of smoke rising from in front of the shelter, and seated on a log next to the fire was a man. Robert stopped sixty yards distant and waited for the man to acknowledge him. The man had seen Robert from far off and raised his arm in a welcoming gesture. Robert did the same and rode slowly into the camp.

The man spoke first. "Good horse."

"Thanks," he nodded. "Name's Robert."

The man was still seated and gave no indication of rising. "Hello Robert, welcome to my home. Are you hungry? You may share my meal."

"Obliged." He slipped the saddle off Station and led him to a grassy spot to the side of the draw. He made sure it was in site of the camp then hobbled Station.

The man was reheating a stew, turkey Robert thought, in an old iron pot. The fire pit was lined with rocks, and the pot's side hung over the edge of a flat rock, allowing the flames from newly added wood to lick the pan's side. In another shallow pan, cooled fat was beginning to melt. He placed this pan on the edge of a flat rock on the opposite side of the pit. He then took a large handful of corn meal and mixed it with a little water. When the fat began to sizzle, he dropped two dollops of the mix and began to fry the corn flapjack biscuit sort of thing. The fat gave it a sweet smell and Robert's curiosity and hunger almost tempted him to forsake his manners, but he held his mug and spoon still. The stew was hot and the man lifted the pan using leather gloves and motioned to Robert to bring his mug close. The man poured a generous helping and filled the mug with stew. He plopped a corn flapjack biscuit on the top and nodded for Robert to begin. The man ate from the pot of stew using his knife to shovel the mix into his mouth.

They ate in silence and were finished in a few minutes. Robert took his mug and the empty pan and pot to the water source for the camp, a small spring that surfaced for a few feet then disappeared again into the earth. He rinsed each thoroughly and returned to camp. The man said, "Thank you, Robert."

Robert studied the man for a moment. He realized he was much older than his first impression. His white hair was in a double braid extending past each shoulder. An intricate beaded band tied each braid at the end. He was wearing leather hand sewn pants and moccasins, but a faded store bought heavy wool shirt. It had once been red, but retained only a sense of its original color. The old man sat very erect and stared at Robert with one dark eye and one sightless eye glazed over with impenetrable greyness. It moved in its socket and followed the dark eye's lead, but took a moment longer to stop its movement. It made Robert uncomfortable at first, then not at all. It seemed to Robert that the grey eye maybe just saw things differently. His face was deeply wrinkled. Robert thought he could hide a pencil in his wrinkles but also noticed that excepting the wrinkles, his skin was remarkably clean and of one color. If the wrinkles could have been smoothed, Robert imagined he would have the face of a child. The old man had yet to stand, but Robert figured him a few inches shorter than himself. He was trim, with no gut and no facial hair. His English was good, better than Robert's. Robert was aware of his own limitations with grammar and wondered where the old man learned to speak so properly.

"I am *Di-de-yo-hv-s-*q*i*. I am Cherokee, *Tsa-la-gi-yi*"

Robert tried to repeat it a few times but mangled it. He slowed down and repeated, *"Dee-day-yoh-huh-sge?* Can I call you Dee-day?" he asked meekly.

"Yes. Your horse had no brand."

The simple declaration took Robert by surprise.

"Haven't had the time," was his quick reply and as soon as he said it, he knew that it raised more questions than it answered. "I won Station on a fair bet back in Missouri. Figured it a good time to set out on my own."

"Your horse has no brand. A horse like yours makes a horse thief proud."

"I'll look into it." Robert walked to Station and led him to where the spring entered the earth. He found a thin flat rock, quickly dug a small depression, and watched it fill with clear water. After a minute, the small pool of water was splashed by Station's mouth, and he drank while looking at Robert. Dee-day watched approvingly. When Station's thirst was satisfied, Robert brought him back to the grassy spot and rejoined Dee-day. The day was still warm and the ground felt good to Robert as he sat near Dee-day's log.

Robert figured his own story was of little interest to his host, but he had many questions to ask and no intention of asking any of them, but finally managed a weak, "How long you been here?" Dee-day looked his guest over, and to Robert's surprise, he began to talk slowly.

"I was very young when your President Jackson told us to leave our land. We had a farm in the low hills of the eastern mountains. Our family and others like us nearby counted over one hundred. When gold was found, men filled with anger and lust came to our farm waving paper. They killed my father. It was winter. They gathered us and forced us north to Tennessee then through Illinois. We walked. We fell and when we could walk no more, we walked more. The soldiers were cruel, save one, Sergeant Peters. He carried me sometimes on his horse. In Illinois, the streams were ice but sometimes would break open and take a Cherokee. My mother died there. The morning was quiet and I was in her arms, but her arms did not hold me. They were cold. We could not dig a grave. The earth was frozen. The wolves following the Cherokee knew this. Two aunts and an old uncle sheltered me and I walked with them. Our ways were lost on that Trail. The Cherokee call it *Nu na da ul tsun-yi*, 'the place where they cried'. My aunts were good women. I never took a wife. I would not have family if I could not be on my land. This land is not the Cherokee's. It is White Man's land. I have no home. In winter I stay with nephews' families and show the young the old ways taught me by my aunts and the old uncle. It is not the true old way. That is gone. So I wander in this strange land. I am alone. They call me *Di-de-yo-hv-s-qi*, teacher. Some call me a wise man. If I am wise, Robert, it is because of what I see, not what I say."

Robert knew his own story was an uneven trade so he didn't tell of his journey from Missouri. Instead, he wondered what fifty years on the prairie would do for a man. He wanted to stay with this old man for a time.

"The White Man harmed you, Dee-day. Yet, you welcomed me to your camp, fed me, and told me of your past. Why do you show such a kindness?"

"You too are a stranger in this land. It is what I must do."

The next morning after a breakfast of quail eggs, potatoes, and coffee, Robert spoke.

"Would you like to ride my horse, Dee-day? His name is Station." Dee-day did not reply. "It's good by me. I'd like you to ride him."

"Yes, Robert, I would like to ride your Station."

"I'll saddle him up then."

"No saddle. Just your halter."

They walked together to Station and Dee-day placed the halter as Robert untied the hobbles. Dee-Day rubbed Station's ears, kissed each one, and then swung effortlessly on the great horse's back. He sat tall and proud and with a touch of his heels, they galloped east. Robert watched his horse and his friend disappear over a low rise and reappear a quarter mile beyond. Station had slowed to a rocking lope and was tracing wide loops as Dee-day laid the reins on alternate sides of his neck. Robert sat cross-legged on the grass and waited. Station returned snorting and proud with Dee-day on his back. Station lowered his neck and the great horse's nose touched Robert's.

Robert stayed four weeks, until the morning chill stayed long after the sun had shortened the trees' shadows. Dee-day taught him to read game trails and how to snare. Dee-day had no gun but he was an expert at catching rabbits and bobcats silently with no marks to the pelt. Robert mastered the craft and also some rudimentary leather skills. Pouches and lightweight shirts could all use rabbit, but for moccasins or heavy items, a tougher leather like deer or cattle would have to take the place of the once plentiful buffalo.

One afternoon, Dee-day announced that he wanted fish for supper. Robert led Station with a simple neck rope and the three walked the short distance to the river. Dee-day studied the water and selected a pool at the tail of a curve in the river. Standing below a cut bank, he reached into his rabbit-skin pouch, took a fishing line of twenty feet, and tied a single iron hook. Three feet above the hook he tied an irregular two-inch rock for weight. He took a rabbit liver he had wrapped in willow leaves, cut it in half and speared it with the hook. Standing downstream, he tossed the weighted line at the top of the pool. The rock took the slack out of the line, but the current was just enough to keep the rock bumping along the bottom, out of sight. Before the line reached the end of the pool, it tightened and then twitched violently. Dee-day remained calm, wrapped the line firmly around his weathered wrist and in one smooth movement pulled the fish onto the muddy bank. It was a fifteen-inch catfish, flopping fresh. Dee-day killed the fish with a quick blow of his knife handle. With a few deft strokes he cut two large pieces from each side then delicately separated the skin to leave four perfect catfish fillets. He washed the meat in the river, wrapped them in wet willow leaves and gathered his gear in the pouch. He was half way up the riverbank when Robert finally spoke.

"You're done?" The brevity of the experience left him little to say.

"No need for more fish. This is a good fish."

Robert took Station's rope and they trotted up the riverbank. He thought he heard Dee-day give a little laugh.

There was plenty of daylight left as Dee-day began the meal. His kitchen was sparse, but he had a collection of spices plus corn meal and flour and the potatoes his nephew would bring every few weeks. Robert heated last night's rabbit stew while Dee-day breaded the four large fillets with a mixture of spices and corn meal known only to him. He chanted while he prepared the fish. After they finished the stew, Dee-day dropped a large dollop of fat into the cast iron skillet. After a few minutes, it began to sizzle and the fillets were placed carefully into the hot pan. He turned them once and in a few minutes, Dee-day announced them done. Robert's first taste of the fish brought him great pleasure and surprise. It was a delight of new flavors and aromas.

"Tell me how you make this so good, Dee-day."

"Mexicans cross the Red River from Texas and we trade. I give them beaded leather and pelts and they give me peppers and spices. You like my fish?"

"Best I ever ate."

After the meal, the two men sat facing south towards the river and the gentle rise beyond. They would often sit silently watching the shadows lengthen, saying little, but this afternoon Dee-day had an action prepared.

"Can you keep your horse calm?" he asked.

After a pause, Robert answered, "Yes. Why?"

"He has no brand. Are you sure you can keep him calm?"

Robert was aware of the problem. He was lucky the great horse was not carrying a brand when he'd won the bet. It would have been too easy for someone to challenge his ownership, but now he had to declare his proper ownership of the great horse and he had to do it before he crossed the Red River. "I can't brand Station. Don't think he'd ever forget."

Silently, Dee-day took some dark berries and few hard seed-pods that Robert couldn't identify and began crushing them with a rock in the still hot fry pan. He added wood to the fire and kept the concoction hot, and it began to reduce. He took the same steel fishhook that had caught their meal and straightened it by careful blows with a smaller rock against a large hearthstone, then sharpened it to a fine point. He dropped a small bit of fat on a flat hearthstone, and while it was melting, he instructed Robert to bring his horse close.

"I will tattoo your horse. What will be your sign?"

Robert's answer indicated immediate agreement. "My initials are RJ, but just do a 'J'."

Robert walked Station near the fire and talked in soothing tones. Dee-day remained seated and began to stroke Station's back right leg. On the inner thigh, where the fur is fine and the skin is thinner, he dipped his finger in the melted fat and rubbed it in a circular pattern, working it into the skin. Station remained calm. Dee-day took his sharp knife and gently shaved a four-inch square. Robert stroked Station's neck and spoke soothingly to his great horse. Dee-day took a finger and wiped the dark residue on the clean skin and, with the sharpened hook, began to stipple a three-inch tall "J". He wiped the excess residue off, added fresh dark residue, and then stippled again the shape of the letter. He did this seven times until a dark and unmistakable "J" had become part of the horse. The lower part of the "J" flared out like a hook. Robert inspected the tattoo and gave an approving smile.

"It's a 'Fishhook J'."

The next morning Robert saddled Station and loaded his pack-saddles. He mounted silently then turned to Dee-day. "Thank you, friend."

"To-hi-du, U-we-tsi."

CHAPTER 13
DARLINGTON

Darlington Indian Agency was only two miles west. Robert figured a short stopover was in order so he could catch any news up from Texas and purchase a little flour and ammo. The agency was established in 1869 and its first superintendent, Brinton Darlington, had selected this site just north of the river's floodplain. It was on the east edge of the Cheyenne and Arapahoe land. These Plains Indians were relatively new to the Indian Territory and had a mixed history of trouble with the overlording whites.

Robert figured the agency grounds covered fifteen to twenty acres. The two most prominent buildings were the three-story commissary and the Indian school. Scattered in no discernable order were a few neat houses for the superintendent, his assistants, and a nice home and office for the physician. The superintendent's and the physician's homes had well-kept fences enclosing gardens and fruit trees. There were a number of young Indians standing along the fences of both homes. To one side of the commissary was the smaller trading store, and radiating out from this core, were multiple smaller buildings, sheds with pens, and more modest homes. All of the structures needed paint and Robert thought the agency had an air of neglect and despair. Most of the grounds had been grazed close and there was more exposed dirt than vegetation. Robert knew that a simple rain would leave a muddy mess and the deep wagon ruts, now dried as furrows, gave evidence.

Robert saw two horses tied in front of the trading store. As he rode closer, he saw a large barrel-chested man exiting the front door. Robert dismounted, and as the man came down the few steps, Robert moved to meet him.

"Mornin', Sir. You live here?" asked Robert.

The man seemed a bit surprised by the question and laughed a hearty, "No. Name's Kurt." He held out his hand in greeting and Robert gave his.

"I'm Robert Jennings. Pleased to meet you. I'm on my way to Texas. Lookin' to hire on a ranch and in time have my own."

Kurt looked the young man over and the great horse beside him. With a slight wave he beckoned Robert to follow. A short distance south of the building was a fire pit with two long logs rolled close to sit on. It was early in the day, but as Robert took a seat Kurt rummaged through his packs and brought out a small jug. He took a swig and passed it to Robert. He dutifully took a small swig and promptly choked. His experience with alcohol had been slight, but he found the slow after-burn quite pleasurable. He took a smaller swig and held it against his palate. After the tears stopped, he swallowed slowly.

"What are you looking for?" Kurt asked, amused.

Robert exhaled, feeling proud of the way he had handled the whiskey. This man had an unusual accent that Robert couldn't figure, but his welcoming smile and now the invitation to his camp told Robert he could trust him. "Like I said. A ranch in Texas. I want to ranch."

Kurt said nothing for a while and took the time to look his guest over. Robert thought he must have seemed naïve and inexperienced to the man and was starting to feel uncomfortable. The discomfort passed as Kurt settled on the ground and used the log as a backrest. Robert sat down and wriggled into a comfortable position.

"So tell me, Robert, what you have in mind."

"Been planning all along to end up in Texas. I'm pretty good with horses and stock and I like this land. I can drive cattle and work hard and buy my own spread after a few years."

"Those days of long drives to Kansas ended years ago, Robert. But you knew that, didn't you?"

That was news to Robert, but he didn't want to let on how little he knew.

"Sure."

"Nowadays, the railroads are all over Texas. The longest drive wouldn't last more than a few days. Most all of the big spreads are laced with fences now. You know how to mend a fence, don't you? They got a new thing down in Texas. Call it a stockyard. Ranchers sell their cattle to a middleman. He pens up the cattle and fattens them on grain. Marbles the meat with fat and makes it taste better. It's what all the markets back East want now. Then they ship the cattle east and they're slaughtered there. It's big business and you need a big spread. Is that what you have in mind?"

"Don't need a big spread. Just big enough to raise a family. Sure, I'll raise some beef, but I'd like to have horses and a few acres under plow." Robert felt meek, and for one fleeting moment questioned his vision.

Kurt continued. "Me, I think that's a good plan. A man's got to see things as they are. A man like you can make that all come to being. How long you been thinking like that?"

"A while now. Ever since I got Station."

Kurt studied the great horse for a moment. " Bucephalus."

"Bucephalus? Name's Station. Who's Bucephalus?"

"Ever hear of Alexander the Great?"

"Don't guess so. Who is he?"

"The greatest warrior ever. Lived over two thousand years ago. He was Greek, and in his short life, conquered a big part of the world. Defeated the Persians and changed the world forever. He rode a great horse like yours, Bucephalus, a big black stallion with a white star on his nose. Legend says the horse was his confessor and confidant. When Bucephalus died, Alexander gave him a state funeral and named a city in Asia after him."

"That's a good story, Kurt."

"It's a true one."

"Well Station and me won't be doin' any conquerin'. How about you, Kurt? You do any conquerin' on your way to the Indian Territory?"

"I saw things a different way when I was a young man, Robert. I wanted to come out West and see the Indians of the Great Plains. Took me a while to get here and along the way, I found out things. This land you're sitting on is Arapahoe, but the Arapahoe are from Colorado, moved here by the White Man. Before them, this was Comanche, but the Comanche tell of their origins up north. So whose land is it? Arapahoe? Comanche, maybe Kiowa, or whoever was here before them? Who walked this land first? Why'd they leave? I actually thought I would find these people, pristine and pure, but I found them bruised and torn. Do you know what some of the Arapahoe do with the cattle given to them by the Agency? They hunt them. They mount their old broken horses or walk up to them on foot and stab them with a spear or shoot an arrow into their side. Instead of the great tandem dance with the buffalo, they stab a cow. That's what's happened to these people. But Robert, there's more to these people than feathers, beads, and bows. This is as far west as I'll ever go because I found it here."

Robert was fascinated with Kurt and the deeply personal story he was telling. "What did you find here, Kurt?"

"Not often, but sometimes the first breath of a myth is revealed. The story people read today in stupid books and newspapers is not the myth. It's crap. I speak Arapahoe, Cheyenne, Comanche, and a few others. Can't understand a people unless you speak their tongue and speak it well. I came to know these people, the source. That's what was given to me."

Robert was struck by the power of these words and the depth of feelings expressed by Kurt. He wanted to say something, to learn more from this man, but he couldn't come up with words that wouldn't seem out of place. He was relieved when Kurt took a slow breath and looked Robert in the eye.

"Head south. Follow the Chisholm Trail. Beyond this North Canadian is the Canadian, then of course the Red. You can find fords on all three this time of year, but there's a ferry across the Canadian if you want. You'll pass through cattle being run by the Press Addington Ranch here in the Indian Territory. I'd stay clear of that outfit. The Indians are contesting them. Shouldn't be there. No, I'd head to Wise County. There's a big spread there, the Waggoner Ranch. Owner's Dan Waggoner. Hear he's a fair man. Foreman's name is Coulter. Met him once. There'll always be a need for a good man with a good ride. He'll hire you and Bucephalus." He laughed. "Come with me tonight for supper. I gave some salted beef to an old Arapahoe friend. The supper is his thanks."

That evening, the two rode a few miles to the home of an old Arapahoe man, his wife, and the wife's younger sister. As they rode towards the house, Robert saw the old man point towards him then wave his hands over his head and disappear quickly inside. He was not pleased by Robert's appearance.

"Stay mounted," Kurt said to Robert. Kurt dismounted and walked to the door. The man remained inside, but Robert could see him standing in the shadows. Kurt explained in Arapahoe that Robert had shared the camp with *Di-de-yo-hv-s*-qi for the past month. The old man waved his guests inside his one room home. It was a square of twenty feet with beds on one side and wood stove kitchen on the other. It was very neat and nothing seemed out of place. It's sparseness allowed the five to concentrate their attention on each other. There was a small table with two benches, so the men sat and were served first.

The two women, who spoke mainly to themselves, served the meal of roasted beef, flour biscuits, and potatoes. The younger sister, White Mare, seemed to keep an eye on Kurt and when their eyes met, she held her gaze long enough for Robert to notice there was more than courtesy at play. After they had finished the meal, the three men retired outside and shared a pipe. The rough leaf tobacco was new to Robert but after a few meek draws, he began to inhale deeply and enjoy the warmth in his lungs. Most of the conversation was in Arapahoe, and after one lengthy exchange, Kurt told Robert that many Indians had heard of a man staying with the wise Cherokee. The old man was proud to welcome Robert, a friend of *Di-de-yo-hv-s-qi.*

Kurt excused himself and went inside to thank the women and, Robert imagined, to say a special thanks to White Mare. He returned and they mounted their horses. Robert asked Kurt to translate a warm thank you.

The old man said in English, "Safe ride, young Robert."

"Obliged," said Robert with a tip of his hat.

That night Robert slept on the open ground and before the morning shadows grew short, he was headed to Texas.

CHAPTER 14
WAGGONER'S RANCH

Just south of the Canadian River, Robert found the Chisholm Trail and its broad path to the Red River and Texas. He soon spotted cattle bearing the Press Addington brand. This was the land Kurt had spoken of, no fences and no clear border. He came across two riders and, after assuring them he wasn't there to rustle cattle, found they were hands of the Press Addington Ranch. He rode with them for a day as they meandered generally south toward the Red. He helped them bring a few head of cattle out of thickets before the fall drive. For his help, the men shared their supper and their evening camp. Robert was open about his plans, and the two men seemed encouraging. They reinforced what Kurt had said back at Darlington. He would be best served to go on to Texas instead of staying in the Indian Territory. The Oklahoma Indians were beginning to press their claims to all lands north of the Red, and even though these two men were not sympathetic, they couldn't deny that the Indians had a legitimate claim. Robert thanked them and early the next morning, rode on to the Red River.

The outer banks were over a mile apart and the braided flood plane was dotted with cottonwoods and sandbar willows that had trapped dead trees and brush at high water, making some of the sandbars impenetrable. In the spring, the river could be a torrent and impossible to cross, and the risk of a heavy upstream rain could cause a flash flood downstream, even on a cloudless day. He was relieved to find the main channel a modest stream that Station could cross with his belly staying dry. The only danger was the mud that could grab Station's legs and pull him down. It could prove fatal. They crossed without incident.

Once in Texas, Robert's avoidance of people and towns was gone. Robert no longer felt the threat from the law, and in fear's place he found a new freedom. He had survived, prospered, on his long journey to this land of North Texas. He had money in his pocket and he rode the great horse. There was no doubt he was the rightful owner of Station, and the Fishhook J would put a fight into Robert if challenged. He had the skills and a young man's innocence, enough to give him confidence as he looked for work.

Robert found Wise County to be typical North Texas, with scattered wooded low hills of limestone, drained by deep tree lined creeks. The prize here was open grassland where great herds of Longhorn, Hereford, Santa Gertrudis and mixed breed cattle grew fat. Robert saw the land was beautiful and lush, but it was obvious that it had lost the open sweep and uninterrupted vistas of the Indian Territory. It was settled. Small towns and farms and ranches laced together with hundreds of miles of dirt roads and along most of these roads, barbed wired fences were their parallel companions. The exception was the Waggoner Ranch and its hundreds of square miles of pasture, spread over four counties. In the interior and its western holdings the fences were few, and the ranch reflected a vestigial sense of wild.

The Waggoner family was Texas royalty and lorded over their domain like New York industrialists living on their Hampton estate. The old man, Dan Waggoner, had just completed his new mansion, El Castile, overlooking Decatur. He was tough but respected in Texas and beyond. He had traveled into the Indian Territory the year before and dined with Quanah Parker, the famed Comanche warrior who had terrorized much of Texas not so long ago. Waggoner had been criticized for the meeting, but he told the press, curtly, that he just wanted to meet the first owners of his ranch. He was actually negotiating a large lease of pasture in the Indian Territory with the old warrior.

Robert found the Waggoner foreman, Jim Coulter, at the ranch headquarters near Decatur.

"How'd you do, Sir? Kurt, up at Darlington, said to look you up. Name's Robert Jennings. I'm lookin' to hire on."

"That so? How's Kurt these days?"

"Seems fine. Shared a camp with him. Said you was a good man and was always lookin' for the same."

"That's a fine mount you got there, Robert, and I'm sure you know how to ride. What do you know about cattle?"

"I know stock and horses, but I never worked on a big spread. Rode down from Missouri. I'm a good worker, and I got no bad habits, Mr. Coulter."

The foreman slowed the conversation and used the quiet to look Robert and Station over. That's all he needed to see.

"I go by Coulter. If you're an honest man, there's a place for you. A buck fifty a day. The bunkhouse is two miles back on the road you came in on. If you don't tarry, you can make supper. I'll be down after dawn breakfast."

"You made a good hire, Coulter." Robert shook his hand.

Coulter liked Robert from that first meeting and rode with him the next two days, meeting other cowboys and getting a feel of the ranch. After that, Coulter knew Robert was a man deserving of his trust. The only skills Robert lacked were roping, branding, and midwifing a troubled heifer dropping her first calf. He learned fast. The bunkhouse camaraderie, the food, the work, it was Robert's place to be, and he reveled in all of it.

He worked with two men he spoke of fondly throughout his life. Shug was the black cook from Mississippi. He was sixteen when the Civil War ended and headed west to enjoy his new freedom. Southern recipes from his mother and an ability to make friends brought him fairly regular employment on his journey. He said the old man Waggoner treated him okay, and he was just fine staying in Texas. Robert thought him the happiest man he'd ever met. He couldn't figure out why this man, who carried scars on his back from his days as a slave, could always offer a story and a laugh. After a year, Robert finally asked him, "Why, after all you went through, are you so damn happy?"

"When I left Mississippi, my ma told me to bring Jesus along. That's jus' what I done."

Robert didn't know about riding with Jesus. Robert's best cowboy friend was a Sauk Indian named Qeetop. His people were originally from Michigan, but had been relocated to the Indian Territory in the 1870's. Robert had been through their land and remembered a few words. This impressed Qeetop, and they became immediate and fast friends. Qeetop explained that he had run afoul of his clan's elders and had to leave. He gave no other explanation. Robert thought he was the finest horseman he had ever seen and would always ride with Qeetop if given the choice.

When duties slackened and the cowboys weren't backed up with seasonal duties, Robert would be sent by Coulter to ride the line for a few days. He always remembered riding the line as his best days on the Waggoner Ranch. He would take a packhorse along with Station and ride the perimeter checking for any trouble, usually broken fences but occasionally a squatter. Robert would chat up the hunter or those traveling through, but any shelter or structure built showing some sense of permanence would find the squatter face to face with this representative of the Waggoner Ranch. Robert sat tall on Station, his .22 now replaced with a .45 caliber Winchester 1876. Before riding up close to investigate, he would slip the Winchester out of its leather scabbard and lay it across his saddle, then make sure the dark handle of his Colt cavalry revolver was not covered by his coat.

He didn't need a badge. Robert learned that authority had two components. He could calmly state his legal case with gentleness and straightforward talk, but how it was received was not in his control. Once he had established his official position, the foe bent on trouble, would counter with cussing and threats, but these threats were never acted out. Robert found them a required response, allowing the threatened man to reestablish his manhood. Robert learned to never insult that aspect of the intruder and could soon manipulate the conversation back to civil talk and coax a mumbled apology from the transgressor. As long as Robert treated even the roughest of the men with a little Western respect, he would come out the victor and the Winchester would never leave its resting position. Robert knew that once a weapon is drawn, a man must decide if he can pull the trigger, and he best know the answer before he draws his gun. Robert thought he could. He found solo men in two groups, honest travelers in search of a port, and outlaws. Robert became a good reader of the two types and looked for how they held themselves and looked him in the eye. There were other tells that Robert would learn in time.

On a cold January night, Robert was alone deep along the south perimeter of the ranch. The line camp was a welcome harbor to a cold and hungry Robert. After tending to Station and the packhorse in a holding pen with hay and water, he prepared a hot and simple supper of stew and biscuits. The small cabin had two bunk beds and a central wood stove next to a wooden table with a bench on each side. He took a fast sleep before the cabin fully warmed from the wood fire that had heated his stew. Deep into the night, he was awakened by the sound of a lone horse approaching. He rolled out of the bed and slipped the Colt from its holster and opened the door. The lone rider dismounted, tied his horse near the pen, and walked politely towards Robert.

"Can I share the camp?" he asked.

Robert sensed no threat and would query the man about his intentions in the morning. "Come on in. Fire's still hot. I'm turnin' in," Robert said and returned to his bunk. He was asleep again in a few minutes.

In the darkest part of the night, Robert was shaken awake by yelling and threats from outside the cabin. There were several men's voices all in a state of high agitation. In the faint light given by the stove's last embers, Robert saw his new camp mate pacing from one side of the cabin to the other.

"Bastards, you Bastards!" He cracked the door and fired three or four rounds into the black night and then slammed the door. The cabin walls were still vibrating from the door slam when a fusillade of multiple rounds, all large caliber rifle bullets, raked the cabin walls. Some rounds found their way through small slits in the planking and entered the interior. Robert's initial confusion and shock were replaced by the stark realization of the mortal threat facing him.

"Hold there!" he yelled with all the force his lungs could muster. "Waggoner Ranch hand here. Stop!"

The men outside must have heard his pleas, seen the three horses, and realized there were two men inside.

"Lawful posse here. You come out now, Waggoner Ranch, you got two minutes."

Robert looked the outlaw in the eyes. He was sitting on the floor next to the door with his back against the wall planks. One more fusillade from the posse could easily find its mark. Robert pulled his pants and boots on, grabbed his rifle and saddle and gear and stepped to the door. It was quiet. The two men stared at each other for a moment. Robert saw that the anger released with the "bastard" rant was gone, replaced by a sad resignation.

Despair clouded the man's spirit and Robert sensed his fatal flaw. The man would not help himself, but in a final act of kindness, waved Robert out the door by flicking his long barreled revolver toward the door to freedom. Robert tipped his hat.

He slowly approached the posse. He made out at least six men, all with guns pointed towards him. One stepped forward and examined Robert's face with light from a match.

"Ain't him," he said, turning to a tall man with a US Marshal badge on his coat.

"Go now!" the Marshal barked.

"Obliged." Robert quickly threw the saddle on Station and was loading the packs on the packhorse when an extended volley rang out, then silence. Robert rode softly into the night, a rising crescent moon gave light. He was still in the saddle as the first golden crest of the sun showed on the eastern horizon. He was thankful for the light.

Robert liked everything about his new life. He mastered all the skills asked of him and would take jobs some of his fellow cowboys shunned. He enjoyed an occasional Saturday whisky in Decatur and would smoke a pipe with his friends, but neither became a habit, and the long periods of solo work did not bring a craving for these pleasures. He became a trusted man for Coulter, and Coulter's first choice for any job that required analysis or a way with people. The two men would ride together, and Robert began to share his plans with his friend. Coulter was at least twenty years Robert's senior and seemed satisfied with his foreman position. He had recently married a younger, Robert thought comely, but kind woman and bought a small house in town. She was now pregnant, so at mid-life, Coulter would start his family.

Robert pondered it all for a while and figured he would take a different path. He wanted his own ranch. He knew this land, its value, how many pairs an acre could carry, and he knew cattle. He could tell by a young heifer's rump width if its calves could safely drop and he knew a good bull. He was always aware of body shape and the ability to put on weight the first year, and he also tracked survivability of the first calf. He knew he could select a good core of heifers to stock his new ranch.

After seeing the Waggoner Ranch through four turns of the seasons, Robert had a good feel for the country, and his eyes and heart found a spot to set his brand. Denton Creek, east of Decatur, flows generally southeast into the Elm Fork of the Trinity River. The narrow flood plain is filled with cottonwoods and alder, and just above the high-water mark, grow tall pecans, scrub oaks, and a few black walnuts. From the creek, the land slopes up to the west and along this broad ridge, was a new county road roughly paralleling the creek. This was good land with high grass, water, and timber. Robert imagined a house and out buildings near the road with views down to the timbered creek. He figured he could make a go of it with less than a section. Two hundred acres, maybe less, would do it. He'd keep most in grass for cattle, but figured he'd dry farm some of the bottom land for a cash crop. He'd heard from Coulter that land was going for around four to five dollars an acre, and in another three years, he could buy a good parcel free and clear. A loan from the Decatur Bank, they always seemed nice, could give him seed money for a core of heifers. He would build the house and barn himself. It wasn't a sophisticated plan but was thought out as well as most, better'n most he thought.

He remained straight to this purpose and spent his earnings on essential things only. Essential things being only things, he hadn't counted on meeting Ida Emma.

CHAPTER 15

IDA EMMA

Robert rarely told the story of the Myers and his courtship of Ida Emma, and he told it only when his children or a son or daughter-in-law was present. He knew he was the safeguard of the truth, and he felt it was his obligation to tell his and Ida Emma's children about their mother and her family. It had taken many years to collect all these experiences and weave them into a fair telling, and this story of Ida Emma and the Myers was told with no exaggeration or embellishment, as if he had written the story on parchment, to be unrolled when called upon.

Newton Myers was only sixteen when he first tasted battle, fighting for the abolitionist cause in Bloody Kansas. He saw death first in Lawrence. When the Civil War began, he didn't hesitate and enlisted in the 4th Kansas Regiment, the "Democrat Fourth", which was soon reformed as the 10th Kansas Infantry Regiment, the "Moral Tenth". He quickly rose to Corporal and color bearer. To bear the colors was a great honor given only to the worthy and the brave, and those who accepted the honor also accepted the target placed upon them by the lines of rifles they would face in battle. Newton survived and earned his Sergeant stripes. He fought in the battles of Fort Wayne, Cain Hill, and Prairie Grove. He chased the Confederate raider John Morgan and never caught a bullet or a canister of grape shot. He became the Lucky Sergeant, and his men would always want to be near him in battle to share in his fortune. He was spared, but his men were not. He was stained by their blood and their brains, and after two years, he began to retreat into silence and brooding introspection.

He married Carrie Turner in 1862, and nine months later, their daughter Rachael was born while Newton was on campaign. He knew his luck would not last the war, and he began to think he would never see Carrie or Little Rachael again. His men knew this too and granted him his time alone to walk the camp in silence.

Newton's enlistment was up in the summer of 1864. He was given a recruiting commission and sent to Leavenworth to raise a company of volunteers. He and Carrie rented a small house, and for the first time, had a life together as a young family. They would take long walks with their daughter, pushing her in an ornate wrought iron baby carriage. Slowly, the sound of battle receded. It was a respite for Newton, and his spirit was reawakened by Carrie and Rachael, and each morning's sun brought newfound happiness to this scarred and battered man. He and Carrie would sit on their front porch and talk about their future, its risks, its adventures, and of peace. The peace they spoke of was not the quiet between wars, but of coming together, a place where they could share their dreams and fears and create a life. It became their vision and they would share it, if Newton survived the war.

A volunteer company elected its officers and Newton, three months after he began recruiting, was unanimously elected Company Commander, a Captain of the Volunteers. This was expected but nevertheless, a great honor for Newton, and his chest swelled as his new company gave hearty cheers to their new Captain and his Lieutenants. He looked at the hundred and five young men. A few had completed high school, and a few had traveled more than a county distant, but most were still in their teens, and their faces reflected their innocence and their excitement of adventures to come. Newton's speech to the volunteers spoke of honor and duty and the Founding Fathers' belief in liberty. He wove his own weft of Christian sacrificial ideals in the mix. This was his only reference to death in battle and he felt he was withholding reality from these boys. If only they knew what he knew, their cheers would be muted by the future's grim face.

That night he didn't sleep, but spent the dark night on the porch with his memory as his mate. At sunup he walked to the camp of his second in command, Lieutenant Ralston, and handed him a letter, a one-sentence letter of resignation, shook his hand and walked home. As he climbed the front steps, Carrie greeted him with eyes full of question. The time for bravery and risk of a sudden leaden death was over. He had survived the passage.

Newton and Carrie stayed in their rented home and began to enjoy the civilian ways. Newton took a simple job in the Smithson General Store, and Carrie was soon pregnant again. It ended in a late term miscarriage and a second miscarriage followed four months later. She suffered deep melancholia and withdrew from her family for three weeks. Carrie slowly recovered, but even months later, would have days she could not leave her bed.

After the war, Newton's company returned to Leavenworth. Eighteen never came home. Others had missing limbs and eyes. Newton was quick to extend credit to his boys, and on a few occasions, an ink spill would remove the debt of a veteran out of money. Newton and Carrie became restless and moved to Fort Smith Arkansas, following a lead by Mr. Smithson and the availability of a store to purchase. In 1872, Ida Emma was born in a small rented home in a place Newton and Carrie found they did not like, far from family and friends.

They moved back to Kansas and bought a small store in Cowley County and a nice butter yellow home nearby. Carrie had sold most of the railroad bonds, given to her by her parents when she married, to finance the move and the new house, but retained a few for the future. There in Winfield they planned to set roots and grow their family, but they had no more children. Carrie had two more miscarriages. After Carrie's parents died, Carrie's little brother, Kirk John, fourteen years younger than his big sister was welcomed into the household. As Ida Emma grew, she and Uncle John became very close and John thought of her as his little sister.

Carrie began piano and violin lessons for her girls when they were six, and Ida Emma practiced with dutiful daughterly obedience. Rachael did not. Carrie was well read and began an early program of poetry and literature for Rachael and Ida Emma and also emphasized composition and rhetoric. Ida Emma learned fast, but Rachael grew into a dark eyed and dark haired beauty with a heart that never opened. That's how Carrie explained her aloofness and inner anger that Carrie felt Rachael directed at her. It was a poor explanation. Rachael would obey her mother to the exact letter, as if to say, "I've done all, and given all, and I can take anything you hand me."

The relationship worsened and fell into a whirlpool neither could escape. Rachael was the smartest child in her school, and when she finally told her mother that she hated her, the hurt was amplified because Carrie knew it was more than just screaming angry words. In Rachael's heart, she meant it. Restrictions and punishments were doled out and met with steel-faced determination by Rachael. Newton was helpless, and any words of counsel were met by anger towards him by both antagonists.

Rachael broke the impasse. The week before she was to begin her last year of high school, she ran away with a slick talking gambler who moved to a new town every few weeks to stay ahead of the law. Newton and Carrie never met him. It was a terrible time for the family, and Newton and Carrie never really recovered. Newton felt he had failed the two women, and Carrie felt that Rachael had failed her. Rather than address the actions that led to the rupture, Carrie made Newton, John, and Ida Emma take an oath to never to speak of the events to anyone outside the family.

Newton withdrew into a brooding silence. In addition to the loss of Rachael, he was troubled by thoughts of despair and a lack of future goals. He countered these thoughts with newfound energy. He must create something unique and worthy of his life. He reflected on his infantry experience. Boredom was the largest component of an infantryman's life, punctuated by focused moments of great terror and confusion. Newton slowly came to the realization that it was these few moments in life that energize and inspire. He would not talk about this with any of his friends at the Grand Army of the Republic Lodge, but he knew that those men that did well in leading men in battle and survived the war, were those same men that were the most successful, adjusted, even happy. Maybe their shirts didn't hold the bloodstains as fast as his.

One evening after supper, Newton and Carrie were sharing a single glass of port wine. Newton took a sip and set the glass down softly and looked Carrie firmly in the eye. He wanted to move to Texas. He knew of land for sale in Wise County and with the sale of their Winfield properties, they could purchase enough to have a fine farm and build a lovely home. They would leave Kansas and find their peace in a Texas garden.

Carrie was silent for a long time then finally raised the glass and finished the wine. "Fine by me," was all she said.

Newton, Carrie, Ida Emma, and John Turner left Kansas in 1881. The Waggoner Ranch had sold land near Decatur, as speculation and waves of new migrants had begun to increase the cost of unimproved land. With money in hand and a newly built home on forty acres on the edge of town, Newton and Carrie established themselves in Wise County as part of a growing and respectable middle class. Newton began to make new friends, but kept them at arm's length. He and Carrie were welcomed into this old Confederate state, but Newton was referred to as the quiet Yankee.

Had Robert known Newton and Carrie well and understood what had driven them to Texas, he would have taken more time and effort to establish a better relationship. But what twenty-year-old would go to that effort at a time when life spins so fast? Every particle of his emotional energy went into Ida Emma. She was only fifteen, but had the maturity and grace of a woman. She was very comfortable with older men and women, and she and Robert had begun conversation easily, as he held the door open for her at Sam's General Store one Saturday.

Robert was six feet two, skinny, and reflected a little wildness from his deeply set blue eyes. His bushy eyebrows could sometime shadow his gaze and once, Ida Emma thought she noticed he was looking at her bosom. She liked that. He was usually clean-shaven, but a few months each year, grew a moustache that drooped over the corners of his mouth.

Ida Emma was nine inches shorter than Robert, her long dark hair, tinted with auburn, was gathered into a wavy tail leaving teasing tufts falling loosely around her forehead and in front of her ears. Her eyes were crystalline, and Robert couldn't tell if they were blue or green, maybe their own color he thought. Her face was framed by the soft lines of her cheeks and her full lips seemed to reveal a perpetual smile. She held herself erect with her shoulders always straight and a little to the back. Her firm bosom tapered to a small waist. Ida Emma was modest, but what harm is there in showing a small waist even if it accentuates other parts? Ida Emma was a lovely girl. Too fine for a cowboy, thought Robert.

Why a girl like Ida Emma would respond so suddenly to Robert's kind words and fast smile he never knew, but even that first day he felt she might have a place in her heart for him. She felt the same, and with few spoken words, they let their eyes do most of the talking. The next Saturday, Robert rode to Sam's General Store and waited for the hour that he had met Ida Emma the previous Saturday. Sure enough, she and her Uncle John came around the corner. It couldn't be a coincidence they both thought.

"Pleasure to see you again Miss Ida Emma. Hello to you, Mr. Turner." He didn't know what else to say.

"Why Mr. Jennings, what a pleasant surprise. You're here for some particulars from Sam's?"

Her Uncle John smiled and walked alone into the store.

"Yes Ma'am, that's why I'm here." A very awkward silence followed, as Robert struggled to say what was on his mind. "But I was hoping I might see you here."

"Why Mr. Jennings, you are a bold one. Are you always so direct?"

"Don't know no other way, Ma'am. I was just thinkin' that as I rode here today, I might see that pretty girl again. If that's too direct, then I'll say I'm sorry."

"Well, Mr. Jennings, truth telling compels me to say what was on my mind. I too, was thinking it would be nice to see that tall cowboy again. And you will extend your forgiveness to me, if you think a girl should not talk as such. And please call me Ida Emma. I will call you Robert."

Robert later admitted it was love, but at that moment the sweep of emotion was so overwhelming he could not use words. He was silent for a moment and closed his eyes, hearing again her warm and welcoming words.

"Robert, are you all right?"

"Yes, Ida Emma. Yes."

"Let's walk while my uncle is inside, Robert."

Ida Emma placed her hand inside Robert's elbow, and they began their first dance, walking slowly along the raised wooden planks of the sidewalk. She told him of the Myers' journey from Kansas, and he told her of his journey from Missouri through the Indian Territory. Robert thought they talked for hours. It was only a few minutes.

"Do you and your uncle come here every Saturday?"

"Would you like it if I could?"

"I have duties most every Saturday. Don't know if I'd be free or not."

"I'll talk with Uncle John. I think we need to come to Sam's a little later on Saturdays. On Sunday, we're at the Methodist Church. Will I see you there?"

Robert and Ida Emma and Uncle John began to meet with regularity on most Saturday afternoons in front of Sam's. They would walk together while John would take as much time as he could purchasing the week's needed dry goods.

Robert became a regular churchgoer. He discovered that theology and love were from the same tree. His mother, Martha, was his first teacher. Her religion was a little God, a little Jesus, some vague sense of Good versus Evil, and ultimate reward and punishment. These memorizable tidbits told Robert little, but he was inquisitive enough to think there may be more. His lack of formal education was no impediment to the Reverend Bailey Stone's sermons. Reverend Stone didn't talk down to his parish in the usual mix of heaven, hell, sin and forgiveness. He gave Robert a window into understanding his mix of emotions and the love he felt growing for Ida Emma. Reverend Stone spoke of God, not as a robed super being, but as something all could experience on earth in different encounters. Love is the breath of the Divine, to be experienced as pleasure and grandeur. Robert could grasp that. Reverend Stone also spoke of God's presence in the world enveloping all. Robert thought of his long rides on Station, his eyes closed while he felt the sensual world he was moving through.

One Sunday, Reverend Stone read from a letter of St. Paul. It closed with a stunningly timeless treatise on Love, the greatest gift, the essence of God. Robert was staring at the back of Ida Emma's head, four pews in front. She turned. Their eyes met. In that moment, timeless, their future was set like flint. That was in April of 1888. After the service, Ida Emma was standing outside the church with her parents and Uncle John. Robert and Ida Emma's eyes met and stayed focused as he confidently approached.

"Good morning, Miss Ida Emma. Beautiful spring day to come, don't you think?"

Without answering directly, she turned to her parents and with no hesitation said, "Mother and Father, I want you to meet my friend, Robert Lee Jennings."

Robert tapped his hat's brim towards Carrie and extended his right hand to Newton and gave him a warm handshake. "It's a pleasure to meet you Mr. and Mrs. Myers, and Mr. Turner, good to see you again." He shook John Turner's hand.

So far the manners taught him by his mother were working just fine. Carrie Myers had known who this young man was weeks ago and knew well who her daughter had been meeting on Saturdays in town and where the targeted gaze of her daughter was now focused. She also knew he was nothing more than a Waggoner Ranch hand with little education. She knew she would never allow Robert to court her daughter. She had shared all of this with Newton and thought he was agreeable with her early decision.

"How nice to meet you, young man," she began slowly. "Did you enjoy the Reverend's sermon today?"

"Reverend Stone always talks a good story. I think St. Paul and Reverend Stone understand each other, don't you?"

Carrie was surprised by this artful response and quickly agreed. "Reverend Stone is an educated man and very knowledgeable in the Word of God."

Ida Emma didn't want to talk about the sermon. "Oh Mother, I would like to invite Robert for dinner today. I have bragged so about your Sunday fare." She tried to hide her excitement but couldn't keep it wrapped in the matter of fact tone she had rehearsed.

Carrie replied slowly and deliberately with more than simple words. She intended to blunt this ambush from her daughter. "You know, Dear, you must always plan well before inviting another into your home."

Her brother John's intervention caught her off guard. "Robert has offered to help me with Red's split hoof. He tells me he can trim it properly to help it heal. Old Red's your favorite now isn't he, Sister?"

There was no doubt the three, on an earlier Saturday meeting, had carefully planned all this. With John's thumb on the scale, she graciously agreed.

Ida Emma was seated between her parents on the single bench of the open buggy. Robert and John followed on horseback, Robert sitting tall and erect on his great horse and John, with slightly hunched shoulders, riding the ailing Red.

"She doesn't like you," John stated the obvious.

"I know she don't."

"She's a proud woman, always felt the world should take more notice. I've seen that the world doesn't care much about Wise County so it's up to us, her family, to do the noticing. My little niece notices you, huh Robert?"

They both laughed so hard that the three Myers all turned around to see what was so funny. Robert just smiled at Ida Emma.

When they arrived at the Myers' home, Carrie and Ida Emma went immediately inside to prepare the meal. It would take at least an hour and the men would stay clear. Newton took his reading glasses and a glass of sweet tea to the front porch and began reading the Saturday Decatur paper and the Atlantic

Monthly. There was an article on the Indian Territory he wanted to read.

John and Robert unhitched the wagon from Rosy, their old mare, and loosened Station's saddle. Robert led Station and John led Red to the small barn.

"I see you don't use a bit on your horse there, Robert. Why's that?"

"It's a good tellin' John, but don't have time today. Could you show me your shoein' tools?"

John started towards the barn to retrieve the tools, but first directed Robert to a small pen. Robert led Station to the pen where water and hay were available. While Robert was attending Station, John brought a wooden case of tools for Robert, and they met in the barn with Red. Robert didn't place Red inside a stall, rather positioned him in the open area of the barn. He had Red stand alongside the stalls so that he and John were on the same side of the horse. He didn't want Red to bolt inside a small stall and put them all at risk of injury. Robert turned his attention to Red and lifted his right front leg to examine the problem.

"Hold him steady now. He might get skittish." Robert took the nail tongs and pulled the nails out of the shoe and tossed the shoe aside. The split was clearly visible and no doubt the source of the problem. "Who'd shoe a hoof like that?" Robert spoke with a little disgust, and then realized he might be criticizing John. "Probly just didn't see how far it went," he added as a modifier. "I'm going to trim it as far as he'll let me. Hold his head tight and talk to him." Robert's instant assessment and treatment plan impressed John.

"Go ahead on, Doc," said John.

He quickly cut the entire hoof back farther than John had imagined possible and only then did Red begin to twitch. Then with a swiftness that surprised both Red and John, he cut a notch another half inch into the split. Red slammed his foot to the ground and would have reared up on his hind legs if John hadn't kept a firm grip. Robert knew when to stop. He stroked Red's nose and said a few gentle words. He took each leg and removed the old shoes and trimmed the other three hooves, but not as severely as the ailing one.

"Now don't shoe him for a week or so and when you do, keep the short nails way clear of the notch. Have him reshoed every two weeks and don't ride him until I say so, and even then keep him on soft ground. He'll heal up fine. Just can't hurry him."

John took the prescription as the fact it was and knew the eighteen-year-old horse would still have some good years in him. "I see it, Robert, what Ida Emma sees in you," John replied.

Robert wondered why his knowledge of horses made him appealing to his new love, and then he realized John's comment was not about horses.

John continued, "My sister is a strong woman. What she says usually goes. Newton's spirit was partly broken in the war. Conflict is now something he avoids. I think Carrie sees this as a weakness."

"Mr. Myers fought for the Union, saw battle?"

"Doesn't talk about it. He's got two friends in town that were Union too, and sometimes they meet for a whiskey, comes home all red eyed. He wants me to think it's the whisky, but I think some of it's tears."

"I suppose the past stays around," Robert added.

"Ida Emma sees strength in you, Robert, not the bullying type or the yelling type, but the kind she can lean on, build on. If I saw my little niece falling for some crude ol' cowboy or slick talker, I swear I'd find a way to sour it. But if I see her happy and cared for, well then, I'm with her." Robert looked John in the eye. He didn't need to say a word.

John was smaller than Robert and didn't hold himself with the confidence Robert had developed. He was ten years older but they seemed almost the same age. John seemed comfortable with his life's position, but Robert couldn't understand why a man his age didn't just strike out on his own. There was a passivity about John that Robert didn't much admire. Robert thought he spoke with an accent but then realized he was the one who probably spoke a little funny. They had met and had a few simple conversations in town, easy things like the weather or some horse going by. Robert knew enough about people to recognize that differences weren't something to stay clear of, and he thought they would be better friends in the future. For now, it was good to have another supportive voice in the Myers' house.

The midday dinner was a simple one. Carrie was not about to go the full effort of a Sunday best affair. Fried chicken, corn, green beans, and biscuits with a pitcher of sweet tea was the fare. Carrie's canned peaches and cream provided a simple dessert. Robert knew Ida Emma had breaded and fried the chicken and that the peaches were a special pride of Carrie's, so effusive compliments were offered. Robert did an acceptable job of copying the Myers' table manners and felt satisfied with his efforts.

Carrie began the inquisition. "Ida Emma tells me you're a vital hand at the Waggoner Ranch?"

"Yes Ma'am, been there four years now. Work under Jim Coulter." Silence followed, so he continued, "Coulter and his wife, Eudora, just bought that blue house on this same end of town. Maybe you met em? Him and Eudora just had their second baby girl." Robert had plenty of topics in mind to prime the conversation, but Carrie had only one.

"So Robert, where did you learn ranching? In school?" she asked sarcastically, her voice rising.

Robert knew to just tell the story. "No, Ma'am, I left Lebanon, Missouri when I was sixteen. Didn't finish school. Headed here to Texas to ranch. I've been saving money every month. I don't have no bad habits. Got my sights on some land on Denton Creek, east of here." Carrie showed no indication she would interrupt, so Robert took a slow breath and continued. "Two hundred good acres with some bottom land for crops and plenty of grass for pasture. I intend to make a go of it. I've got over half saved."

Finally, Newton spoke up. "These drier plains take more acres per pair than up Missouri way. Can't run too many head on two hundred acres."

"You're sure right about that, Sir, but here's where I got the edge. I'll breed only the best cows and horses, and not just work horses. No, Sir, I aim to raise the finest ridin' and cuttin' horses in the county. People say I got a good eye, so by keepin' or tradin' for the things ranchers like in their stock, they'll come to know the Jennings' horses and I'll be able to sell 'em for more. Maybe just for breedin'."

Newton sat up straight and opened his eyes a bit and looked his young guest over. This young man had spoken with determination and showed his intelligence, book wise or not. He gave a gentle smile. "Sounds thought out."

Dinner was a success. Robert had won over the two men, and he had hopes that he and Ida Emma could wear Carrie down. After the peaches were eaten, Robert thought he might have seen a small smile after he complimented Carrie again on the fine meal.

A great victory was achieved when Newton turned to Robert, "You must come again, young man. We should talk more about brood stock."

Robert was not looking at Carrie but could see the effect of her ice dagger glare as Newton's face changed expressions. He didn't change what he said, and Robert saw there was only so far this man would be pushed.

"Mr. and Mrs. Myers, thank you for your kindness. Miss Ida Emma, it was a pleasure to share a meal with you and your family."

Ida Emma was beaming. "Robert, I'm pleased that we could offer our hospitality. Mother so likes to entertain guests."

Carrie had to grudgingly give Robert a credit for manners. She ended the conversation. "Ida Emma, we must clean the table now. Good day, Robert."

"Thank you for treating Red's hoof, Robert. John says you did a fine job," Newton said, as he pulled his chair back from the table.

"I'll walk you out," John said, and together they exited the front door and walked around back to the barn. He slapped Robert on the back. "You did good, cowboy."

This sudden emotion shown by John was pleasing and Robert broke out in a big grin. "You think so?"

"Newton was serious. He wants to hear more."

"Thanks John. Appreciate your words." Robert tightened the belly cinch on Station and swung his right leg over and mounted the great horse.

"This is a fine animal you have here. Maybe the best in the county. How'd you come by him?"

"He's the finest in all of North Texas, but I'll save that story for next Sunday."

An effective conspiracy developed with Ida Emma and her Uncle John. Newton may have been officially neutral, but Robert felt the quiet man liked him. This was a great victory for Robert and Ida Emma, because if Newton sided with Carrie, their courtship was doomed. Instead, a proper courtship it was, and each Saturday Robert would try to find his way to the front of Sam's General Store and meet Ida Emma. If Robert was working on the west side of the ranch, he might not be able to meet Ida Emma for a few weeks. Many Saturdays he would ride twenty or more miles to Decatur, arriving late at night. He kept a change of clothes at the livery where the owner would let him wash up and sleep with Station. If the weather was cold, he would stay at the nearest Waggoner bunkhouse, three miles from town. Sunday mornings he was clean and excited and standing outside the Methodist

Church, waiting for the Myers. Ida Emma invited him to sit with her and her family in the same pew every Sunday. Unless the Myers had been invited elsewhere, he would land an invitation for dinner. Further weakening of Carrie allowed Robert and Ida Emma to spend time alone on the front porch. Talk with Newton and John also helped solidify his friendship with the men, and Robert's intentions with Ida Emma became clear to all. This intention had not yet been spoken, because Robert still hoped for a thaw in Carrie. He found something quite unexpected.

CHAPTER 16
CHOICES

Across the Red River and in faraway Washington, changes were coming that would shape a land and its people forever. By 1888, most of the American West had been settled with railroads, towns, and fences, yet the great push continued, fueled by a swelling population and its quest for land. The Indians of North America had been compressed and abused and were now reassigned smaller land allotments within their own territory, the very territory promised them by President Jackson. This allowed the opening of great tracts within their land to be reassigned by the US government. A quarter section, one hundred sixty acres, was to be awarded not by a sale or by any previous method of claim, but by a run. Reward was to be granted to those who could claim the land first. Title was to be awarded after five years of residence and improvement of the land, or the claimant could purchase the quarter section outright for a dollar twenty-five an acre, two hundred dollars. The idea intrigued the nation and the world and the Myers.

In Decatur, events were taking a more romantic course. Ida Emma was scrupulously keeping all of her obligations to her parents including her piano and violin lessons, her education, and her domestic duties. But on her Saturday afternoons with Robert, her independence was manifest. With her Uncle John's assistance, she was able to meet Robert, first with her uncle as chaperone, then later unaccompanied. Their meetings were usually hand holding and walking but even this modest contact was reported to Carrie, often in exaggerated detail. She was not pleased. Carrie was an intelligent woman and from her own youth, she could still remember the power of love and its ability to influence and cloud, what she considered, sound judgment. She felt Robert was a nice enough young man, respectful of her daughter, but just not the man she should marry.

One evening, after a light supper, she sat Newton down. He had seen her like this before and was not looking forward to whatever words were to come.

"Newton, I'm sure you're aware of what Ida Emma and Robert have in mind?"

Newton figured this was to be the topic. At least she wasn't upset with him. "I expect his request to come soon."

"Well, she's only sixteen and," she stopped. "I don't think a semiliterate Southerner is her given calling in a husband."

"His father's sympathies don't play here, Carrie."

"Lord's sake, Newton, his name is Robert Lee Jennings, named after the rebel Robert E. Lee," she blurted out her long held opinion. She realized it was an overreach so she immediately restated the obvious. "He's a semiliterate cowboy, Newton."

"His father didn't fight for the North or the South, probably paid his draft. Our daughter's sixteen and strong willed. I can't forbid her to see him. You know she'd choose him over us. You know that as fact. He paused and further strengthened his resolve to prevent another fracture of his family. "Carrie, I understand your feelings about Ida Emma and Robert, but our daughter sees the world different from you and me. She's in love with that young man and you're not going to alter her feelings. You don't have that power. And Carrie, we can't lose Ida Emma. I'm afraid the bending is going to have to come from you."

Although not tenderly delivered, Newton had given his wife one more opportunity to open her heart, to keep the family together and not repeat the failures of pride and hubris that had led to the terrible loss of Rachael. Carrie felt a great shudder of pain, but no regret. She could have said, " Yes," and found a new freedom.

"I think you should forbid it," Carrie said matter-of-factly.

"Not going to do it."

Carrie was taken back by the strong response. Newton's sudden display of decisiveness was a trait she had not seen much of these past few years.

Upstairs, Ida Emma sat alone in her room reading Elizabeth Barrett Browning. Robert had told her last Sunday evening before he left her house, "I'm gonna make you mine." The only way to interpret that was as a proposal, but an odd one and come to think of it, not all that clear. She pondered the phrase over and decided, yes, that must have been what he meant. He was just a bit awkward and it must have been quite an effort just to utter those few words. Next Saturday, she would respond accordingly.

Saturday was a cold day. A norther had blown in Friday leaving the ground crisp and frozen hard. Thirty degrees in Texas will cut through a man like English steel, and the wind and humidity will make even a fat man shiver.

"You think about what I said last week?" Robert asked Ida Emma. She was sitting in front of him, sharing the saddle. He had his arms wrapped securely around her, pulling her tightly so he could feel her ribs through her heavy wool coat. They were riding to Denton Creek, where he would show her again his plans for the Jennings Ranch. They stopped on the high land where the open grass sloped to the cottonwoods below, their bare branches moving rhythmically in the cold wind. Ida Emma pushed Robert's arms aside, and using the saddle horn as a pivot, deftly swung a leg over then the other and in a split second was face to face with Robert.

"Robert Jennings, I am your girl, and I'm that for as long as I live." She kissed Robert more deeply than ever.

"Ida Emmy, don't know what made you say yes, or why you'd fall for a man like me, but I swear to God above that I'll forever do right by you. I love you."

"I love you, Robert."

Above the creek and their future home, above the towering cottonwood limbs, they swore their futures together. They would announce their intentions the next day.

Sunday broke clear and cold but the winds had died down revealing a brisk and fresh winter's day in Texas. As the family was preparing to sit down for the midday dinner, Robert and Ida Emma were exchanging short glances and smiles. Robert was nervous. After the blessing, Carrie took command.

"Mr. Myers and I have an announcement," she said. "We are selling this little parcel here in Wise County and we're going to make the Run in the Indian Territory." Everyone was stunned. No one more so than Newton. He had been blindsided and now in front of the entire family, his wife had dictated this extreme action. She continued, "With money saved and the sale of our home and these forty acres, we can build a grand home on a full quarter section of American prairie. Take our part in a great historic event. We're very excited." Silence.

After a few breaths, Newton spoke. "Well, we've spoken of the Indian Territory. I was not aware of your final decision." He could not appear to be pusillanimous, but he couldn't call her on this unilateral action. She had boldly put him in a corner, and he could either speak his mind clearly and rupture the family or take a side step and try to salvage the relationship. Carrie had played her cards boldly. This was no bluff.

Newton had left the war twenty-three years ago and wanted little else but peace of spirit. It wasn't Carrie's fault that she never understood this need, even Newton didn't fully understand it. He just knew that he felt an aversion to conflict. Fear of battle wasn't Newton's cross. He had led his men against lines of Rebel muskets, heard the lead pass him by and never hit their mark. He had seen one of his boys have his head taken clean off by a canister of grape shot, the boy collapsing in death's motionless embrace, and still Newton walked on, telling his men, "Forward," towards the puff of distant muskets, forward towards their death. No, it wasn't fear of death. It was deeper. Newton never understood his inner turmoil and would live his life between pain and revelation, beyond words. He just knew that his insides were tortured and a rift with his wife would only make it unbearable.

Newton took a long sip of sweet tea then turned to his brother-in-law. "You know, John, two quarters together would be three hundred twenty acres? That's quite a spread."

Carrie's muscles relaxed and a broad smile crossed her face. She knew her husband, and he had responded just as she thought he would. She didn't admit to herself that she had manipulated Newton, but all in company knew it, and from that moment on they felt differently toward her.

"With one last year of schooling, Ida Emma, there'll be a need for teachers in the Territory."

Ida Emma looked her mother squarely in the eyes. "I won't be accompanying you to the Territory. Robert and I are to be married."

"Yes Ma'am, Sir, we're askin' for your blessin'." Robert tried to stay with the script he and Ida Emma had prepared, but now all he could do was say what came to mind. "I'm fixin' to buy those two hundred acres on Denton Creek and start my ranch. Ida Emma's said yes."

"All this announcing, Robert, don't you think you should have asked properly?" Carrie's tone was laced with reproach.

"Seems all this plannin' was goin' on without Ida Emma knowin', so I just felt it proper to tell you what we're plannin'." His tone was polite but took on resoluteness to equal Carrie's.

She had met her match. She tried one last parental thrust. "Ida Emma, you will go to the Indian Territory with us and finish your education. After Robert buys his ranch and is established, he can then ask for your hand in proper fashion."

Ida Emma ended the discussion. "I'll not be going."

Robert took her hand and stood up slowly. "Walk me to the door, Ida Emma?" Then he turned to the Myers. "I hope it all goes as you wish. Thank you for your Sunday hospitality. Good day."

Alone on the porch, oblivious to the cold, Robert held Ida Emma tightly.

"You see what will happen, Ida Emma? You'll be alone here in Texas without them," Robert said. "Is that what you want?"

"Robert, you've given me more than I ever thought was possible. I never knew a person could feel the love I have experienced with you. It is a gift that I'll hold forever. It must have been what St. Paul was writing about. That's how I feel. My sadness isn't so much that my parents will move away, rather, it's that they don't have the love we do."

"Ida Emmy, I wish I could say things as good as you, but you just have to know that I feel the same. I'll always take care of you and that big heart you got there." He touched her chest then kissed her deeply.

When Ida Emma returned, she took a biscuit from the table and started to go up the stairs to her room. She turned and with straight-backed determination looked her mother directly in the eye. "Whether you know it or like it, Mother, your daughters always have choices. I have made mine."

CHAPTER 17

ROBERT'S GIFT

During that fall and winter of '88-'89, the Myers and Robert and Ida Emma walked on separate but equally focused paths. The Myers had multiple interests and assets and had signed a sales contract to be executed before the Run. Robert and Ida Emma continued to meet on Saturday evenings and Sundays at church then spend the afternoon together. He was no longer invited to Sunday dinner. That was fine with Robert and Ida Emma, and they were able to spend hours alone and free to experience their new love. If the weather permitted, they would take long rides on Station and would usually end up near Denton Creek, where they would lay out the proposed position of the house, barn, and sheds. Ida Emma would prepare a simple lunch of canned fruit and sandwiches, spread a blanket on the dry brown grass and listen to Robert's plans. They became her plans too.

Robert was allowed to see Ida Emma on the Myers' front porch but was not allowed inside. This was Carrie's pettiness and proved no barrier for the young couple. Finally, one cold evening, Ida Emma simply announced to her parents that she and Robert would be coming into the parlor. Carrie led Newton to their room and the couple was alone.

Ida Emma began to teach Robert the violin. He called it a fiddle and showed some aptitude for this new and wonderful instrument. He never would have sought this artistic endeavor on his own, but it became an expression of his love for Ida Emma and he loved responding to her gentle instruction. She would play a few notes, carefully showing Robert the proper finger placement and how to draw the bow. He would copy these placements and slowly begin to coax the notes from the instrument. After a dozen lessons, he could play a few measures of Ida Emma's favorite waltz without interruption.

"Ida Emma, I never knew I could play a fiddle. My ma would be proud of her Missouri boy."

"Well I'm proud of that same Missouri boy too, Robert. I believe you've quite a knack for the violin. Play it slowly again, and let me dance for you."

Robert began playing the waltz slowly. His fingers flowed gracefully along the thin neck of the instrument, and with the one-two-three-one-two-three of the waltz, Ida Emma began to move. She wrapped her arms around her waist and took her first steps, dipping and flowing with the sensual vibrations of the violin. She closed her eyes as she danced, then as she passed by Robert with her head bowed, she opened her wonderful eyes to meet Robert's.

"Ida Emmy, you are the finest woman in all of Texas."

Her returning smile came from deep within. He forgot the composer and called it Ida Emma's waltz.

It was a busy and dizzying time for the two, and they were not shy showing their love to each other and to anyone in town who cared to watch. Robert and Coulter became closer friends and Coulter assured Robert that old man Waggoner was willing to sell. Robert wanted to get married after the purchase. He planned to build a temporary and very simple shelter on the land, then he could marry his girl and have her a place to live, all proper and in keeping with prairie protocol.

Uncle John entered the small sphere of Robert's friends and became a sympathetic conduit to the Myers' household. John was genuinely fond of Robert and found Robert's lack of education no barrier. In fact, he noted Robert's always curious mind and keen observations of the natural world whether it was livestock, especially horses, the weather, soil types, even the night sky and its seasonal changes. One evening, Robert told the tale of Orion the Hunter and the nearby Seven Sisters. John wondered how Robert knew of such things, but simply sat back and enjoyed the telling. It was that same evening that Uncle John revealed himself in frank honesty to Robert and Ida Emma. The three were seated on the Coulter's front porch sharing a single wool blanket and sipping hot cider ale offered by Eudora Coulter.

"Robert, you know I'll never be a rancher or farmer. I don't have the fire you do," John calmly stated.

Robert looked up with a question on his lips but John continued.

"Nope, I just don't have the connection to the land like you do. I think I'd rather run a business or maybe teach at the new State Normal College they're starting up over in Denton County. I'd need to study for a few more years though. I'm just not so sure my sister and Newton have it in them to start anew from scratch."

John had covered a lot of ground and Robert and Ida Emma were silent, expecting more.

"But you're still gonna make the Run, aren't you?" Robert finally asked in the same serious tone set by his friend and confidant.

"I'm not fully sure, to tell the truth, Robert. I don't think Newton would do it if it weren't for Carrie. You know she's pushing him. He'd be happy to stay here in Decatur. He's got his church and those few Union buddies. I don't understand the push to go to the Indian Territory except," he paused and swallowed, "except to take Ida Emma away."

Robert of course knew this thinking, but Robert and Ida Emma's plans were fixed and wouldn't change, no matter where her parents decided to live.

John continued as if speaking to himself, "Truth be told, I'm weary. Not just with my life here in Decatur, but in all those things that matter most. I'm afraid I can't find that spark that you two have. Maybe if I found a girl, I'd feel different. I just don't have a fire in my belly, a reason to greet the sun. A man's got to make a place for himself and here in Texas, well I just don't see a road for me. If I don't make the Run, I don't know how Newton will get along." There was a long pause then he tossed his head side to side and lifted an eyebrow. "Well, I guess I'm going to the Oklahoma Territory."

Ida Emma took a short sip of the now cold cider ale. "Uncle John, you're right about taking care of Mother and Father, but I just know you'll find that spark you're looking for north of the Red."

John nodded, resigned, but with no enthusiasm.

March in North Texas can still make that fat man shiver or make him sweat fast. On a warm day a cotton shirt is all a man needs. The lengthening days start to coax the buds to swell and open, and the rocks' warmth can bring lizards and snakes out to bask. Morning's cool moist air fills the lungs with awakening, and if a man like Robert pays attention, the earth teaches him. But if a blue norther races south over the plains and mixes with the moist air, a man can freeze if unprepared and caught in the open. The cold humid air penetrates all but the warmest clothes and a temperature of forty can kill a man or a new dropped calf. A good cowboy will ride the herd and keep an eye on the widening heifers, ready to drop their first-born. If the weather turns, he'll try to bring the heifer to a sheltered spot, out of the wind.

There was such a spot on the south sector of the ranch. It had, over many years become a favorite calving ground for the experienced older cows. It was a large depression two hundred feet across and ten feet deep. The rim was crowded with scrub oak along the north side, giving an effective windbreak to the depression. The cowboys called it the old buffalo waller, but more likely it was formed by the collapse of an underground limestone cavern. Robert was alone that day in early March, and was herding two very wide heifers to the waller. He hoped other cows would be there with new calves and help calm the new mothers to be, sort of a bovine midwifery.

He was surprised to see a whiff of smoke rising above the bare oak branches. He figured a fire could only mean warmth and warmth must bring good news. Then again, maybe it was some outlaw on the run. It was Coulter. The two heifers entered the waller and found some forage. Robert rode over to Coulter and dismounted. Coulter was sitting on a log and had a nice fire going. The embers told Robert he had been there a while. A pot of coffee was on a rock beside the low flames along with two metal cups. Robert could smell the rich coffee and mixed with the humid cold, teased Robert of the pleasure to come.

"Coulter, you're a welcome sight. What brings you out here?"

"Was out checkin' the new bridge over south of here. You know the new farm to market road? Wanted to make sure those boys set the bed to the embankment so as not to wash out with the first big rain. Thought you might be out this ways so swung over on my way back. Thought we'd like a coffee in this cold."

"I even like coffee on a hot day, Coulter," laughed Robert as he poured the two cups full and took the first sip. Coulter held his without drinking and Robert got the first sense he had news to tell. "Why you here, Coulter?"

Coulter took his first drink, and then said directly, "Spoke with Mr. Waggoner three days ago. Had a meetin' with the assistant foremen, Eli, and me. After the meetin', Eli followed up with a firm offer to buy a full section to start his own spread. The old man lit into him. Told him he wasn't breakin' up the ranch. Told Eli he could stay as an assistant foreman, liked his work, but no sale. Ended as fast as it started. Eli just walked away."

Robert felt the heaviness of the telling, but he wanted to fully understand its application to his own plans. "You didn't mention then my wantin' the two hundred acres along Denton Creek?"

"Like I told you before, last fall we spoke and he nodded but made no firm commitment." Coulter spoke deliberately, trying to be as accurate as possible. "Took that as good, but don't know how he feels now. Didn't think that was the right time to bring it up again."

There was a long silence as Robert sipped his cooling coffee. "Well, he hasn't said no." He spoke with just a hint of optimism. "My offer is hard cash and fair. What do you think I should do?"

"You've got a lot happenin' now, Robert, not sure. I get along good with Mr. Waggoner, so maybe I should ask for you when I think the time is right."

"Yea, I guess that's best for now," Robert answered softly. "I have another thing to ask of you, of you and Eudora."

"You name it, Robert."

"Now don't say yes 'til I ask. Myers are headed to the Run next month. Place is sold. You know Ida Emma and I are marryin', but I wanted to have title to that land in my hand on that day. Could Ida Emma stay with you and Eudora for a time?"

"Of course," Coulter said with no delay. Guess you didn't know your Ida Emma and Eudora already spoke about that?" he asked with a smile. "If Eli decides to leave, the assistant job is yours."

"Thanks."

Robert shared the unsettling news with Ida Emma that evening. He no longer waited for an invitation to knock on the Myers' door. This cold evening she invited him inside without asking her mother first. They sat in the parlor and spoke in soft tones.

"You know I'll marry you tonight if you ask?" Ida Emma spoke with strength in her voice.

"I believe you, Ida Emmy," Robert said. "After Coulter told me the sale could have a glitch, he offered to have you stay with him and Eudora till I have title," Robert said. "But you already knew that," he added with a welcome laugh.

They sat side by side on the divan in silence when John burst into the room with an infusion of energy, very unusual.

"Robert, you know the Indian Territory. Look at this map I got here." He spread the map on the small parlor table and traced the boundary of the Run. Robert couldn't easily read the small print but he immediately recognized the two wavy lines as the Canadian and the North Canadian Rivers. Along the straight west border just above the North Canadian was an outlined square and writing he couldn't read.

"What's this here say?"

John looked closely. "It says 98th Meridian."

"No. I mean right here. What does that say?"

John found where Robert was pointing. "This area of the Territory, the part the government is opening up here for the Run is labeled 'unassigned land' and this little square here says 'Darlington Indian Agency'."

"What do they mean by unassigned land?"

"Not sure, Robert. Must be land that wasn't assigned to a particular tribe."

"So the government is givin' the Indians' land to you? I don't understand. That land is full of people. It's theirs now. I know that land. How can they take it from the tribes?" Robert's innocence had run squarely into reality. Robert was not aware of the legal maneuverings that had set this all in motion, and he had no idea of the lands to be opened. His initial confusion graded into a simmering indignation.

John sensed it. "Robert, don't know how you feel about all of this. Sounds like you have thoughts running counter to the government and those thousands of people fixing to make the Run for their quarter section. Can't tell you it's right or wrong, but I can tell you it's going to happen. Every piece of land, every acre offered will be taken the first day, and no one there will care about Robert Jennings or his thoughts on the fairness of it all. It's free land, Robert, and people's memory is short. It'll be up to the ones writing the history to try and make sense of it, and up to us to tell our children the truth."

Robert tried to think about these things, but it was too much to sort out. He studied the map a bit longer. He thought again what his friend had just said and just stared at the map. He felt like a lone leaf on a tall cottonwood, high above but unable to control the mighty tree. He would talk with John.

"That's good land there. All along the North Canadian. It's where I'd go. Spent some time there. It's near perfect."

John's mouth opened slightly and his eyes sparkled clear. "Sister, Newton, come in here right away!" he nearly yelled.

Newton and Carrie soon entered the parlor and looked at John then at Robert.

"Why all the excitement?" asked Newton.

"Robert knows this land. You have to listen to what he says," John answered.

Robert didn't like the sudden attention and the forced sharing of his knowledge of this land he knew so well. A simple touch of his knee by Ida Emma told him a give here could yield harmony in the future, or at least start a slow healing. He understood immediately without a word spoken by Ida Emma.

"I come through this country on my way from Missouri. Spent a few weeks just east of the Darlington Agency. I know the land."

"What would you recommend, Robert?" asked a very polite Newton.

Robert was now committed to full disclosure so he held nothing back. This was Ida Emma's family and surely that counted.

"Well, it don't matter what you hear or whatever you're told, make your way to the Darlington Agency," he said. "That's where you start. At the gun, you ride due east as hard as you can. Follow near the top of the long slope leanin' south to the river. You can always tell the river by the cottonwoods. Keep it on your right. It's all good land. Pick a claim that's got the lay for farmin' if that's what you want. Find one with good timber. You'll need the timber. But there's a spot, better than most. After 'bout two miles there's a large grove of trees, alder, gum, and oak I think. The draw below the trees leads down to an ox bow of the river pointin' up to the north. Don't know how the lines gonna split this all up but it's good land, good land. It's good land there." He slowed as his memories of his time with Dee-day caught up with his spoken words and he stopped to remember his gentle teacher. He was thankful that Dee-day moved his camp each year. Maybe he wouldn't see the coming Run.

"Go on please, Robert," asked Carrie in a new and polite tone.

He looked up at Carrie then continued, "It's only a short distance. It'll be a full gallop and the best horse'll claim the best land. Don't take a wagon at the gun. Ride a horse and gallop like hell." Carrie gasped at "hell". "Sorry Ma'am, but I'm tellin' you no wagon's gonna claim a good piece that day. You stay with the wagon and let these two ride," he paused, "like hell." They understood.

"Thank you, Robert. May I offer you a slice of peach pie?" she asked.

Robert loved Carrie's pies, but her coldness these past months had shown him a side he didn't like, and he wasn't about to sweep it under a pie offering. "No thank you Ma'am, Ida Emma and me got to talk."

April in North Texas is a delight of colors and new growth and moist air laden with the sweet aroma of opening buds. That's if that particular day is between barn rattling storms and tornados that snake across the prairie like a mad cottonmouth. This April day's ending was still unknown. A dark sky was threatening, but the wind's stillness was giving no clue to the afternoon's final say, clear and bright or driving storm.

Robert was resting on Station outside the Myers' home, as he studied the Myer's preparation for the Run. Most of their belongings had been packed and stored, to be shipped north after a homestead was claimed. The items needed for the Run and temporary shelter were loaded on a large wagon. The sides were sturdy and a good three feet high. There was no arching wooden skeleton like the old Conestoga wagon. The load would be covered with a heavy canvas tarp. Newton had sold all of his livestock. He would buy new stock after the Run. He didn't want to drive animals north and place them at risk. Money in his pocket or in the bank in Decatur was safer. He had his favorite gelding, Red, saddled and two mares and two old plow horse geldings to pull the wagon. Newton would ride Red, and John would ride the best mare the day of the Run. Newton had done a good job paring their belongings for the arduous trip. He was in much better financial shape than most of the families making the Run and could afford to carry a light load. Many of the hopeful families would bring everything they owned on strained and overloaded wagons.

Robert surveyed the new pilgrims. Red was certainly adequate, assuming his hoof held up, but the four other horses were a problem. All were past prime and now were being asked to pull a loaded wagon two hundred miles over rough road. He wondered how Newton could have done such a poor figuring. Maybe if Newton had been able to cool Carrie's heat, they would have talked more and Newton would have asked for Robert's help. Newton and John were binding their success to one of four horses. None was up to the task.

Dinner that night was at the Decatur Inn and Robert was invited. The evening was punctuated with Carrie going on about her new country and the lovely home she, she kept saying she not we, was going to build and how she would invite educators and musicians and artists to populate the Oklahoma prairie. It was to be a grand adventure culminating in the establishment of a shining Chautauqua community, a torch of civilization.

Carrie kept talking. "I believe once the railroad is connected to the East, I can persuade artists and writers to make the Indian Territory a regular stop on their travels. Won't it be fine to bring such learned people to the Territory? Yes, I believe that's what I'll do. Oh, and dairy cows, Newton. I think I should like a few dairy cows. They are such gentle creatures. Why, did you know Marie Antoinette had a dairy at her palace?"

"She gave her head for it," Newton added dryly.

Robert had had enough. "There's already people there you know. Any way you want to see it, legal or not, you're takin' their land. They was already Indians there long before President Jackson forced other Indians from all over the country to the Territory. Must be fifty tribes and all got their own idea of what's civilized. Some from the plains, some from the Rocky Mountains, and some from the East. They're all different. Speak different languages. Some farm and some don't. Some friendly and some not. If you know one, fine, but it don't mean you know more'n one. Readin' about somethin' don't tell you what you need to know or what's true." He stopped, unsure if he was making any sense or just sounding frustrated.

"Thank you, Robert," John said sympathetically. "You're the one man here who has actually experienced the Territory. I hope my sister and her family recognize the stark truth of what you say. The future isn't written yet, Carrie."

Carrie was silent. Newton closed the discussion.

"Robert, we here want to thank you for your advice and counsel. I know what you say is true and I know your feelings are strong. I respect a man who lets his heart speak. Our success in this great adventure, if we are to achieve success, will be, in part, because of you."

After dinner, Robert, Ida Emma, and Uncle John walked outside. Robert was to ride with Ida Emma to the Coulters' where she had moved two weeks ago, and then he would ride alone to the bunkhouse and his corner bed. Instead he lingered with John.

Robert was direct. "John, you're puttin' you and your run up for a bad outcome cause of your horses. Red's okay, but you really think you're going to make a run with one of those others? Seems a poor idea."

"You said it's only a mile or two from the start point. Seems I could get a short run from one of them."

"I said it was two miles but it could be more. You don't know where the government's drawin' the startin' line. What if a hoof splits, or one has a bad leg, or one is stolen, or if those close-in quarter sections get taken before you, and you gotta run ten miles? There's no tellin' what could happen to foul you up, then what have you got? You got nothin'."

There followed a very long silence.

"I want you to take Station. Ride him and you'll claim that quarter or a good one like it."

"I can't take Station."

"Hell, I ain't givin' him to you. I'm just lettin' you borrow him. You'll bring him back to me by fall."

John appeared stunned both by this gift and by its simple truth. He needed a horse and Robert just offered his great horse to claim his quarter section.

"But Station?"

"You've seen how I ride him and how I care for him. You never tie or hobble him out of your sight. Do you understand? Never out of your sight. You talk to him like you're talkin' to me. And if there's a storm, you stay with him. Never leave him alone in a storm."

"I'll do just as you say, Robert. And I'll bring him back to you this fall. You have my word. Thank you."

Robert unhitched the saddle and slipped it to the ground. He handed the modified halter reins to John. "You don't use a bridle. I never put a bit in Station."

Robert stroked Station's nose then spoke softly to his great horse. Robert shouldered his saddle and walked Ida Emma to the Coulters. The next morning at day- break, Ida Emma kissed her family good bye. Robert was miles away, riding a horse from the Waggoner herd.

CHAPTER 18
THE RUN

The Run was front-page headlines in newspapers all over the country, and even the foreign press ran stories of the great land rush. America was captivated. The press reported multiple aspects of the Run and many individual stories caught a reporter's eye, so that a curious reader from a faraway state could get a parcel of first-hand accounts. Later historians would traverse these morsels of the participants and again hear the stories of courage, and risk, and greed and avarice, mixing fact with legend so that a reader might grasp a tiny crumb of the experience. But it would remain only a small shard of the reality. Great events, like wars, exist in the frozen memory of those who experience it. It was like that with the Run. Ten thousand stories, like a prism, reflected and altered the day for those that weren't present. You had to be there.

Newton and Carrie and John were there. Two weeks after the Run, Ida Emma received her first letter from her mother dated April 25, 1889, postmarked Reno City, Indian Territory.

My Dear Ida Emma,

I am writing you as I gaze upon our quarter section of this great land. Your father and I have shared in a wondrous thing, and I am not sure I can convey to you in this first letter our true experience, but I must try.

Our journey north was uneventful to the Red River. You know I haven't spent a night out of doors in many years, but I think I adapted well. I was able to prepare quite nutritious and tasteful meals on an open fire and sleep on the ground. I saw a glow in your father's eyes, absent for years, and each morning as he and my brother broke camp, he seemed to move with a fluidity, lost for twenty years. We were fortunate that the spring rains have been mild, so upon reaching the Red River, we were able to find fords over the two ribbons of the river channel. If the rains had been heavy, we would have been forced to travel farther east to a ferry. Once into the Indian Territory, we continued north and skirted the Arbuckle Mountains on their west side. We encountered our first Indians here, Chickasaw we were told, but they kept their distance and we felt no threat. By our third day in the Territory, we assimilated with other pilgrims into a small eight wagon train group and followed the Chisholm Trail to the Canadian River. Here the flood plain is much narrower than the Red and the channel more regular. Where the Trail met the river, we were ferried across at the most exorbitant rate of two dollars. I shall address this injustice once the Territory's courts are established. The country is beautiful between the rivers, with large trees shading parts of this lush prairie. I tell you, Ida Emma, we could have stopped anywhere and found our garden.

We arrived and camped with others near a place called Reno City. It was really just a collection of tents and few wobbly wooden buildings. The people there say it will be the new county seat, but we all know the Rock Island Line will determine the county seat once the railroad lays their line west of the new Oklahoma City. Any county seat must have a railroad.

You would not have believed the mix of people those days near Reno City. There were so many foreign accents. I think German was the most common, and there were dialects from all over America. I had the most difficult time talking with a family from Union County, Georgia. Lovely people but hard to understand. We met an artist from New York City, a Mr. Remington. He was a very large man with huge hands. I couldn't believe how beautifully he could paint Indians and their horses. He said he was just sketching and would return to his New York studio to finish his paintings. I will never forget his wonderful art.

Two days before the run we paid another ferryman two more dollars to cross to the north bank of the North Canadian River where we made our way the short distance to the Darlington Agency. We found it to be as your Robert had described, and we spent these days before the Run talking to the Whites and Indians about the lands east. The three of us pledged to keep Robert's description of the land he visited to ourselves. As more people gathered the night before, I became quite concerned that there were not enough quarter sections for all. I was proper in my concern.

The morning of April 22 was crisp and the air was light as were our spirits. We broke our simple camp and loaded everything onto our wagon. You father and uncle were saddled and ready, and our four-horse team was cinched to the wagon. I do say that Station is a fine animal. I was to hold the team steady when the cannon fired. I was to keep them in place as your father and John raced east. It was our bit of deception to our fellow pilgrims. I know Robert first suggested running with horses only, no wagon, but I tell you, Ida Emma, I don't know what these otherwise intelligent people were thinking. There was no circumstance in my mind that would allow a wagon and team to race east and have any chance of a good quarter section. I must assume they were inexperienced with the ways of the West and the uneven ground they were to traverse. I pray God may forgive us if our not telling our plans was the same as a false witness.

At noon, the cavalry sounded a cannon and the Run began with yelling and noise and such commotion. A number of men discharged their firearms into the air, and this added to the chaotic scene. As I had prayed, Newton on Red and John on Station were easily near the front as the dust finally cleared. I could just make them out far to the east. The scene revealed to my eyes two overturned wagons. The men were trying to unharness their horses and ride on alone. I also saw a number of men running on foot far behind the now departed rush. I fear their efforts were not rewarded.

Our plan was for me to wait two hours then drive the wagon due east. I was to look for two signal fires, praying the columns of smoke would guide me. Ida Emma, for a time, I was all alone on a roadless prairie following my compass and the path of your father. It was a moment of golden clarity for me. I alone was riding to claim this land, and I am unable to adequately convey my thoughts in simple words. You must see this yourself. Not a house, not a building or fence, or any sign of habitation, not a plowed field, or a windmill. The grass was high along the sides of the wagon and scrubby plants scratched the bottom of the wagon and tried to catch the reins. I could have ridden for days, then suddenly, I saw the two smoke columns. I continued with alacrity to the spot and there your father, holding his claim flag, was as tall as the day we first met. What a grand piece of land we have, my Ida Emma. I think we can put to plow most of it, with one twenty-acre corner in heavy woods the exception. The whole piece slopes south to the river beyond. You uncle has a claim south and west of us, only one quarter section between us. I do believe he may have claimed the land your Robert spoke of.

Your father and John returned last evening from the claims office in the new settlement of Kingfisher, and we are both now legal on these parcels. At the claims office they heard tales of deception. Men had ridden in early and were already sitting on claims when the Run began. This led to conflict with those striking legal claims, and at least two men were killed in this area alone. Seems our two quarter sections were so close to the starting line that these criminals must have felt the cavalry would have discovered them too easily. These deceivers were more common farther east of us.

Well, Dear, you can see my hand can't write as fast as my mind can talk. There is so much more to tell you, but Ida Emma, you must see this land. Please give our thanks and regards to Robert. Write soon of your plans. Has Robert purchased the Denton Creek land yet?

With our love,

Mother and Father

CHAPTER 19

SILENT RIDE

Ida Emma read the letter quickly, reread it and then waited for Robert to arrive. A little past five, he rode up and tied his horse in front of the house. Ida Emma was standing on the porch and beckoned him to hurry inside. He was puzzled.

"Robert, I received my first letter from Mother. You must hear this."

He kissed her tenderly, and they walked inside to the parlor.

"Did they claim a quarter section?" he asked.

"Patience, Robert, I'll start from the beginning."

She read it slowly then Robert asked her to read it again, and a third time as he tried to figure out where they had made their claims.

"She thanked me, Ida Emma. Sounded fair about it all. Not sure she was ever gonna climb that mountain."

"Seems so, Robert."

"Can't be sure where along the North Canadian they've lit. I knew Station would run strong for John. Knew he would."

They sat silently for a few minutes watching the sky darken and twilight have its last color burst when Coulter rode slowly up and dismounted. Robert excused himself and walked directly to Coulter, whose stance telegraphed conflict.

"Evening, Coulter," Robert said.

"Evening Robert." There followed a long uncomfortable pause. "Just came from headquarters."

Robert didn't like the tone, but remained silent.

"I have some tough news, Robert. The old man won't sell anymore of the ranch. He still remembers the Panic of Seventy-three and thinks land's the only good thing to own. Thinks the days of five or even ten dollars an acre are past. Sees big prices in the future. Won't sell." These last words were spoken in a barely audible whisper.

Robert said nothing, but sensed heat building quickly inside. It boiled and rose and boiled again and turned white filling him with rage, a white rage of such intensity and pain that it frightened him with its sudden blinding onset. The pain didn't go away but lingered and tortured Robert until he could not contain it.

"Goddamn him!" he roared. "Goddamn him to hell!" The emotion in his voice frightened Ida Emma and alarmed Coulter. "Goddamn the sonofabitch!" he said to no one as he stalked to his horse. He didn't say a word to Ida Emma or to Coulter. He swung into the saddle. "Goddamn him!" he screamed a last time with his head back and his eyes fixed skyward.

"Robert, don't do nothin' stupid!" yelled Coulter. "Think of Ida Emma," he said as Robert was riding away. It may have saved Robert's life.

Riding at a full gallop for fifteen minutes, Robert arrived at the lane entrance to the Waggoner Ranch home and headquarters. He stopped, allowed his horse to catch his breath, and finally gave himself time to calm and to reflect on this terrible news. Robert heard again Coulter's warning words, and he slowed his breathing and began to think more clearly. The lights in the house were being lit and the inner warmth of the home shined. Robert saw people moving in shadows preparing for the evening meal and the day's recap. It was a ritual observed in most homes, and the old man and his family were the same as the Coulters or the Myers and, Robert hoped, someday would be the same as the Jennings. He laid the reins gently across the horse's neck, turned his head, and rode slowly to the bunkhouse. After a few minutes, he saw Coulter riding towards him. Robert rode slowly past. He would talk to no one tonight.

For the next ten days he rode alone, withdrawn. It was not the proper thing to do to Ida Emma, but he trusted that she understood his need to be alone. Robert had no say in this action. He simply responded to an inner fire that he knew would only damage a relationship if he had the poor judgment to reveal it. So he stayed away from town and people and simply rode. He fixed a few fences along the way, but mostly he just rode. He decided he'd ride the entire perimeter of the Waggoner Ranch. Along the north side he spent a quiet cold night with no blanket, only a fire to keep him warm. He rose the next morning and gazed north, knowing he had missed an opportunity across the Red. Missed a shot at his own land because he was too proud and too stubborn to recognize the land didn't care about the feud with Carrie or for a man named Robert Jennings. It just didn't care. The land was simply there, and Robert had been so fixed on being independent of the Myers that he had failed to see his independence was granted by himself, not the Myers. He would never again allow a conflict to cloud his best judgment, never.

That bit of painful clarity made him feel better, so he reheated the coffee and poured a second cup. He began to take stock of himself, his strengths, and his possessions. He counted the four hundred eighty dollars in the bank and thirty in gold coins, over five hundred dollars. He had two rifles, the old single shot .22, an 1876 Winchester .45, and two Colt .45 army cavalry revolvers. He had plenty of ammo, three changes of clothes and winter wear, but only one pair of boots, a good saddle and tack, a few tools and of course, Station, somewhere in the Indian Territory.

The nontangible side of the ledger was strong. He had a poor education and only read haltingly, but he could do simple math and he understood crop yield and what it took to graze a cow and calf. He knew horses and cattle and how to judge them and he knew how to treat injured animals and how to pull a calf stuck in mid-labor. In fact, he reasoned, he knew a hell of a lot about animals. He knew hunting and carpentry, and he could build a house and barn when the time came to start his ranch.

As the coffee cooled, he turned inside. He realized he had other skills some people didn't. He could make a friend easily, and his word was his bond. He had developed a simple yet profound idea of God, one of redemptive encompassing love. He would be hard pressed to put it into words. He wasn't sure just how wise he was, but he had plenty of wonder. And he had Ida Emma. She had placed her love and trust in him and now was the right time to act, to move ahead. He figured the best plans don't always work out and his charge was to find another one. "Just need a new plan," he said to himself, pleased with this new line of reasoning. So what was the plan?

Robert had no place to be and was in no rush to saddle up and head back to Decatur. He traced the events that had brought him to this patch of North Texas prairie and wondered of the decisions he had made and those he had passed on. He thought of the drunk cowboy with the great horse. What a thing to happen to a sixteen-year-old. What would another man have done? By God, he thought, I took action right then. A moment later everything would have changed. Why did he and the cowboy meet up right then and there? What would Bailey Stone say? Hell, it was Robert's quick thinking that opened his entire life. Where would he be if him and Station hadn't left the next day for Texas? And what about Dee-Day and the time spent with the gentle Cherokee? "By

God, I've done some pretty good things and I'm only twenty-one. And Ida Emma. I got Ida Emma and we'll partner up and just do what we have to." He didn't realize he had spoken these last thoughts out loud.

The coffee was gone, and the fire's embers were getting cold. He didn't know how long it had been, but the sun was far above the treetops and their new green leaves. "Now what?" He repeated the question three times, and the answer came. "I'll head west."

He figured to follow the Canadian River west to the New Mexico Territory. The land west was drier and higher and the soil thinner. It took more acres to run a cow and calf and Robert knew he couldn't afford enough land to run a big herd. He'd heard stories of where the Canadian River left the Sangre de Cristo Mountains, where it was a small clear stream gathering smaller creeks. There at the piedmont the grass was thick and fewer acres needed for a pair. That's where he'd set his future.

The hardest part of most decisions is the making it, not the doing it. Robert's cloud had been storm laden by Carrie Myers and the old man Waggoner. Two people Robert couldn't control, but whose actions had controlled his. No longer would he allow anyone to step in front of his light. A man made his own. He stood and stretched his arms overhead meeting in an arc and rotated his neck to feel the warming sun on his face. He saddled the black horse quickly and rode south in a determined gait. He left his old coffee pot and cup by the fire. Maybe some young cowboy could use them.

Robert rode back to Decatur and arrived at the Coulters' before supper. Ida Emma was on the front porch.

"I see a sparkle in your eyes, Robert. I just knew I'd see it when you came home," she said before they embraced warmly.

"Hopin' you'd understand, Ida Emma. Got some ideas to talk over."

"It's odd, Robert. I knew you'd be away for a time, but I also knew you'd come back with a new face. So tell me about these ideas you have." She took his arm, and they sat together.

He told of his plans to move west, to New Mexico, as soon as they were married and the sooner they were married, the better. At supper, they brought Coulter and Eudora in on their plans and their kind friends suggested they could marry in their home. Ida Emma and Robert quickly agreed, and would ask Reverend Bailey Stone to officiate. A wedding date was set for early June.

In those few weeks, Robert had a full plate, and no task more important than riding to the Indian Territory to bring Station home. Coulter agreed to allow him the continued use of the black gelding he had been riding. The joy of the young couple was palpable to the Coulters and others. They appeared as young marrieds, only to separate each evening as Robert returned to the bunkhouse. He once stated his displeasure with the arrangement, but a gentle look from Ida Emma dissuaded him from further petitions.

Ida Emma wrote a letter to her parents after she and Robert had set their plans, and advised them he would riding north soon for Station. She assumed that they would not travel back to Texas for the wedding. She was surprised when she received a letter from her Uncle John in reply. She read it quickly and exclaimed, "Oh my Lord." When Robert arrived for Supper, she gave him a glass of sweet tea, and on the front porch read aloud to a curious Robert.

May 10, 1889 Reno City, Indian Territory
Dear Ida Emma and Robert,

I read the letter to your parents last evening at supper. They have constructed a simple lean-to with rough-hewn small trees and lined it with tarpaper. It is crude, but surprisingly dry from the rains. They have ordered a nice house from the Sears and Roebuck and expect delivery to Oklahoma City within the next month. I will help them assemble it with additional help from our gracious neighbors. I tell you, Ida Emma, these people are the finest you could imagine. This country is beauty in a bud.

Ida Emma, your parents are not young. They are infused with this land's energy, but I fear they cannot sustain the strength to build their farm or keep it going year after year. They need me daily and I know with the new house and outbuildings to come, I will have little time for my own.

Robert, I am sure I have claimed the land you described. Your Station easily covered the distance ahead of all others, and I recognized the very copse of trees and the draw and the deep oxbow of the river. Your description of this land was simple and pure, but your words could not capture its deep and silent beauty. Robert, you and Ida Emma must come north. I will deed this land to you, and you can buy it outright for a dollar twenty-five an acre. I want no profit. Your Station claimed this land, and it should be yours. If this is acceptable, please notify me so that I can dedicate my time to my sister and Newton. Keep in mind that a planting of wheat on the north area above the draw should be in the ground by June if you are to have any expectation of a yield.

I await your reply and look forward to being your neighbor on this prairie.

Your loving uncle and friend,

John

After a short pause Robert said, "Please read it again for me, Ida Emmy."

She read it slowly, emphasizing the description of the land John had claimed. "Sure sounds like the land I spoke of. What do you say, Ida Emmy?"

She turned, her eyes level with his. "Yes," she said. "Yes."

CHAPTER 20
LANTERN NIGHT

Robert's immediate concern was to purchase a team of four horses, a wagon, and just the right mix of implements and household goods to take on the twelve-day journey to the Indian Territory. Robert was paid his last due wages the next day, and he counted out forty dollars for Ida Emma to purchase the needed household items for the kitchen and house to be. He advised her to keep the purchases small. There was only so much room, and he was sure that most items could be purchased at Reno City, although he figured the prices would be higher.

Robert spent the next two days buying a wagon and tack for a four-horse team. He concentrated his efforts on his first big stock purchase. There was a small-time horse trader near town, Zeno, who Robert liked and respected. Robert had appreciated some of Zeno's animals and his horse knowledge. He had seen a set of filly twins born eighteen months ago that Zeno had up for sale. Twins are rare in horses and their difficult birth had almost killed the mare, Zeno's favorite. As foals, the fillies were considerably smaller than normal, but Robert had noted this size difference had narrowed the past two months and he thought they looked promising. There was a saying that Robert had heard.

One white foot buy him,
Two white feet try him,
Three white feet and a white nose,
Take off his hide and throw him to the crows.

Robert knew this to be nonsense, but some men actually put a little faith in this or other sayings. Zeno wasn't a believer in such a folk tale, but he was willing to sell at a good price to Robert because he wasn't sure that their initial low weight wouldn't mean future trouble. Robert figured that whatever made an animal grow right was determined by something other than their birth moment. Besides, he knew the sire, a large well-proportioned stallion. He saw good lines and he knew he wanted these two fillies. He negotiated a deal with Zeno for the two fillies and two older black geldings that, while past prime, still had a few good years left. He needed the geldings for the plow and wagon. For three hundred dollars, he had the beginning of his horse ranch.

The only problem, and a big one, was that the fillies were not broken for either saddle or harness. For the next four days, Robert worked hard to make them ready for the journey. They were young and spirited, but he found that once they were harnessed behind the two older horses, they would calm down and respond to their lead. Robert proclaimed the team ready. The journey north would be a proving.

While Robert had been working on their new team, Ida Emma had purchased and boxed their new household goods. The young couple was to be married by the Reverend Bailey Stone on Saturday and would depart early the next morning. The spring window would remain open only so long and Robert felt there was not a day to waste. This resolve met its first test when they learned their simple plans of a wedding at the Coulter's wouldn't happen. Reverend Stone was called away by a family illness and sent his regrets to Ida Emma along with his blessing. The Wise County judge wasn't available on the Saturday either, so the two had their first working it out. Robert didn't want to delay until Monday and Ida Emma refused to cross the Red River as an unmarried woman. Robert's frustration was neutralized by the cool reasoning of Eudora.

"Why don't you two leave Sunday just as you planned?" said Eudora. "You can travel north, and on Monday you can have the judge in Montague County marry you. How you arrange other things like Sunday night is yours to figure. Coulter and me would like to be with you when you marry but that not being the case, Saturday evening we'll have a special reception in your honor right here."

Robert would have agreed to just about anything at that point. Ida Emma's thoughts of a simple but sweet wedding officiated by their friend, Reverend Stone, faded by necessity. They were replaced by the excitement of the great journey and her Robert forever at her side. Seemed the thing to do.

"Let's leave on Sunday the twenty-first as we planned, Robert."

The Saturday evening reception was a simple affair. Chug, Qeetop, two other cowboy friends, and three of Ida Emma's schoolmates were the guests. Eudora prepared a table of pastries and chocolate candies, and Coulter opened a bottle of fine Kentucky whiskey. He poured everyone a finger's worth in their glasses.

Coulter offered a toast. "May you always travel with the wind at your back and the one you love, 'aside you."

Sunday morning, before daylight, Robert and Ida Emma said their last good-byes to Coulter and Eudora. The road north to Montague County was in good shape and they traveled hard to be near Montague, the county seat, by nightfall. They slept under separate blankets. As planned, the judge performed the simple ceremony the next day, and before noon they were headed to the Indian Territory as Mr. and Mrs. Robert Jennings.

Robert knew a spring day could be the most sensual of pleasures. Warm humid air fills the nostrils with waves of flowering aromas, and together with sights and sounds, they fill a man with delight. Memory is only memory and can't fully recreate these waves of pleasure, so each day's task is to recall them and try to remember how it made a man feel. It's never fully satisfying, but it drives a man, seeking to feel it and smell it and hear it again and again. But a woman who is with you every day can put the need for memory aside, as her presence surrounds and fills you with its pleasures. She loves you as much as you love her, and the world is experienced in its purest form. There are few times in a life when a man can say things are perfect, Robert thought, but the night after they were pronounced man and wife and Robert and Ida Emma stretched the canvas tarp between the wagon and the trees, and set a simple lantern at the head of the blankets, and listened to the whippoorwills and the coyotes and later the moon rose and shone on these two alone with only the heavens as their witness, it became perfect. Robert and Ida Emma knew it was so, and swore to each other that they would always remember the night and to talk of it often and be as honest and free with each other as they had been that first night.

Ida Emma, educated and smart, tried to write things down in a simple journal but was constrained by her chosen words. The third day of their journey, Ida Emma was making an entry in her journal. She placed the pencil to her lips and sighed.

"Watcha writin' there, Ida Emmy?" Robert asked.

"I was trying to write about all the greens I see. Every bush, tree, and clump of grass is a different color, so I just wrote 'verdant greens'."

"Don't know what verdant means, but how do all those greens make you feel?"

"Why, just wonderful, Robert."

"Then maybe that's what you ought to be writin'."

He knew how to employ his senses, unfettered by language, to fill his interior with those pleasures and memories. He would call on this practice throughout his life, long after Ida Emma was gone.

The last night in Texas, the newlyweds camped above the flood plain of the Red River. The next morning, before daybreak, Robert discovered his horses had been stolen. He remained silent as he fingered the cut rope. His brief anger at himself for somehow allowing such a calamity to occur was quickly replaced by a white-hot resolve for justice. He armed Ida Emma with one of his Colt revolvers and extra rounds.

"Give me two nights," he told her. "If you feel threatened, take all six shots and shoot to kill. I love you Ida Emmy."

"Be careful, Robert." She didn't know what else to say.

Robert had his 1876 Winchester, a Colt revolver, plenty of ammunition, biscuits and water. He was on foot tracking riders. The odds were not in his favor, but calmness had returned and he was up to the charge.

Within a half-mile of their camp, he came across other camps of travelers. They had stayed the night there, like Robert, to ford the river the next morning. He talked to all the travelers that he that came across and soon had his first lead. Two men, on old sorrels, had been seen riding through that same morning, headed east. It had been obvious to the families in camp that the men were not settlers, and one man told Robert they looked like trouble to him. Robert thanked the man kindly and set off west to find their trail.

"But they went east I told you, Son," said the man.

"They was without my horses when you saw 'em. Not interested in where they was goin'. Interested in where they'd been. Obliged." Robert knew he would kill the men if he found them with his horses, but he had to have his horses today. Justice would have to wait.

Robert had picked up decent tracking skills with Dee-day and that, along with the soft clay and a little common sense, revealed the trail of two riders. He ran when he could, and when he was winded he ran slower. He tracked most of the day, stopping only for a drink, a bit of biscuit, or to confirm the still fresh trail. At dusk, Robert came upon a rope enclosure. The enclosure held eight horses. Four were his.

He squatted and surveyed the layout. On the far side, he saw two men preparing a meal and enjoying a laugh. They were unaware of his presence only fifty feet away. Robert took the Winchester off his shoulder, silently chambered a round, and cocked the hammer. He grasped the rifle's walnut stock just behind the trigger guard so that the gun pointed straight ahead. His finger was only a muscle twitch away from the trigger. His left hand rested on the handle of the revolver, his elbow cocked and slightly to the side. He moved silently, and when he was ten feet away he made his presence known by clearing his throat. The two men were startled and instinctively shifted their bodies away from Robert. Their handguns were holstered and their rifles were still in their scabbards, too far away to be reached.

"You got my four horses, two fillies and the two black geldings. I'll be takin' 'em with me," Robert said directly to both men, his feet squared with his shoulders. At six feet two, he was taller than most and standing on a small rise, he must have looked like a giant to the seated men.

"Well, Mister," the older of the two said after his initial surprise had passed, "them horses belong to the Wells Fargo. Issa and me are agents duly charged to purchase horses."

"Don't know about that, but I'm takin' my horses."

The older man in charge no longer caught off guard, put up a defense. "See here, Mister. We purchased them horses for the Wells Fargo. You'll have to take your gripe to them."

"Here's what I know." Robert said, never taking his eyes off the men, ready to raise his Winchester if challenged. "I know you bought them four horses from two men this mornin' early. They was ridin' two old sorrels. I know they told you some story you didn't believe, so you paid a low price and them two was happy to get whatever you paid 'em. I know those two are fillies, never foaled, and they all four got a small brand like a crooked Z on their rump. I know I got a bill a sale in my pocket and even if you stupid lyin' horse thief sonsofbitches can't read, you'll see the same brand on the bill." Robert didn't move a muscle. He had stated his case and continued to stare at the men.

The two men turned to each other as if to say, "What do we do?"

Robert removed all doubt when he added, "And I know I'll blow a hole in any goddamn horse thief, if I catch him."

At eleven that night, Robert rode back to Ida Emma, still awake by a roaring fire. "Quite a day, Ida Emmy," Robert smiled.

"I knew you'd get those horses back. I just knew you would."

He joined her by the fire.

After saving their great journey from disaster, the remainder of their trip was a pleasant ride in the country. The grass had greened and was shooting its flowering bodies past the gunnels. The leaves of the trees had fully opened yet maintained their new green sheen so that even their shadows were green. Robert knew this land and he knew he was returning to where he belonged, that he had become a part of this prairie years ago.

Ida Emma was to Robert, the perfect mix of child and woman. Every new rise or bend in the rutted road brought exclamations of beauty or a simple sigh of discovery. They realized, on their journey to the Indian Territory, that their discovery was of each other and the new world they were creating.

It was a Tuesday when they were ferried across the North Canadian River and within the hour, they arrived on the north side of John Turner's claim. Robert showed Ida Emma the lay of the land, the crease down the middle, and the large copse of trees at its head. She looked raptly at her husband as he spoke of his days spent here with Dee-day and showed her the old campsite with soot-covered rocks still marking the old fire pit, now grown over with new grass. Farther below and a little east on open grass was John's shelter, a poor sight. It was his flat wagon with a canvas tarp on one side stretched to the ground. It was obvious that John had spent little time here and the land had no improvements at all. His letter was accurate. He could not maintain two claims.

Robert hobbled the horses and they began grazing the long grass. He and Ida Emma then unloaded most of the wagon as if to claim this land as their own, and when finished, they sat on the grass, their backs to the north, silent and thankful and blessed and in love.

Robert didn't recollect the time passed, but blinked and shook his head when he heard a horse approaching from behind. He rose and saw John and Station loping towards them. As he came closer, Station's ears became erect and his nostrils flared. He knew Robert.

"Thought that was you," John exclaimed as he slid off the great horse. Ida Emma rushed to give him a welcoming embrace. Robert waited his turn by gently stroking Station's nose. John and Robert shook hands and Robert's left hand grasped John's right shoulder. It was the warmest greeting Robert would ever give another man.

The next day the three, on horseback, left before daylight and rode to the claims tent at Kingfisher, a good ride north of twenty miles. Robert gave John two hundred dollars, one hundred sixty acres at a dollar twenty-five each, in paper money and gold coin. Ida Emma provided fifty dollars of her own money. They had already spent most of Robert's savings and she had told Robert that she wanted a share in the land. John paid for the claim in full and was given the deed to the quarter section free and clear. They walked across the street to a tent with a hand painted sign that said simply "Law Office." Sidney Baker, fresh from law school in St. Louis, had come with the intention of making the Run, but decided he could do just fine bringing the law to the Indian Territory. His mother was half Cherokee. For three dollars, Baker had John sign over to Robert and Ida Emma a quitclaim deed and the land was theirs.

The next day, Robert and Ida Emma laid the outline of the soddy that would see them through the winter and where Ina would grow in Ida Emma's womb.

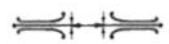

The evening had long given way to night. The cicadas played their summer's hum and beyond the light of the porch, fireflies traced circles of flight. The chipped ice in the tea had long melted, but Robert took a last drink then stretched his hands behind his neck to loosen his arthritis. The older men, Estep, Shaw, and John had heard most of this story, but the younger men and boys had not. Estep wasn't sure if Robert told the story to give some sense of this land to the younger ones or if maybe Robert just liked to tell stories. He was so good at it.

Jesse didn't want the story to end. He had been taken back to 1889 with this telling, and he wasn't ready to return to 1914. He cranked up his courage from the light's edge.

"So Mr. Jennings, what happened to Station?"

All the men turned to Jesse as if to say, "Silence, don't ask." Robert waved a hand. It was okay.

"Well Jesse, in April of '99, a dry front came down from the north. I can feel the change in my skin and so can a horse. Station was on the north forty with other stock. The flash and clap was at the same time. Knew it was close, and the damned dry lightnin's the worst. Knew somethin' bad. Went straightaway up there and found him. Struck dead. Buried him where he fell. Don't plow the spot. The tall grass and some dogwood grown over. I can see the dogwood from the house."

"Wish I'd known your Station, Mr. Jennings," Jesse said.

The men rose as the women walked past and gathered the children. Each said their thanks and goodbyes and complimented Mary on her cooking and the fine gathering. The cars slowly wound their way down the short lane, then turned on the section road. Jesse was in the back seat alone with his thoughts. In the front seat, Ina cradled the sleeping Helen.

"Quite a story you heard tonight, Jesse," Edwin said over his shoulder. "Old Estep and Shaw, they've a tale to tell too. Quite a story."

A light rain had begun as Edwin pulled into his parent's lane. Jesse said his thanks and entered the front door. His parents were in the parlor.

"Night," he mumbled as he climbed the stairs.

CHAPTER 21
LAMENT

Robert's Sunday routine was rarely interrupted by church. He would walk Mary, Alice, and Buck to the car, wish them a good ride to the Oak Chapel and then head down to the barn. This October Sunday in 1923 was such a day and Robert was anxious to take his new filly, Windy, for a long ride. He had recently traded for the one-year old, but had delayed halter and saddle breaking longer than he should have. He'd only ridden her with a saddle twice, and Robert knew more training was due. She had a lot of spirit and Robert hoped he could work that into her riding nature. The eyes of this dappled grey filly stayed fixed on Robert as he cinched the saddle's belly strap.

"Steady there, Windy. You and me gonna have a nice ride this mornin'. You got nothin' to complain about. The weather's good and I got to show you the river. You'll like it. Soft on your hooves. Keep an eye out for moccasins and old rusted barbed wire. My eyes ain't as good as yours."

He swung his right leg smoothly over the saddle and sat straight-backed. He rode slowly due south over his land, three hundred twenty acres and no debt. Robert rotated his crops of wheat, cotton that he never made his children pick, and corn. These crops grown on the north forty acres gave them a modest cash income as long as the rains and the prices held, and the hail stayed away. The formal registration of horse and cattle bloodlines was not much practiced in Oklahoma, but first with Ida Emma's help and now with Mary's, they'd written every stallion, mare, cow and bull that contributed to his stock. He amassed a considerable record of bloodlines expressing those traits he deemed best. Easier calving, fast weight gain and the ability to withstand winter's freezing weather were three traits he valued highly, and he found the English and Scottish breeds met these critical measures. This was no secret to the cattlemen of the region, but Robert continued to look for the subtle differences among individuals that could improve his stock and his profits.

Fine horses were always his first love. Most horses in rural Oklahoma were work animals for the fields or for hauling wagons. Now the automobile and tractor were taking over those roles. There was little demand for lean muscled beauties like his Station or even his new filly, Windy. Robert knew that only a few men had need of a fine horse, but a few were all the market Robert needed. He could still sell a fine riding horse and sold several as far south as Collin County, Texas.

He kept the big draw on his right and passed the site of the Arapahoe summer camp. He always figured Kurt had told his Arapahoe friends that Jennings wouldn't mind if they set up a camp just above the old ox bow. Robert told the elders that it was fine with him and offered his implements from the barn if they were needed. That was the only talk he had with them. Each summer six or eight men would set up a temporary shelter and bring some of the young boys to spend the summer in a still pristine spot to share stories and show them the old ways. Robert never called on their camp and was never invited to a meal. This morning there were a few of his stock grazing around the site. Robert saw that the Bermuda grass had taken over here. The old ways of the Indian and the buffalo and the tall grass, gone. Robert never knew what happened to Dee-day.

The tall grain elevators of El Reno were still visible just above the cottonwoods along the river. He'd been a part of the city from its first days when the little shack town of Reno City was bypassed by the Rock Island railroad and faded from memory. The new county seat dropped the "City" and added an "El". Just what the hell is "The" Reno? He smiled. He thought about turning west to the Darlington Agency then riding into town to check on his three rental houses. The largest had been purchased with Ida Emma's encouragement to serve as a weekday boarding house for the Jennings' children while they attended the high school. Weather made the ten mile round trip impossible many days, so the weekday Jennings' boarding house assured that the children's studies were never interrupted. A nice couple, the Princes, lived on the first floor and looked after the children. Now only Alice and Buck were staying there, and they rarely caused trouble. He would visit the Princes some other Sunday.

Robert turned east to follow the high trail along the river. He closed his eyes and recalled the long rides with Station and the sounds and smells of this old river. He heard a broken cottonwood branch rub against another in a slow creaking, like an old saddle on a good horse. He opened his eyes as a red-tailed hawk, harassed by a few crows, swooped low overhead.

He remembered the promises he'd made to Ida Emma and those she'd made to him on that lantern night long ago, promises he made again as he held her hand that last summer day of 1909. The doctor said the surgery had gone well and that she would be fine. He said it was a bad appendix. The neighbors had all come by and brought food and well wishes, and Ida Emma was beginning to regain her strength. The fever came with wicked dark speed. The last day she couldn't open her eyes, but she squeezed Robert's hand as he spoke those same promises softly in her ear.

Alice sobbed in Edna's arms, and Ina held little Buck. There was no one to hold Robert, and the rain fell as he walked alone to the barn.

Robert's mother, Martha, had come straightaway from her new homestead near Tucumcari, New Mexico. She and her youngest son, Thomas, had tried the homesteading way after her husband had died. Martha and Ina kept the family cared for and it was Martha who figured the widow Mary Hawkins, a close-by neighbor, would be a good wife for her widower son. The two families were joined in a solid marriage and with her four, these two North Canadians counted twelve children. Mary loved Ida Emma's family as her own. Robert called her Mary. She called him Mr. Jennings.

Robert grew to understand this time of his life and the personal peace he had attained. The great anguish of Ida Emma's death became, oddly so, a source of strength for Robert and his family. His Ida Emmy remained an inspiring memory for all.

Windy snorted and tossed her head as Robert gently laid the reins on her neck. Robert set her in a rocking lope and they covered the two miles to the Oakland Cemetery in a few minutes. At the base of the cemetery's low hill, he dismounted. He tied Windy with a long rope and left her to graze the seed tops of the browning grass. He found a fall blooming aster and picked four little pink flowers. The short walk to the middle of the country cemetery brought him past the granite markers of some of the North Canadians. He knew them all. At the top of the little hill there were five cedar trees on the south side of the Jennings' plot. He had brought his mother's remains from New Mexico, and she was buried to the left. Ida Emma was to Martha's right, and to Ida Emma's right would lay Robert. Robert placed the flowers on Ida Emma's stone then sat cross-legged at her feet.

"Hello to you, Ida Emmy. We all miss you and your carin' for us, and we miss your easy smile and your soft voice. I try to keep mine soft, like you said once, but I don't always remember. Our kids are all doin' good. Mary's a good woman. My ma said she'd love our kids too, and she does. Yeah, our kids are doin' good, but Newt's still bothered by that shrapnel in his shoulder. Damn that wilted ol' Kaiser. Doctor says it's best just to leave it be. Guess so. That gas really hurt Newt's eyes. He can't stand the bright sunlight and his head hurts bad sometimes. He wears these darkened glasses when he's in the sun, and from afar he looks like a black-eyed demon, then when he gets closer, why it's your same sweet Newt. Him and Vi be welcomin' their sixth in a few months.

"Ida Emma, I got a shamin' I got to tell you. I stopped at their house last week with no invite, just to see the family. Newt was outside cleanin' up after workin' in their garden. I saw his back. Ida Emma, he's still got the scars from the whippin' I gave him when he ran off to Bertha. I didn't say nothin' 'bout what I saw. Had a nice time talkin' with him and Vi and those five kids. That night I couldn't sleep and just sat on the porch. Figured maybe he wanted me to see those old scars. As I sat there in the dark, a smallness swept all over me like a black cloud and closed me in, till I was no bigger than a seed. Damn me! I did the same thing my pa did to me, and I didn't have the sense to find another way. It's a shamin' on me. I'm here to tell you I'm sorry.

"The other thing I wanted to talk about with you is our Alice. Remember when she was a tiny baby and she used to get those ear pains? She'd be crying so loud. You'd give her a crushed up aspirin while I fired my pipe. I'd hold her in one arm and you'd cover her crying eyes with your hands while I'd gently blow hot smoke in that ear. In a minute all that pressure and pain would be gone. You'd look at her asleep and say, 'Little Belle, sleep. Sleep in your daddy's arms'.

"I still call her Belle, Ida Emmy. No one else calls her by that, just me. She's seventeen now. She's got soft skin like you, but Lord, she's tough. She may be the toughest of the eight. Don't know if I'll be around to see her story played out, but I know she'll have a good one. Well, she'll be getting' her diploma from the high school come spring. She's a fine girl, yes she is Ida Emmy. I don't know how to raise such a girl, when to hold her and when to let her go. You and I together could make that ear pain go away, but there's things now I can't shape. There's lots of boys that show a favorin' to her. Mrs. Prince tells me a couple of 'em walk her home, and they stand around and talk and laugh. You know she's the age you was when we married.

"I'm getting' old now. Make a lot of noise when I move around and don't heal up fast like I used to. Ida Emmy, my life's in two parts, the one before I met you and the one come after. We did real good together, didn't we? Wish I had those words that always come so easy for you, but it's the damnedest thing. Your leavin' was the saddest thing ever happened to me, but just thinkin' 'bout you still puts a smile on my old wrinkled face."

Robert rose slowly and stretched his arms overhead. His shoulders creaked then loosened. He walked slowly down the hill and called for Windy. She looked up but kept munching the grass. He'd train her to come when called some other day.

CHAPTER 22

THE CEDAR FLAT

Alice enjoyed and cultivated the interest shown to her by her classmates. She had an air of confidence and certitude in her manners. She never shied from an encounter in the classroom or the hallway and was thought of as an independent young woman. Her teachers encouraged her to continue her studies after high school and spoke to her about attending the Teachers College in Edmond or even the Oklahoma University near Oklahoma City. She could have been the first Jennings to attend college. But she also enjoyed the attention the boys were sending her way. She played the flirtation game as well as any, and mimicking the silver screen's leading ladies, she learned to pout and tease and forgive all, with a quick smile and a toss of her head.

Alice had a little free time after school before she would walk the few blocks to her boarding house and report to Mrs. Prince, and she used this time as her social hour. She became a regular at Patterson's Drug and Fountain or McClennan's Five and Dime. Her stage center was a counter stool at Patterson's or a green vinyl booth at McClennan's. The jukebox was kept fed and the energized melodies of the Jazz Age began to resonate in this little Oklahoma town.

She said she'd always known him, didn't remember the first time they spoke, but one fall afternoon she saw Jesse standing at the counter. He was leaning back on his right elbow and staring at her. She didn't break and turn away. She returned the look. With his left hand, he swept his dark blond hair back, and with this simple move, the courting dance had begun. He was a grown man and he was different. He was just under six feet, flat bellied, and she swore his eyes really did twinkle. They must have. The high school boys, in their plumage display, would often engage in a round of arm wrestling and Jesse needed no encouragement to enter the competition. He would feign disinterest in such juvenile games, but would agree to take on the winner. He put a lot of nickels in his pocket and the boys would use his strength as a marker of their own. If an obviously stronger opponent challenged Jesse, he would taunt the larger foe and praise his superiority and strength. This would go on until Jesse was clearly the underdog, so that even in losing to superior strength, he would win the approval of the crowd.

"Well, Jesse Sheets, you finally lost a match," Alice said.

"Can't win 'em all. How you doin' today, Alice? This your last year of school? Can I give you a ride home?"

And so there was only one boy to meet Alice after school, and only one boy to bring her home. And he was no boy. Alice's classmates saw they were being shut out of the sweepstakes. They couldn't compete with this dapper young man with money, a car, a quick laugh, and the inside track to Alice's heart. He saw himself as a man-about-town, even if the town was El Reno, and cultivated it with his brother Floyd's circle of friends and his hunting buddies. He was loyal to his friends and polite to the women. He talked a good game and knew how to dress for a night on the town. Alice always said that if Adonis himself had broken flesh free from an old marble statue, it wouldn't have mattered. She was in love.

Alice knew that for her to be happy in love with Jesse, he would have to meet with her father's approval. So instead of the man asking for the father's permission, she reversed the process by talking first with her father.

"Daddy, you know I've been seeing Jesse Sheets after school some days," she said politely after a Sunday supper.

"Mary and me talk with the Princes, so sure we knew. What's on your mind, Alice?" he asked directly.

"Well, I just you wanted to know that," she paused, "to know that I find him very likable."

Mary spoke up. "Likable? Come now Alice, you can speak more clearly than that."

Alice laughed a little and it seemed to free her up. "I'm in love with Jesse, Daddy and Mother, and I've just got to tell you how I feel. Never experienced such a thing before, but I know it's real and it grows more every day."

"Belle, Mary and I been there before you," said Robert. "Think I can say it's a powerful thing, love, but sometimes it pushes everything else to the side. Just be careful what gets pushed aside."

Alice knew of her father's conflict with his mother-in-law, Carrie, and took his comments as general and not as a specific warning. Still, she wasn't sure.

"Jesse is a good man, Daddy, and he loves me. I think we can have good life."

"Belle, I'd like you to slow up a bit, and enjoy this last year of your schoolin', but you're a woman now and you'll be makin' your own future. There's lots of ducks in that pond and I want you to be sure he's the right one."

"Thanks Daddy. I'm sure."

The following Sunday, Robert and Mary hosted an afternoon supper to celebrate a big promotion for Hill Elliot, Edna's husband. He had been promoted to foreman with an oil well service company and was now overseeing three drilling crews, even had a company furnished truck to visit the sites. Jesse was invited, and Alice knew that even though Hill was the featured guest, eyes would be on Jesse and Alice. All of the Jennings' and Hawkins' children were to be there, except little Carrie who had married an Estep and moved to Kansas.

"Jesse, do you remember when you played the dashing knight in Edna's play? I think you were sweet on Edna back then," Alice teased.

"Sure, I remember. You was the unicorn. You was magic then and you're the same still. You'll always be magic to me, Alice."

She loved his answer. "Well, do think you could spin a little of your own magic with that harmonica I see in your pocket?" She knew Jesse needed only a little prodding to entertain the children.

He called the little ones together and started playing his few songs with loud confidence. The children were swaying and he encouraged them to go on ahead with their dancing. He started a little Irish step and soon the little ones were following his lead. After a few minutes he stopped his music and broke into a big laugh as the children's glee spread to him and to the adults nearby. Mary Jennings clapped her approval and nodded to Alice. Robert, in the distance, just watched.

After the men had eaten and the children and women were in the kitchen, Robert asked Jesse to take a walk. Jesse obliged. They opened the gate near the draw and walked down into the trees where only the leaves brushed by the wind made a noise.

"Nice place you have here, Mr. Jennings. Hope to have a place like this myself someday," Jesse said sincerely.

"Ida Emma and me built this, and now with Mary, we've pretty much raised all our kids. Hope I done right by 'em. They all different and they all got a different place in me. Jesse, my Alice says she loves you and I know what that means, so why don't you take the here and now and tell me what you're thinkin' about for the future."

Robert spoke with directness and kept his eyes focused on Jesse. He was looking for a tell. He told Alice later that he knew Jesse was telling the truth by the way he never broke his gaze. The two men's eyes met, unbroken.

"Mr. Jennings, you're true about all that. Your Alice is different from any girl I ever knowed and yes, Sir, I love her. Know she's still in school, so we're agreed to not do anything official till after the spring."

"Jesse, Alice's heart is hers to give, and I got nothin' to say about that. Bein' in love is about givin' your heart to someone, but that man better make sure that heart is never hurt or broken. Just 'cause she's with another man, don't mean I can't still protect her."

Jesse didn't respond, but nodded his head up and down. "Say, Mr. Jennings, hear you got a fine new filly. I'd like to see her."

"I've seen you ride, Jesse. You're welcome to ride Windy some Sunday, if you'd like. Be easy with her 'cause she's with foal." They walked to the barn.

Later, when the evening was given to darkness and most of the guests had left, Jesse kissed Alice goodnight.

"What did you two talk about down in the draw?" she asked.

"You."

"Come on now, Jesse, you have to tell me."

"Your daddy's fond of his Alice and he let me know that I better take good care of you. And your heart."

"Seems like good advice, but what did you say?"

"I told him right out that I loved you. I'm not sure your daddy trusts me or any other man. I'll take good care of you and then your daddy can rest easy. You bein' the last girl and losin' your mother, well he feels a special thing 'bout you."

Alice knew Jesse was struggling with his feelings and the right words to express them. She heard his words of love and protection and care and knew their life together would be wonderful.

That fall and winter, Alice and Jesse continued their courting dance and as the summer of 1924 approached, the courting turned to planning. Robert and Mary were still hoping Alice might continue her studies at the University, but when the Elm Glen School needed a teacher for the coming school year, Alice said a quick yes, and Robert gave his approval. A judge in Kingfisher married them.

Robert and Mary hosted a reception that afternoon at the farm. Mary decorated the house with all the flowers she could find from her garden and lined the fence along the lane with hollyhocks and daises, Alice's favorites. This second union of a Sheets and a Jennings seemed joyous and the celebration afterwards was great fun. Jesse pulled out his harmonica and entertained the young children with his robust singing, dancing, and laughter. Alice was entertained and in love. The newlyweds spent the night at the Kerfoot Hotel, and on Sunday evening, they moved Alice's things into Jesse's parents' home, just a mile east of where Alice was born.

That first summer was a happy time for the young couple. They would escape the noisy bedsprings and disappear down the hill east of the house, and within a dense circle of cedars and on the broad green leaves of the soft new grass, make love. They would fall asleep, and the first to wake would hear the slow rhythmic breath of happiness and peace. Each listened to the other, and those soft days of grass and cedar would imprint on their forever memory its sounds and scents to be recalled throughout their lives.

Alice's heart was always open and, that first summer she and her new mother-in-law, Anna, became close friends. While Jesse was working, Alice and Anna spent a lot of time together. With two women in the house, any chores or meal preparation took half as long and the two had hours of talk, serious, fun, silly, and profound. Alice felt she had a third mother and Anna loved sharing her home with her young and energetic daughter-in-law. One day Anna confessed that Alice was the daughter she had always wanted. Her youngest, Grace, had married and left home, but Anna and Alice both knew that indiscretions begun in her youth would continue.

One weekday in June, Anna was to drive into town for a little shopping and asked Alice if she would like to accompany her. Alice asked instead if she would drop her off at her parents' home for an afternoon visit. Anna was happy to comply and they waved to each other as Alice climbed the steps calling for her mother Mary and her daddy.

Alice found them both sitting at the kitchen table.

"Afternoon, Mother and Daddy. Don't usually find you inside the house during this time of day, Daddy," she said with a smile.

"Mary called me up to try out a new pudding. Can't say no to that, now can I? Good to see you, Belle."

"I'm so pleased you dropped by, Alice. You have to try this. I added a little maple syrup," said Mary.

Alice took a taste. "It's delicious. Didn't think you'd ask Daddy to come up if it wasn't."

Mary poured some hot tea and the three enjoyed the midmorning break. Alice felt so comfortable in this kitchen. She studied her father with a glance over the top of her cup as she took a sip. He was still an imposing man, but Alice saw the years climbing his countenance. His face was now deeply wrinkled and his mustache drooping over the corners of his mouth had significant grey to match his thinning hair. His forehead was deeply tanned but one inch below his hairline the skin was white, shaded from the sun by his ubiquitous cowboy hat. She noticed his hands were very wrinkled and tanned with large dark spots among the crusty knuckles. He walked tall but would shift his weight from side to side as he extended his frame.

"How's Jesse and Floyd's business doin'?" he asked after finishing his tea.

"He and Floyd have work every day, and with fall coming, they're talking about hiring a third man. He works hard, Daddy," Alice said.

"That Jesse is a hard worker. Always knew that, Alice," Mary added.

"Say, Belle, did you know I leased five acres to a family from Tulsa a few weeks ago? Down along the west side of the new quarter section. Met the man, Fredrick James, at Edwin's Automobile Shop." Robert had changed the topic and his tone was serious.

"News travels fast along this river, Daddy. Of course I knew that. I also know they're a colored family with two girls," said Alice.

"Hope I did right by Mr. James. I know there'll be talk, but the man said he needed to be in the country. Had enough of the city. Since when do I give a damn about talk?"

"Daddy, you're the strongest man I know. Don't know all that went into that lease for Mr. James, but I know once you make up your mind, there's no stopping you," said Alice.

"Your daddy's a galloping ride, Alice. Sometimes he's hard to stay on, but what a ride he is. I'm not one bit worried, and I don't think there'll be anything more than talk. Your daddy and I can handle that." Then Mary added an afterthought. "And more if we have to."

Robert nodded his head in agreement. "Mary, you and Alice better know this. The Klan's been meetin' regular in town. I'm told their numbers growin'. Can't ignore that. If you two hear things, you gotta tell me. Don't regret what I did, but can't close my ears to anythin' that would threaten us."

Alice knew her father and could tell he wasn't finished. He was troubled.

"Daddy, there's something else, isn't there?"

Robert was silent for a moment then took a long silent breath. He stretched his neck and rubbed his temples.

"Yea, there's more. You should know everything." Robert began slowly with a determined tone. "I went into town after I signed the lease and made a call on Cecil Anderson. The Klan's supposed to be secret, but everybody knows he's the Grand Lizard in Canadian County. Told him straight up what I'd just done and that I didn't want no trouble. He just stared at me, his temper rising, but before he could talk I looked him up and down. I could tell he wasn't used to bein' talked to like that, and I sensed his weakness. I read his tell. He's a coward. I told him any harm comes to the James or the Jennings by any of his white sheeted goons, I was gonna slay me a dragon. Told him it wasn't just me. I'd have all the North Canadians with me."

Robert seemed relieved. Alice looked up at her father and a sense of calm and security embraced her as he put his arm around her.

"Belle, I always liked your Granddaddy Newton. Now your Grandma Carrie and me never saw things the same way, but that Newton was a fine man. You know he fought for the Abolitionists in Bloody Kansas before the Civil War? And do you know why a seventeen year-old would put himself in front of a minie ball? An idea. Just an idea. He figured a person should be free. That shouldn't be so hard to figure out. He was only seventeen, the same age I was when I left Missouri. Took me longer to see things that way, but I come to know that an idea is more important than some goon trying to take that all away."

The three were silent for a few minutes as each pondered the implication of Robert's action. Mary, in her calm manner, broke the silence.

"Alice, I have two quarts of canned peaches here. Why don't you take these over to their place and introduce yourself to the James and meet the two girls? They'll be in the Elm Glen School this fall."

"Thank you, Mother. That's a wonderful idea."

"Would you like me drive you over, Belle?" asked Robert.

"No thanks, Daddy. I'd like the walk. Oh, and Daddy, I'm proud of what you did."

Alice kissed them both and thanked them for the tea and pudding. She dampened her cotton scarf at the kitchen faucet and wrapped it around her neck. The day was getting warmer. She walked west, above the draw, then south to the almost completed three-room house. She expected to see Mr. James working on the house, but saw no one as she climbed the wooden stairs and knocked on the door. There was no reply so she knocked again. She heard footsteps from within, then a loud response.

"Who's there? What do you want?" a stern female voice asked.

"I'm Alice Sheets, Robert Jennings' daughter, the new teacher at the Elm Glen School. I was hoping to meet you and your daughters."

The door opened fully. Donelda James stood in the doorway but did not beckon Alice to enter. She was a large woman, taller than Alice, dressed in a cotton housedress and black lace-up boots. Her coal black hair was gathered in a bun and beginning to show streaks of white above her ears. Her eyes were intense and not welcoming. She looked Alice over and then began to relax.

"Mr. James told me to never to let anybody in this house if he's not here."

"I understand, Mrs. James. It's a pleasure to meet you. I'll be teaching your girls and I thought I'd come by before the school starts."

"My girls are six and nine. So that's the first and fourth grade. They're good girls and smart too. But they're scared. They the only colored at your school?"

"Yes, Ma'am, they'll be the only ones. But I give you my word I'll take good of them."

"So a woman, a girl, not twenty says she's going to take care of my girls," she said with her voice rising. Donelda took a breath and tried to calm herself. "Do you know why we moved here, to this place out in the country, away from our friends and family, to a place we don't know and a place that may or may not be safe for our girls? Do you know why we're here?"

"My daddy just said you moved from Tulsa, Mrs. James."

"Do you know what happened three years ago in Tulsa, Mrs. Sheets?"

"No Ma'am, I guess I don't."

"Figured so. Our Greenwood was burned to the ground."

"Greenwood?"

"The colored part of Tulsa. It was a real nice place. We colored had our own schools, a hospital, and plenty of good businesses. Mr. James and I had a furniture store, sold and repaired. We lived above the store. Mr. James is handy with wood and can make anything. That's why he knew he could build us this house. I tell you Mrs. Sheets, we had a good life back there. People said Oklahoma was made up of good people from all over. Maybe so, but evil people came out those days. Mrs. Sheets, they killed Mr. James' brother. No reason. Went on for two days. We lost everything. Papers said thirty or forty people died, but we know it was hundreds. You can count the graves. It was hundreds." Donelda stopped and touched her eyes with a handkerchief. "I wanted to stay, rebuild, but Mr. James said he wouldn't live there ever again. Why move to a new place where we don't know anybody and don't know how we'll be looked at? Mr. James says maybe that's what we're supposed to do."

"I'm sorry to hear that bad story, Mrs. James. I should have known all that, but I didn't. I'm sorry."

Telling the story of the Tulsa riot drained some emotion out of Donelda and she gave Alice a warm smile.

"Please come into our home and share a cup of coffee with me. The girls are down by that old ox bow looking for crawfish. You ever eat steamed crawfish, Mrs. Sheets? Spiced up, they're delicious. I come from Louisiana and know about those things."

"Thank you Mrs. James. I'd like that."

Alice entered the unfinished home. The framed sides and roof were weather tight but the interior walls were incomplete and open. The kitchen cabinets and counters were made from a variety of woods, mostly pine, but the large table was solid oak, finished in a light stain and sanded glassy smooth. There was a cast iron pot on the wood stove and Alice could tell by the wafting aroma that the coffee was ready. Donelda poured the hot coffee into two white ceramic cups and offered a small pitcher of cream. Alice poured the rich cream into her cup and stirred it to a caramel color. She took a first sip.

"That's good coffee, Mrs. James."

"That's my Louisiana roots. Think maybe it was my coffee that made the sale when Mr. James was courting me," she laughed.

Alice laughed too and remembered her father's tales of hot coffee on a cold day.

"My daddy loves good coffee too. Passed that on to me. Thank you for your hospitality, Mrs. James."

"Who's Shug, Mrs. Sheets?" asked Donelda after taking a full swallow.

"Shug was a cook on the Waggoner Ranch down in Texas. My daddy was a cowboy for Mr. Waggoner before he met and married my mother, Ida Emma. She's been gone for thirteen years now."

"Sorry to hear you lost your mother so young, child."

"Daddy married Mary two years later, and she's a good mother. She gave me these two quarts of peaches as a welcoming gift for you and your family."

"Thank you Mrs. Sheets. I hope to meet her soon," said Donelda. "But I was wondering if Shug was a colored man."

"Yes, he was. Daddy always said good things about ol' Shug. He called him ol' Shug. Said he was the happiest man he ever knew."

"Knew it must have been so, because when my Fredrick asked about land, your daddy said Shug would've wanted him to help my Fredrick. That's all he said, but Fredrick and I figured he was colored. You see, Mrs. Sheets, just like when the evil came out in men back in Tulsa, there's good that comes out too. That Shug was a spirit for the good. That's how I see things."

Alice rose and extended her hand to Donelda. "You stop by the Elm Glen School any time. Anything happens, I'll come right over."

"Thank you, Mrs. Sheets. I believe you'll do fine by my girls."

That fall of 1924 and the following winter and spring were as close to perfect as Alice would ever remember. She loved all of the twenty-six children in her class and organized each day with lessons and activities for each of her eight grades. It was a daunting task, but she was up to it, even when her belly grew. All but the youngest children knew she would not return the next fall. Alice and Anna grew close and their quiet time alone at the kitchen table with a cup of coffee was a warm memory they shared.

Iris Jeanne was born in the early summer, only weeks after the end of the school year, at the Sheets' home with Dr. Womack attending. It was a good delivery, and Anna asked Jesse to tie a pink ribbon around the mailbox as a sign to anyone driving by. Jesse was a proud and attentive new father, excepting diaper changes. Their future looked promising, and the loss of Alice's income was not a blow to their finances because the coal business was good and winter, with its increased demand for the black rock, was only a few months away. Jesse worked hard through the summer and was able to trade for a newer Model T. If a heavy rain made the roads impassable, he would stay the night in town with Edwin and Ina. Jesse would call home and have Alice hold the phone up to Iris Jeanne's ear for a good night wish.

Anna was visibly distraught when Jesse and Alice announced that they had rented a house in town and would be moving. They had found a neat two-bedroom house on K Street with a garden and an old carriage shed for their new car. Alice and Anna knew this was inevitable, but they both cried as they hugged each other the afternoon that the last of Alice's things were loaded into the Model T.

Alice learned to drive and would take the car over the river to see her parents and the Sheets regularly. Her house was never locked, and the grandparents always felt welcomed. Jesse was welcoming to all, but a distance remained between Robert and him.

In 1928, Alice miscarried a boy. Her family was supportive and tender, but it left her wounded for longer than anyone knew. Friends tried to console her and tell her she would be pregnant again in no time and recounted how other young women had had similar experiences. These words were meant to give her comfort, but Alice felt they minimized the loss she felt. One Monday, she drove with Iris Jeanne the forty miles to Cement to see her sister, Edna. Edna greeted her warmly and Iris Jeanne played with her two little cousins, Kathleen and Bud. Over the kitchen table, Alice poured her heart out.

"I can't get over this like people say I should, Edna. Is there something wrong with me? How come I still feel the loss like it was yesterday?"

"You've been listening to other people instead of your heart, Dear."

"What do you mean by that, Edna?"

"People sometimes feel they have to say something, thinking it's what they should do before they think about the actual words they're saying or who they're saying it to. They're trying to help, but they really have no idea what to say. Just by offering something they think it might make you feel better, knowing others care. Do you understand?"

"I always appreciate their concern, and I thank them, but I don't feel better. Sometimes I feel worse."

"Alice, that little boy took a part of your heart with him when he died. That piece will always be gone. It's never growing back.

You'll live with that forever and you shouldn't ever feel like it's supposed to heal up. But it's how it should be, to carry that with you. You'll be happy again and maybe you'll have another, but you'll have that piece of sadness the rest of your life. You and you alone will remember that little baby, and he'll know you loved him."

Alice grew stronger after that talk with her sister and began to understand a bit of her private self. When Iris Jeanne was napping, Alice would walk the rows of her garden and run her hands along the lengthening vines and stalks and ponder things she'd been told by her father and her sister.

Alice loved her life, and the move into town was any easy transition, quickly absorbed by new friends, old friends, and brothers and sisters of the Jennings and the Sheets. The home of Edwin and Ina was common meeting place on Sundays and at least once a week, Alice and Ina would meet for coffee and talk. Edwin was doing well with his Automobile Repair and Texaco Gasoline Station. He was the proud owner and would puff his chest to fill out the freshly starched and ironed shirt Ina would have for him each morning. Jesse and Floyd were doing fine and the regular hours gave Jesse evenings and Sundays off to enjoy his family. He would sometimes hire himself out to help his father, who was winding down his own freight business. Jesse was beginning to enjoy his time off, and some Saturdays or weekday evenings after work while the sun was low, he would take off with his hunting buddies and supplant the meal with dove or quail. He was always a good shot, and a bird on the wing remained the test of a marksman. After the hunt, he would often stop by a local watering hole and have a beer or two with his friends. Prohibition was never an obstacle in El Reno.

The three couples: Ina and Edwin, Edna and Hill, and Alice and Jesse were best friends and met regularly on weekends. Ina and Edna announced to Alice that their birthing days were over.

Alice didn't sign on. It was obvious to these three women that they powered their families. Edwin didn't know. Hill would have denied it, and Jesse neither knew nor cared. Eleanor of Aquitaine would have been pleased.

CHAPTER 23
DARK CLOUDS

When the market crashed in 1929, these three families, with the Jennings sisters at the helm, hardly noticed. The events of the faraway coast would not affect El Reno they thought. The country would always need food and the railroad. El Reno could ride out any downturn, and what concern of theirs was a problem on Wall Street?

Alice kept the K Street house as she had been taught. There was rarely a thing out of place and no task was too big or too tough. The fence was a bright white and the rows of her garden straight and weed free. Alice had all the skills of a farm wife and even at her young age, showed maturity and sound judgment. She never entertained any alternative and thought it unnatural any observed behavior in contrast to hers. She felt that way until she developed a group of friends outside her family and saw that many families had their own unique problems and tried to do the best they could in such circumstances. Not all efforts met with success. Even her sister Ina had voiced concerns about her marriage with Edwin. She had told Alice bluntly once that she wished Edwin gave her more joy, then reflected that maybe it was partly her own doing. That was all she ever said. Alice reasoned Jesse was damned lucky to have her.

Alice and Jesse had Kendall in 1931. Alice said a prayer of thanks. In Kendall's blue eyes she saw a life given to her and realized its fragility. Jesse insisted Kendall's middle name be Jesse, but Alice was just as determined it would be Jennings. Jesse refused to budge so Alice reluctantly proposed a compromise. Kendall's birth certificate would read "Kendall J. (only) Sheets". A few teased the boy later and would call him Kendall Jonly.

Life had tempered Alice's view of perfection and she realized that perfection was only in fairy tales. She knew she had much to be thankful for and was always fast with a nice word to her Jesse. The national depression was worsening, but Jesse and Alice were living on a cash economy with Jess's income only down slightly due to jobs lost and falling prices. They could manage just fine and the birth of Kendall caused only a small financial adjustment.

The autumn of Kendall's birth saw the last good harvest in Oklahoma for eight years. The fall rains didn't come, but the thick prairie soil yielded moisture from the earlier rains and brought the golden autumn color of harvest. Even though Jesse and Alice lived in town, they were thoroughly integrated with the agricultural base of Canadian County. The Rock Island Railroad and Fort Reno gave only a small sense of the outside world and its money, and every citizen knew that as the harvest goes, so goes prosperity. Prices for wheat, most crops, and oil collapsed in 1932. The thinner soil in the western part of Oklahoma began to crack and its moisture bled out, leaving a parched and brittle skeleton. In the Panhandle of Oklahoma, families began an eight year dance of despair. In the first month of 1932, this dry baked soil was swept skyward and carried east. It was a new event and brought fear and dread to those it covered. There was initial confusion about the cloud's genesis, but soon they knew. The land was dying.

Jesse returned home one evening in January of 1932. Alice was preparing supper with Iris Jeanne's help and noticed an increase in the wind and a sudden drop of fifteen degrees. As Jesse entered the back door, a gust of wind entered the kitchen with him, slamming the screen door and bringing a stinging blast of dust.

"Damn that wind! Must be a strong norther. Didn't hear nothin' about it on the radio." Jesse was coughing and his eyes were watering.

The slamming door and gust of wind startled Kendall and he started to cry.

"Now sweet Kendall, it's fine. No reason to cry." Alice said soothingly. "Iris Jeanne, hold Kendall while I help your daddy." She moistened a towel and handed it to Jesse.

He began to wipe his eyes. "That's a strange blow. Just dust. Not rain or sleet. Just dust. Never seen it like that before. Better check the windows and make sure they're all down and locked."

Just then the wind increased to a howl like a summer thunderstorm, but there was no moisture. The whole house shook and the window frames rattled. Jesse and Alice saw the house suddenly filled with a cloud of fine and irritating dust, and Jesse began coughing again. The dust permeated their little world and filled its corners with darkness. Alice served the meal as Iris Jeanne held and comforted Kendall.

"What's happening, Mother?" she asked.

"I don't know, but we'll be just fine," counseled Alice.

The dinner plates collected a dark patina of dust and had to be wiped clean before the food was served. After an uncomfortable meal, Jesse turned the radio on. It was no cold front or blue norther. It was more than blowing dust. It was something new, a duster.

Collapsing farm prices and unemployment fell hard on many, including Jesse's brother, Edwin. His once thriving business could not hold out, and his bloated payroll of friends and family helped push him into bankruptcy. By 1932, this wasn't new to El Reno and the stigma associated with insolvency had softened. He was able to find a job with the county, and Ina and Edwin kept their welcoming home open to any family or friend in need. There were few businesses that proved to be depression proof.

After a long hot July day, Jesse's reward was a good supper with his little family. Alice freshened his tea and added a few broken cubes of ice.

"You and Floyd must have worked hard today. You came home a little later than you usually do," she said with a little curiosity.

"You know Roy Jones? He's the fella that works for the Massy Fergusson dealer. Well, we was havin' a beer this afternoon and we got to talking."

"I wasn't being hard on you Jesse, for coming home later. Just wondered. What did you and Roy talk about? You seem ready to tell some news here."

"Alice, what's the things that people have to have? No matter a depression. Tell me three things every family's got to have."

Alice thought a moment. "You always hear it's food, shelter, and clothes. Is that the answer you're searching for?"

"You got it first try, Alice. It's food. And what's the food every family with children needs?" He didn't let Alice answer. "Milk! Every child needs milk. There's nothin' can take the place of milk. And that's what Roy and I was goin' over this afternoon."

"I think you're right, but go on. I want to hear your idea. You have an idea don't you? I know you must."

"Just count in your head how many North Canadians there are and how many have a few dairy cows or even just one. Then figure that the North Canadians are only a dozen or so, but there's a lot more farms around that have some dairy cows. If they was to sell any extra milk, then they'd have money in their pockets. Even a few dollars a month be more than nothin'," Jesse said. He had a big smile on his face.

"I see what you're saying. You and Roy would deliver all that milk to one of those processors in Oklahoma City. Even with lower prices, there's still money in it for you and Roy and the farmers. They can't afford to take those few gallons themselves thirty miles and back each day."

"Between Roy and me, I bet we know a hundred farmers, maybe more. Roy says he can lease a big Dodge truck and we can buy it in a few months. He's goin' to the City tomorrow to talk to the processors, and I'm gonna start callin' on everybody I know. Tell me what you think, Alice?"

"Jesse, seems to me you put a lot of thinking into this plan of yours. Makes sense. Would you like me to go with you tomorrow? With Iris Jeanne in school, Kendall and I could help you call on the North Canadians."

"Swell idea, Alice. Those old friends would never say no to you and Kendall."

They struck a vein of gold. After only the first two weeks, Jesse and Roy were breaking even and after that, their success was beyond their most optimistic projections. Jesse traded the old Model T for a newer Model A and paid the difference in cash. Alice had extra money in her pocket, but instead of celebrating, a sense of doubt covered her smile. She would talk with her sister, Edna. She and Kendall drove to Cement after taking Iris Jeanne to school. Edna greeted her sister and Kendall with warmth and an offer of coffee for Alice and chocolate milk for Kendall. Edna was in high spirits and happy to host her sister.

"I'm so glad you drove your new car down here to see me. Please tell me all about the milk run and Jesse." Edna started right away with the questions Alice expected.

"Everything you've heard is true. The run is a great success, and Jesse and Roy see nothing but roses. It's all happened so fast

Edna. I just wanted to talk with you and maybe help me keep a proper view of all this."

"In the middle of this depression, to hear of someone doing so well, Alice I am so proud of you and Jesse. Have you heard how Daddy talks of his son-in-law? We're all happy for you." She paused when she saw a furrow on Alice's brow. "But that's not why you drove down, is it?"

"Edna, I know I don't have to ask, but we are closer than blood. I tell you everything and you know more about me than anyone, but you must never speak a word of this to anyone."

"You know that as fact, Sister."

"I have this fear. A fear of darkness and change. A change that can come with a silence and a swiftness that takes my breath, my very life away. The same swiftness that took our mother and my little boy before he was even born. The same swiftness that brings those dusters. Those that we love can be taken in a moment of random cruelty. I don't understand it, and I fear it. At night, I see Iris Jeanne and Kendall and Jesse sleeping, and in their dreams they carry my happiness. But I can't control those things and just as the promise of money may come with the milk run, it can also bring sudden and unexpected darkness.

"Jesse and I are looking to buy a lovely home on five acres on the east side of town. You know the place on Rogers Street. With the money Jesse is making, he says the bank would give us a mortgage. I'd have never imagined I would live in such a fine home. And Edna, Jesse is bringing home over three hundred dollars a month! That's more than our daddy made in the greater part of a year, when he was a young man."

Edna waited for Alice to finish these thoughts. "Alice, I know the nature of this world seems to be cruel sometimes and you're right to fear the things to come that you don't know, don't have any control over. But you must trust the strength that you and Jesse have to meet these changes and perhaps the darkness that can sometimes lie hidden inside."

"Edna, just as I knocked on your door there was a sapphire blue clear sky and in that sky, just above your house, was a small white cloud. That little cloud gave the sky dimension and scale and seemed so gentle, but that little cloud may be gathering moisture as we speak, and in an hour or so, your house may be shaking with thunder. Edna, I'm concerned that Jesse and his new buddy, Roy Jones, may be drinking, and I mean more than a beer or two. I'm afraid that little cloud may be gathering moisture and I'm not sure I can stop it. That's the darkness, the sudden darkness, that I'm afraid of."

The two were silent for a moment then Edna spoke. "I wasn't sure if you had a particular thing in mind. Now I see your worry is well placed. I know you see his two brothers, Jack and Floyd and the trouble they're having with drink. I was hoping Jesse would be more like Edwin in that drinking habit. How much of a problem is it? Is that cloud still growing or has it started to thunder?"

"It's still a small cloud and, maybe not too much to concern myself at this time, but I see those brothers, even Jesse's little sister Grace, they're all having problems with drinking. Jesse and Roy have a beer or two after the run is finished. There's a place in Yukon, Sissy's, right on the Route Sixty-six. They'll stop there for noon dinner. Jesse tells me this. He's keeping no secrets, but sometimes he comes home smelling of alcohol and sometimes his steps are unsure. He's never angry or violent, nothing like that, but he's not the happy man he deserves to be. Edna, I don't know what to do."

"Poseidon may twirl his trident, but Alice, you're Jesse's Aphrodite. You find a nice quiet evening or a Sunday afternoon and tell him everything you just told me. When he hears the concerns that you have and feels the love in your heart, I think he'll take the right road."

"Edna, are you happy? Forgive me, but are you really happy? You were the smartest most well-read girl in El Reno. You could have gone to college, written books, anything, and you're here in Cement with a well site foreman." Alice paused and embarrassment swept over her. "Edna, that must sound terrible and callous. What I meant was—"

"Don't apologize. We're closer than that. Are you asking about happiness or bliss? Bliss is a moment. Happiness is a state. A state that may have dark moments. You can only take one action at a time and I was given those choices you spoke of, but I chose a good and gentle man and a life in Cement. Hill has no weaknesses and he loves our children and me deeply. I know that even this horrible depression and drought can't change that. You and I are the same, Sister. The reason you're all tied up about some dark future cloud, be it money or alcohol, is that you understand that happiness and peace come from the same source. If we are truly to know peace, our freely given love must be returned."

Alice reflected on these words as she and Kendall drove home to El Reno. It seemed like good advice and she decided to do just as Edna had suggested. There was to be a gathering at her parents' farm this Sunday and perhaps that evening would be the right time to talk with Jesse, but the evening came and she said nothing.

Three months passed and Alice's intentions wavered. Jesse came home each afternoon tired but sober. He and Roy still stopped at Sissy's and had one or two beers.

Alice never had the big talk and she began to relax and enjoy her new life. The loan at the bank came through and the family moved to the new home on five acres. Jesse's day began at three each morning, as Roy would pick him up in the dark. Jesse always brought a thermos of hot coffee to share and the two joked and laughed themselves through the day. They always greeted their farmers with a hearty, "Good Morning," and a quick sharing of the day's events to come and always the weather. The rains didn't come.

Alice kept the new home and grounds spotless. She cultivated her city friends and became forever fast with many. She had the money to splurge for trips to the big stores in Oklahoma City, but she maintained a modesty born of her prairie parents and no one ever said she flaunted her money. Jesse too maintained a frugality, but on occasion would show up with a new silk hat or spats and once, bought a beautiful double-barreled Browning shotgun, ordered from the factory in Utah. Alice never asked him what it cost. Jesse may have pressed his solo purchases when he told Alice he was buying a new Chrysler.

"Jesse, let's slow down here. Show me our monthly obligations, and together we'll make a decision," she said calmly after he'd told her his plans.

"We got plenty of money, Alice. I thought you'd like a new car. You drive all over the county with the kids seein' your friends and family. Thought you'd be happy."

"Jesse, you're not buying this for me. You're buying it because that's what you want. I don't think it's what I want, and I'd rather save some of that money. If you think we need another car, then let's sell the A and buy a newer used one, a Chrysler if you want. Any car man would be happy to make a sale these days." She knew she made good sense and Jesse agreed. Still, the event gave Alice pause and she recalled her afternoon with Edna.

Alice would look back on those early days on Rogers Street as the happiest of her life. Wrapped in a sphere of contentment, isolated from the pain of the depression, this little Sheets family was filled with joy. Alice and Kendall were each other's constant companions around town and at least once a week they would drive over the river to visit with Jesse's parents and with hers. Kendall was treated like a little prince. On a hot summer Sunday in 1934, they were all looking forward to a Sunday gathering at the Jennings' farm. Alice took the children to church that morning then hurried home to change clothes and pick up Jesse, who had started harvesting a few carrots from their garden. Jesse helped his family in the car and they drove the few miles to the old homestead.

They were the first to arrive. Robert and Mary stepped down from the porch and gave big hugs to Iris Jeanne and Kendall then greeted Alice warmly. Jesse shook their hands and asked Robert if he could take Kendall down to the barn to see the new gelding, Hank. Robert said yes, and Alice and Iris Jeanne went inside to the kitchen to help Mary. Robert called Alice back to the porch.

"Say Belle, could you bring me a glass of your mother's sweet tea with plenty of ice? And bring a glass for yourself."

Alice knew from the tone he had something to say. She obliged and sat down on the second rocker after giving her father the tea. She pressed the cold glass against her forehead, enjoying the quiet.

"You picked a scorcher to see your children today, Daddy."

"Hadn't seen the grandkids in a while. Thought they'd like the day. Your Kendall's fixin' to ride. Let's see how he sits on Hank."

They watched as Jesse placed a halter on Hank then gently lifted Kendall onto his bare back. Robert stopped fanning himself with one of Mary's magazines and took a long drink of the cold tea.

"Alice, I'd best be the one you hear it from, so I'm just gonna tell you," he began slowly but with gentle firmness. He had a message. "Jesse is layin' over at Sissy's after the run's finished."

"I know he stops there for dinner some days. May have a beer too," she added trying to convey to her father that she was aware of this pattern.

"Got nothin' to say about a beer, but there's some rough ones there. Make a livin' outa horseshoes and cards. I know your Jesse like's a game of horseshoes. He's been losin' more than not. Alice, I've seen a good man give in to what goes on at Sissy's and places like it. You need to know this thing. Don't be cajoled by Jesse's smile."

"Cajoled? Thanks Daddy, I'll see what comes of it."

"Don't just see, Alice, do what you have to."

Robert nodded his head and turned his attention again towards Jesse and Kendall. Kendall was sitting tall on Hank's back while Jesse had a twenty-foot rope leading the gelding in a gentle circle. Kendall was squealing with delight, and Jesse was giving solid riding instructions between his "attaboys." Robert studied their interaction for a few minutes.

"That's a fine looking boy there, Belle." Robert seemed relieved that he had finished saying what he had to say. "Look how he keeps his back straight." Kendall was only three and riding Hank bareback in a slow rocking gait. "Look how he's moving with the horse. He's balanced there and pushin' his legs into Hank's sides. I say if a boy learns to ride bareback first, then he knows how to ride. A saddle just separates you from the animal and can make a man lazy, can lose the feel. That Jesse is right to start him off bareback."

The compliment to Jesse was sincere but didn't hide Robert's misgivings about his son-in-law. Jesse was a good provider and had given Alice a lovely home with children whom Robert deeply loved. His lack of education had been overcome with hard work and now Jesse was at a point in his life that gave the promise of wealth in these dark economic times. Alice knew her father understood men and their weaknesses.

For the next few days Alice pondered her father's words. She hadn't seen much evidence of Jesse's drinking but she admitted to herself she had been too willing to assume the best when there was early evidence to the contrary. But gambling? Poseidon twirled his trident.

Two weeks later Jesse came home late and the smell of alcohol was strong on his breath. His steps were halting and he refused to make eye contact with Alice as he entered the kitchen through the back door. Alice was there as he walked by without a word.

"You okay? You're two hours late," she stated calmly and factually.

"Okay? Sure," Jesse replied.

After waiting to see if there was more to follow she said, "Jesse, you've been drinking at Sissy's haven't you?" No reply. "Well, haven't you?"

Jesse stopped, turned and raised his eyes to Alice and roared for all to hear. "Ain't none of your goddamn worry!"

Alice was stunned. Jesse had never spoken to her like that before and this explosion frightened her. After a moment, she regained her composure and her courage. "It most certainly is my worry. Jesse, I've got no word against a beer with your friends. You work hard and take good care of your family, but these are perilous times and you can't go mixing alcohol and gambling."

"Who said I was gamblin'? I can throw a few horseshoes if I want. I'm damn good at it too, and you're not tellin' me what to do. No women's gonna tell me what to do, and don't you go actin' like your sister Ina. I ain't no pussywhipped Edwin."

Alice had never seen this behavior in Jesse and had no idea the proper course to take. She decided to defuse the evening, but not before a final word. "It certainly is my worry for your safety, for your health, and for the health of your family. It most certainly is my worry and don't ever talk like that to me again."

That evening at supper, Jesse mumbled an apology to the three and then kidded Iris Jeanne about her freckles. He pronounced Iris with only one syllable, which sounded like 'Arse'.

"Arse Jeanne, them angels been kissin' you."

Alice didn't smile.

By the spring of 1935, even the most optimistic were starting to lose hope. Hope can carry a man or woman for a while but at some point it can collapse and the whole family feels the hard reality closing in. Parts of America's Southern Plains were dead and, for many of its inhabitants, hope was lost. The winter had been cold with more frequent dusters. Many families just left, left behind what they couldn't take and fled to any place they could. Any place was better than the dunes of Oklahoma, Kansas, Texas, New Mexico, and Colorado. There was a new killing disease that struck the young the hardest, dust pneumonia. In a Saturnalian frenzy, the earth was devouring its children.

In the middle of April, the radio station in Oklahoma City, KOMA, interrupted the Sunday calm with word of a duster on the way. The announcer's tone had sense of coming dread. He had just spoken with the station in Boise City. Ina called Alice and told her the news. Alice had heard and was headed out the kitchen door to gather her family. Jesse was preparing the garden for planting. Iris Jeanne was in the apple orchard with a friend. Alice told the little girl to head home right away and watched her cross the street and enter her house safely. Kendall was in the garden hitting the garden rows with a long stick, imitating his father's hoeing motion.

"Jesse, the radio said there's a big, really big, duster on the way. Said to get everyone inside and prepare."

Jesse stood straight and looked up at the blue sky and the few cirrus clouds keeping it from being completely clear. "You take Kendall here and go on inside. I'll join you in a few minutes." Alice took Kendall's hand and with Iris Jeanne on the other, she entered the house.

Jesse drove the Chrysler inside the carriage barn and slid the bolt tight on the swinging doors. The chickens and the two goats were herded into their sheds and anything loose was weighted down or placed inside one of the sheds. When Jesse came inside all the windows were closed, and Alice and Iris Jeanne were placing moist towels around the windowsills. It was all they could do so they moistened more towels and a thin blanket and sat by the radio.

The wind began to pick up and the bright day was overcome with darkness as the sinister cloud rolled east. The electricity went out early, and their home was thrown into near total darkness. The temperature dropped twenty degrees in only a few minutes and continued to drop as the wind raked the strong house. The walls gave a hollow wailing in return as if to surrender to the dusty darkness that penetrated the house. Kendall could not be consoled. The four huddled under a moistened blanket in the center of the parlor, holding each other and trying to sing. Jesse pulled out his harmonica and played Skip-To-My-Lou, the best of the three songs he knew. The terrible noise from outside was louder than the notes coming from the dusty harmonica. Kendall trembled and buried his head in his mother's lap. They became silent and after three exhausting hours, the children fell asleep under the blanket, Kendall in Alice's embrace and Iris Jeanne in her father's strong arms.

The Black Sunday storm was a disaster. It was the worst dust storm the dead plains would ever produce. It swept across the Southern Plains in an arc and was carried by the high winds. Choking dust settled on Washington DC and the eastern seaboard and on ships three hundred miles at sea. It was a convulsion of the dead earth finally heard by the whole country. People and livestock caught unprotected died in the open. The hospital wards swelled with sufferers of the dust pneumonia. For many, small granite stones would be their worldly mark.

The next morning Alice stood at the kitchen window. She took a slow breath and said a simple prayer of thanks. She had weathered this storm and took strength thinking she could weather worse.

CHAPTER 24
MENTAL HYGIENE

The rains never showed, that spring of '35. Around Canadian County there were a few showers but not enough to replenish the moisture needed by the earth. Life in El Reno took on a cloud of constant shadow, but clouds let the sun in on occasion, and in El Reno and Oklahoma there was some light. The nation was finally aware of the disaster. It had an official name, the Dust Bowl. Even though regions of four other states were as blighted, Oklahoma became the poor man of America. They were called "Okies", those desperate families that fled west or stayed on, trying to survive this disaster. The media and a few writers and photographers like Dorothea Lange gave a face to these nameless victims and in an odd way, gave comfort to the unemployed in Chicago, Philadelphia, New York, and the rest of the country. At least they weren't Okies. But the Okies had a champion, Will Rogers. No man since Mark Twain had given voice to this vision of the common American. He was the most well-known, most loved, and most read personality of his day. His weekly column in the New York Times skewered the folly of government and spoke of the sweep of nature's wrath, but he always gave rudder to the struggling mass that he knew was America's strength. Oklahoma had a collective pride in her favorite son.

Wiley Post was Oklahoma's second favorite son. He was the first aviator to fly solo around the world and had established multiple aviation records. His breakthrough of engineering, skill, and daring crowned him one of the great aviators of all time. In August of 1935, Wiley Post's Lockheed Orion Explorer, with his friend Will Rogers sharing the cockpit, nose-dived into a cold Alaska lagoon. A second Black Sunday descended on the nation and centered over Oklahoma. The only moisture that August was the tears of the Okies mixing with the red dust of Oklahoma.

Jesse and Alice shared in the common grief. Two days after the terrible news, Jesse came home very drunk. He was mobile, but his speech was slurred and his walk was unsteady.

"You're drunk," Alice said matter-of-factly.

"Will Rogers is dead," he answered in genuine sadness with his blue eyes red from the tears and the whiskey.

"We're all sad about that, but what does that have to do with you being drunk? Do you really think that gives you credence?" Alice asked with a slowly escalating anger. Jesse said nothing, just lowered his head and walked by. The supper was quiet at first then the silence was broken by Iris Jeanne's excited talk of the new school year.

Jesse settled into a pattern of month long sobriety broken by a day or two or three of heavy drinking. Alice felt herself partly to blame because she had avoided a confrontation. She didn't know what to say or how to comfort Jesse, and she realized that haranguing her husband would not penetrate the cause of his drinking. He might give some excuse that perhaps he thought gave cover, but Alice was embarrassed for him and let him know his excuses carried no reason. If it wasn't Will's or Wiley's death, it was the latest duster, or the death of some neighbor, or the death of a neighbor they didn't know, or some other stretch, then finally fiction entered the play.

Alice was never given a full accounting of Jesse's earnings. Most was in cash, so it was easy for Jesse to keep an extra twenty or fifty for his fun at Sissy's. He considered himself a talented marksman and horseman, so it was only natural that he would excel in horseshoes. Except he didn't, and when whisky was added to his confidence, it subtracted from his talent. He lost more than he made in bets with the locals, who soon learned to throw a game to stroke Jesse's ego and then raise the bets as Jesse continued to raise his glass of whiskey. Jesse became a cash cow for the regulars at Sissy's, and it was obvious to all except the cow. Even Roy tried to get him to slow down, but Jesse was blind to reason. He was usually good for his losses, but he might have to defer a day or two to collect his pay. Two days were tolerable, but two weeks were not.

Jesse returned one Friday afternoon on time and quite sober. He also returned swollen and bleeding and needing Roy's help to come inside to a bewildered Alice.

"My Lord, Jesse, you're hurt! What happened?"

Jesse was woozy and mumbled something Alice couldn't understand.

"Got jumped, Jesse took a beating," said Roy. He and Alice removed Jesse's shoes, shirt and trousers and helped him to bed. Alice brought clean towels and soap and water and began to clean Jesse's swollen face.

"Your Jesse is tough, but no match for those two. Sucker punched him."

"Did you call the police?"

"Well no. We was in a hurry to get outa there. Came straight here."

Alice looked Roy over and noticed he had no signs of battle and his unmarked face could not bring his eyes to meet hers. It didn't add up, and after the shock of seeing Jesse had passed, she knew what had happened. "Thank you Roy. Can you get help for tomorrow's run? I think Jesse needs to heal up."

"Sure thing, Alice, I'll stop by tomorrow to see how he's doing," and with that, Roy was out the door.

Alice continued tending to Jesse who was awake and had heard the talk between Alice and Roy. "Got jumped, huh? Where was this?" she asked.

"At Sissy's, just as we was going in for dinner."

"Why didn't Roy help?"

"He tried, but they was too fast."

There was long silence as Alice completed her nursing and dipped an iodine soaked swab on the deepest cuts. Jesse flinched.

"Don't lie to me Jesse Sheets. How much do you owe?"

The lie was never to be believed and Jesse settled into the pillow, relieved that he wouldn't have to reconstruct an event that had no memory. "Two hundred. Said I had a week to pay or there was more where this come from."

Alice said nothing as she pulled the sheet up and fluffed his pillow. She brushed his hair back with her fingers and lingered, softly touching his forehead.

"We'll figure this all out, Jesse. You rest now." She went silently to the kitchen and began to reheat the morning coffee. She sat on the wooden kitchen chair and sobbed. She had no idea what to do. She started to accept some of the blame. Perhaps if she had spoken earlier, when her suspicions were beginning to gather facts, she could have prevented all this. No! She was not a partner to his drinking, and she was not going to be saddled with the worthless weight of guilt.

Supper was very quiet. Alice told Iris Jeanne and Kendall that their father had fallen off the back of the truck and hurt himself. Kendall stared at his father's swollen face with curiosity. As he continued to stare, Jesse turned and let out a surprising, "Boo!"

Kendall jumped back in his chair, and Jesse and his son shared a hearty laugh.

Jesse paid the debt with the help of all of Alice's coffee can savings and for the remainder of the fall stayed sober and free of Sissy's dinners. Jesse was able to rebuild the trust of his clients, all of whom had heard the story. Roy seemed to honor Jesse's struggles and would save his drinking for El Reno and a different group of friends. Alice and Jesse had a respite, and the Christmas season was a good time for the young family.

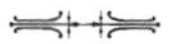

In the dead part of Oklahoma in 1936, the rains only teased. Canadian County had a scattering but not the spring soakers needed by the earth. The regular dusters were dealt with by Oklahoma resolve. Those who remained were, for the most part, to stay and see this terrible time through. Robert and Mary Jennings and most of the North Canadians were getting by. Robert had no debt and was in better shape than most, now that all of their children had left. All had married and left except his second son Jack, who did most of the hard work on the farm. He and his wife, Ethel, and their three children built a modest house half way between the Jennings' house and the river. It wasn't visible from the Jennings' porch, but when the fire was lit, the rising curl of smoke could be seen in line with the grain elevators of El Reno. Newt and Vi and their five children were renting the quarter section just east but were struggling. Newt's brothers and sisters would say that Newt couldn't make a dime with two nickels. They weren't trying to be mean, and Newt would probably agree. Newt was troubled and would spend many evenings alone, hunting with his dogs. He kept his distance from his father and only showed up occasionally for large Sunday gatherings.

These two oldest sons were complex men who didn't trust each other. Just what was between them, the sisters never figured out. It wasn't the sort of thing you would ask over supper, and the sisters' speculation never reached certainty. Ina was always more cut and dried, and she declared to Alice that Newt was too much like their father Robert, and Jack was too much like their grandmother Carrie. Alice didn't know what "too much" meant and didn't think Ina shed any light on the mystery, but would nod in apparent agreement. She always felt tender towards Newt, and if he were to tell anyone why he had become so silent, it would have been Alice. He never did.

Alice and Jesse would visit the farm on some Sundays, but Jesse would often beg off and hunt with his brothers or buddies. The land around the river was still rich in dove and quail and Jesse remained a good shot. His treasured gun was his Browning double barrel twelve gauge. It was a heavy gun, but Jesse loved the balance and the way it looked. It had a raised rib between the barrels and the walnut stock was kept polished and smooth. Jesse paid attention to the appearance of his guns, his car, and his clothes, and his still lovely Alice.

Jesse never confessed his alcoholism to anyone, including himself. Instead of opening himself to Alice, he listened to his friends and other voices, and he began to see his drinking as a measure of his own manhood. If asked, he couldn't really define what manhood meant, but he constructed a map that placed at its center, manly control as its dominant virtue. This would be expressed in his manly pledge to stop drinking, but it also became a force in the marital dynamic. If he was to be strong and manly in one area, then it must encompass all manly realms. It was as simple as it was unworkable, and failure was assured. His frustration led to increased belligerence and a more argumentative relationship with Alice. His slow simmering temper began to surface more frequently without the aid of drink and for the first time, Alice suffered not only the collateral heat of his anger, she became its target.

The summer of 1936 had begun with cautious optimism. The big news in El Reno was a coming fly-in by Amelia Earhart, the most famous and beautiful of the world's lady aviatrixes. She was to fly the futuristic autogyro to the airstrip at Fort Reno. Amelia Earhart was not an Okie, but Oklahomans followed her accomplishments closely just as they had followed Wiley Post. The El Reno Democrat had run stories every day for the previous two weeks, and a great number of the county residents and beyond were expected to show. Alice and Jesse had planned, like most of their neighbors, to take a picnic lunch. Alice was anxious to show Iris Jeanne that there was a wide world outside of El Reno, and this brave Amelia could help Iris Jeanne see what a woman could do.

With that thought in mind, Alice stopped packing the basket for a moment. She realized that she had followed a well-trodden path of options. She had an education and was proud of her teaching, if only for a year. She had no second thoughts about her family and didn't see her care of Jesse, Iris Jeanne, and Kendall as an obligation but as an expression of love. Nevertheless, she reasoned, if Jesse should become injured or fall further under the wheels of drink, then she would have to earn money. There had to be a third way between the wife of an alcoholic and that of Amelia Earhart.

She began loading the basket when Floyd and two friends pulled up in his Plymouth and honked. As she walked to the screen door, Jesse entered the kitchen from the parlor. He was carrying his shotgun in its flannel wrap, had his hunting vest on, and was trying to grab a sandwich from the basket.

"What are doing, Jesse?" She looked his hunting clothes over. "Where are you going?"

"Huntin'," he answered sharply. "I'll probly be home for supper."

"We've been planning this for two weeks. The children are excited. This was to be our day."

"Goddamnit woman! I said I'm going huntin' and don't give me grief. Not in front of my brother and not ever!"

"Why are you acting like this? Why are you so angry?" She asked, her tone now rising in anger to meet his. Iris Jeanne and Kendall heard every word. Jesse grabbed two sandwiches and walked out the door to the waiting car without answering.

Alice finished the lunch preparation and the three left for Fort Reno. The announcer, from a raised wooden platform announced Amelia Earhart's imminent arrival from Tinker Field near Oklahoma City and sure enough, she approached low and slow from the east.

The craft was unique and Alice and Iris Jeanne had never seen anything like it. It had short stubby wings and an engine and propeller in front, but above Amelia rotated a huge four-bladed propeller spinning independently of the front engine. After a few gentle passes, she put the autogyro into sweeping climbs and rolls at such a slow speed that the crowd thought it would fall out of the sky. Her skills and the new aircraft's passively spinning propeller allowed such maneuvers, and she confidently flew the craft over Fort Reno. It was breathtaking. She landed the aircraft on General Sheridan's old assembly ground and taxied to the raised platform. She was swarmed by the crowd and the awaiting press. A few soldiers formed a cordon around the aircraft, and Amelia climbed the stairs to address the crowd. She thanked all those in attendance and for American aero-technology making such a craft possible. She said she would take a few questions from the crowd. Obscured by adults, Iris Jeanne excitedly waved her hand.

That night Jesse and Alice talked.

"Sorry you missed Amelia Earhart, Jesse. She put on a show and your Iris Jeanne and Kendall had a great day. Would have been better if you'd been there."

"Hadn't been huntin' in two weeks. Had a good day. There's five dove cleaned in the ice box."

"You'd said you were going with us. Told the children, then you didn't. Why on earth did you talk to me like that? You had no call to be angry."

"If you're lookin' for an apology, then fine. But you got no sway over me and my time."

"You can puff your chest out when you're with your buddies, but that's not going to fly here. I'm not trying to control or badger you, so don't say it like it's my doing, Jesse Sheets." Alice was getting angry. "And another thing. You were sober and you still got angry with me, in front of the children too. Jesse you've got a concern. More than a concern, you've got a drinking problem that covers you the twenty-four hours of the day, drunk or sober."

"Don't call me drunk!" Jesse said angrily.

"Hear me out. Call it what you want, but you're headed down the wrong road and you're picking up speed. Can't you see that?"

"Here's what I'll do. I can stop and I can start whenever I please. No man with a drinkin' problem can do that. I can. I'll lay off for a while. No more'n a beer at dinner with Roy. I get up at three every mornin', and I'm bringin' home near four hundred dollars a month. A lot of women be more'n fine with that."

Alice didn't buy Jesse's bravado, but saw little point in continuing the talk.

"I'll hold you to your pledge, Jesse. I want to help you."

"Don't need help. You got my pledge."

Jesse was mostly faithful to his partial sobriety for the summer. He would nurse the one beer through noon dinner with Roy, telling himself he could master the drink if he just manned his way about. It worked for a while, but inside, Jesse became increasingly angry and resentful and a powder keg of emotion. He could control it for a time, but the rage would build and when the vent finally released, it was terrifying to Alice and their children.

The perceived precipitating event, whether a lost tool, a dinner not hot, a leaky faucet, another damn duster, a neighbor's barking dog, gave proof of Jesse's illness.

An uneasy truce was observed through the fall, but Alice knew it wouldn't last. Alice concentrated on the children and Jesse worked hard on the milk run. She and Roy said little to each other beyond a simple greeting. She knew Roy had the same problem as Jesse and although she didn't blame him, she knew they formed a deadly alliance of support and excuse. Jesse's anger was always present under a thin veneer, and the perceived threat to his manhood that Alice represented became a daily challenge. He swore to all his friends that he would never be pussywhipped and would toast his proclamation with a beer.

Even the relative calm did not give Alice solace. She decided to seek advice. Reverend McClure of the First Christian Church was her first outside counselor.

"Jesse is angry at the world, Reverend," she pleaded in one short sentence. "He's back to drinking and won't listen to me."

"I know, Alice. I know this is so. Why, do you know how many men are drunk in the street every day right here in El Reno? They've lost their family, and the depression just keeps them down, like a weight they can't get out from under. Jesse is still working and I know you have a comfortable living. More so than many in our congregation."

Alice didn't want to hear how some men had fallen much further than Jesse. She knew that. What she needed to know was how to stop the slide.

"Yes, Reverend, I know of others who are fighting a hotter battle than me, but I need to be able to help, to stop Jesse from going there, ending up in the street, or even dead. Telling me about drunks in the street doesn't give me the answers I need."

Reverend McClure was startled.

"I'm sorry Reverend, didn't mean to sound impatient or rude."

"I see Alice. Well, you must ask God to help Jesse find his way back to you and to his Son, Jesus."

It was a predictable response and Alice had heard it from his pulpit before. She knew there would be no recipe for Jesse's health today.

"Thank you, Reverend. I'll do just that. See you on Sunday."

She sat in her car and reflected. She was very frustrated by the predictable advice. If prayer could save Jesse it would have shown results by now. She couldn't even get Jesse to darken the church door, much less ask God for help. She drove to the Carnegie Library. It was a source of El Reno pride and the granite building, built with a donation from the Carnegie Foundation, was a favorite spot for Alice just as it had been for her sister Edna. She parked and walked slowly up the steps to the office of the head librarian.

"Afternoon, Leana," she said to her friend. "How's your Taylor getting along?"

"Well hello, Alice. Saw you walking up the steps and hoped you would come by my office. Taylor is home now that the fever is down and improving each day, but Dr. Womack says he can hear a murmur in his heart. Says a lot of people have a murmur after the rheumatic fever and do just fine. I think my prayers were answered."

"Well that is good news indeed," said Alice with genuine concern. She figured if God was to intervene, better to help the innocent. She would ask Reverend McClure about that but knew it was too complicated for a Sunday sermon. "Leana, I need your assistance," she asked in a quieter tone. Leana said nothing but looked intently at her friend. "I need the newest thoughts or treatment for," she hesitated then stiffened, "for alcoholism."

Leana, and all of Alice's friends, knew of Jesse's drinking. "Of course Alice, come with me." They walked past three large oak tables and chairs with their seated visitors to an open area of high wooden cabinets. In the middle of the room were six plush leather chairs with curved metal arm rests, and in front of the wooden cabinets were racks of newspapers from around the country and current magazines. Leana found the latest issue of *Mental Hygiene* and handed it to Alice.

"We're not to check these out, but you can take it home and return it when you're finished," she said.

"Thank you kindly, Leana. You give Taylor a kiss for me now."

"I will. Take your time with that magazine."

This new science of mental hygiene, according to an article Alice had read, was becoming the modern way to look at health problems that didn't originate in the physical body. Instead, it was an attempt to uncover those problems that arose in the mind. Sure enough, there was a three-page article titled "How to Render the Drinker Whole".

Alice was crushed. The article stressed a healthy family environment, good food, a clean home and lots of love. What a disappointment thought Alice. She had offered all of these things and more to Jesse, only to find him worsening.

Alice returned the magazine the next day and continued to reflect on the article. She thought that she could indeed do her part to improve the atmosphere at home. Perhaps she should cease any harsh tone with Jesse and cloak her family in a cloud of motherly love. Perhaps it would allow Jesse to relax his inflated sense of manhood and by feeling more comfortable with his masculinity, maybe it would soften his need to drink. She just couldn't understand Jesse's refusal to live in peace. Why initiate conflict? Mental hygiene would have its go.

The next day, Alice spent the time after Iris Jeanne and Kendall had left for school cleaning the house. It had been two weeks since the last duster and Alice began with a purpose. The house was swept and dusted and the cotton window coverings washed in the kitchen sink. The dust from them turned the soapy water dark and when Alice hung them again that afternoon, she was so pleased with the clear light they let in. She straightened every item in the house then refolded Jesse's socks, T-shirts, and underwear. In the closet, she separated the pants from the shirts and arranged them by work or dress, mostly work. That evening and the next morning, Jesse didn't seem to notice. She wasn't done.

She went to Youngheim's Department Store and spent time evaluating the lingerie. She found a light blue bra that instead of covering the breast with a tent, allowed some of her breast and cleavage to show. She found a matching pair of panties and bought it a size smaller so it would hug her curves tightly. She giggled to herself as the clerk placed her purchases in a box with clean white paper. It didn't take much skin to excite a man and Alice knew it had never taken a lot of encouragement from her to arouse Jesse. She figured it might help Jesse to know that he was still desirable too. Then she got a little confused trying to figure out who desired who and finally thinking, "Oh well, fun in bed can only be good, and a little variation can only help. Besides, it's mental hygiene."

She waited until Sunday. Alice and Iris Jeanne and Kendall attended church with Anna Sheets, their usual Sunday custom. Jesse worked around the house and garden and enjoyed these hours alone. After a modest noon dinner of ham sandwiches, she told the children that their neighbors, the Maines, were making ice cream and they were invited. Iris Jeanne and Kendall left as soon as the meal was finished and the table cleared. The two ran out the back door, and Kendall challenged his sister to catch him. The door slammed shut, and Alice locked it before the cotton window covering had stopped moving.

She stood backlit by the sun coming in the door's window. She was wearing a sleeveless simple yellow cotton dress with small white daisy prints. She wasn't wearing a slip. As she turned around she saw Jesse eyeing her. The sunlight, crisp and clean, penetrated Alice's dress and outlined her body. She slipped one strap off her left shoulder then looking straight at Jesse, slipped the other strap and let the dress fall to the floor. Jesse's eyes fixed on the sunlit vision. He stood, walked to her and gently ran the back of his hand over the exposed skin of her breast. He slipped a finger inside her bra and with back of his hand traced the top of her breast. His other hand moved inside the front of her panties and, while touching her, he kissed her deeply. A low sound came from Alice's throat as she put both arms around Jesse's back and brought him closer to her. He picked her up and carried her to the bedroom. The daylight was bright and clear and as Alice tried to pull the sheet up, Jesse in a sweep of his arm, pulled the sheet off the bed so that nothing of Alice would be hidden. They made love as intense and as pure as those afternoons when they were young, on the grass beneath the cedars.

After their breathing slowed and their sweat began to cool, they slept. Alice was the first to wake, and she turned to face her sleeping husband. She gently stroked his temple and twirled the hair behind his ear with her fingers. She remembered him as a young and innocent man, the man who would light up a room as he entered. She recalled the cedar flat and finding grass in her hair at evening supper. She thought of their two children and the way Jesse loved them. She recalled the joy in his voice as he told her about the milk run and its potential. But then she recalled the anger and the swearing and the separation and the stupors and the cruelty. She wondered, of all of these things, which would be Jesse's leavings.

Alice stood and walked naked to the kitchen and returned with a glass of tea to share. With the sheet still on the floor, they lay together facing each other.

"You're still beautiful," said Jesse, sounding a little perplexed by Alice's continued nakedness.

"And I still love you Jesse. You need to know that. You need to know that every day. Our hearts want the same thing, don't they?"

There was a long silence then Jesse opened his eyes wider with a look of sudden understanding. "This is about my drinking isn't it?" he asked with an edge of tension.

Alice rubbed his chest and answered softly. "It's about telling you that your family loves you. Some of us can show it in different ways," she said with a sultry bent. "You like different now don't you?"

"I like it. I like it a lot."

Kendall was banging on the kitchen door. They dressed quickly.

CHAPTER 25
REUNION

There was to be a reunion of the Jennings and Hawkins family in July of 1937. The five sisters and Mary decided it must happen after Robert had suffered two heart attacks. The doctor had given the standard advice of no exertion and nitroglycerin pills for any chest pain. The fine horses once raised by Robert were all gone, save the one gelding Hank. Jack, now running the day-to-day of the farm, kept a small herd of white-faced cows and had recently bought a dozen Black Angus heifers. He was a good farmer and knew stock well, but he had grown up thinking his father had favored Newt. The other brothers and sisters found that not the case since Newt had caused more trouble for Robert and Ida Emma than all their other children combined. Jack held on to this wound, no matter the actual. Maybe Robert saw a little of himself in Newt, but if that was the case, he never overtly showed favoritism; in fact he was hardest on Newt. Jack remembered Newt running away to be with Bertha and figured his father must have admired Newt's spunk and boldness. Jack's life was predictable and honorable.

This Sunday Newt would return with his new wife Bertha, the girl he had run off to be with when he was fourteen. Newt served in the war, suffered a shoulder wound and survived a gas attack. He came home with a Purple Heart and seared memories. He had married Viola Pickard and they had five children and a good marriage. Vi and their sixth child died in childbirth and Newt was devastated. Mustard gas or shrapnel couldn't have caused more damage. He placed, the neighbors said passed around, his five children with friends and family and fled to California. He found work at a dog track and broke off all contact with his family.

While he was in California, Bertha and her husband and their seven-year-old son had moved to Cement and become acquaintances of Edna and Hill Elliott. The marriage failed and they divorced. The day the divorce was final, Bertha's former husband asked Bertha and their son to accompany him to the cemetery to pay respects to his deceased parents. He was leaving Oklahoma and his son the next morning. Bertha agreed but stayed in the car rather than accompany her ex and her son to the gravesite. She was staring in the opposite direction towards a lone sycamore swaying in the wind, thinking about her future, when a loud noise disturbed the silence. In confusion, she turned towards her son and saw him lying motionless on the ground in an unnatural position. Still perplexed, she saw her former husband place a revolver to his temple and looking straight at Bertha, he pulled the trigger.

Edna contacted Newt at the dog track in California and told him the news. Newt and Bertha married a month later. Neither was whole and those who knew them best, Ina, Edna, and Alice, prayed they would heal each other. Newt and Bertha gathered his children and the new family, recently moved back to El Reno, promised they would be at the reunion. Even Jack was looking forward to the day.

The morning of the reunion Alice was in an elevated and very happy mood. She decided to skip church so the four could drive out to the farm early. All seven of her brothers and sisters and the seventeen grandchildren would be there. Adding Mary's four children and their nine grandchildren, it would a great feast.

Highway 81 was a nice two lane paved road with a modern iron trestle bridge over the North Canadian. The rains were still missing over the dust bowl, but scattered showers in the eastern half of Oklahoma allowed a marginal cotton crop to yield a few puffy cotton flowers, providing a little income for Robert and Mary. Robert had kept his long ago promise that neither he nor his children would ever pick cotton so, come fall, he would hire it out. This forty-acre field came quickly into view once Jesse turned his Chrysler onto Hefner Road, the old section line laid out for the Run of '89. It was only eight-thirty when they turned onto the short lane and parked below the house. Robert's Buick was not in its usual place alongside the house. Mary was alone in the house and came bounding from the kitchen and gave Alice a warm embrace.

"Morning Mother," Alice greeted this kind woman and at the same time, Iris Jeanne hugged her waist and Kendall found an open spot and added his own hug.

"How are my precious ones today? Would you like to help Grandma?"

"Sure," Kendall answered quickly, "whatcha need?"

"Iris Jeanne, take the little man here and see if you can gather a few pints of strawberries. There's baskets by the garden gate."

Iris Jeanne was happy to help and she and Kendall disappeared around the back of the house. They knew the farm well and had helped plant part of the garden that spring. With water from the well, the garden was an oasis of abundance and provided the Jennings, their children, and a few neighbors welcome fresh produce.

Mary had become close friends with Theo and Dotty Dickerson, who had purchased the Myers' farm across the road. Carrie Myers had kept the farm going after her husband, Newton, had died the year after Ida Emma's death. She adopted two orphans, a boy and a girl, and raised them well. Her brother, John, stayed for several years then realized he had no future there. He finally tasted love with a girl, sixteen years younger, married her and moved down to Chickasaw. His closest friend, Robert, had tried to find him work in El Reno, but John was determined and said he'd had enough of his sister. After Ida Emma died and Carrie's influence on her children waned, she became a genuinely unpleasant woman to be around. She grew fat and angry and domineering, a combination not even a grandchild could overlook. Her dreams of Chautauqua on the Prairie were forgotten by all. When she sold her three quarter sections and moved to Apache, the North Canadians' response was that of yawning indifference.

Carrie's adopted girl held the close of the story begun in Kansas, long before the Myers' move to Texas. Several years after the Run of '89, Carrie and Newton's disowned first child, Rachel, arrived on Ida Emma and Robert's back porch, dying from tuberculosis and cradling her three-month-old child, Lola. Ida Emma cared for her sister those last two weeks of her life and the day she died, Carrie was with her. Ida Emma later told Edna she had never witnessed such grief. Carrie cried out her failings and her love and unable to separate the two, she collapsed on the bed with her dead daughter. After the tremors and sobbing stopped, she stood up, wiped her eyes and gathered little Lola in her arms. She told all the women present, that she was adopting Lola. She had no sway on those present, but asked them keep these happenings inside the family. She renamed her granddaughter Annie Myers and never told the story outside the family. Carrie loved and nurtured Annie, always a sickly little girl, and tried to show her the love she had denied Rachael. Annie died before her eighteenth birthday and Carrie's adopted son inherited her considerable wealth.

The Dickerson family that bought the nicely improved Myers' farm became fast friends with Mary and Robert. Mary and Dotty spent time helping each other in their respective gardens and would share seeds and ideas. Mary's plot would always have tall rows of hollyhocks along the edges giving streaks of color waving over the dark green vegetables.

Alice looked at the clean healthy rows and said to Mary, "Your garden is just lovely this year, Mother. You and Dotty must have quite a competition."

"Well, I do have an advantage you know. Jack and Ethel help quite a bit, especially when it's time to water," Mary said.

Jack's work on the farm showed his pride and the house had a fresh coat of paint. He had been careful to match the green trim first chosen by his mother, Ida Emma.

"You know Alice, since your father's heart attack, he can't do much around here so Jack is really the one bearing the work," said Mary.

"Is he all right with that, Mother? Sometimes he seems to stew about things."

"Well, they both have tempers and they show it sometimes. I don't think Jack feels appreciated, and now he sees his father so looking forward to Newt's visit today. Kinda rankles him."

"We all love Jack," said Alice, "and know he's why the farm is still doing well, but Mother, we haven't seen Newt in over a year. He stays at his place south of town and hardly ever sees anybody. I hear Bertha's not well." Alice felt ashamed for a moment for sounding so gossipy, but she wanted more news of her big brother and his new wife. She had heard stories.

"You're talking about letting those boys run naked aren't you?" Mary asked calmly. She continued, "Stories are easy to start and hard to kill." As she said this she glanced at Jesse, standing silently a few feet away, listening to the two women. "I know neighbors talk, but those two little ones had a bad rash and Bertha'd read about sunlight curing a skin rash, so she thought she'd try it."

"So you've spoken with Bertha. I should have asked you first instead of believing such gossip."

"A story told ain't always a story happened," added Jesse, with surprising clarity.

The three turned around when Robert drove into the lane and watched him get out of the car with slowness evidencing his heart and the loss he had just experienced. He walked straight to Mary and stared at her, but she felt his eyes were looking some place she did not know.

"Kurt just died," Robert said in a low voice, barely able to escape his lips. Then his voice became stronger and full of emotion. "Me and White Mare was with him. He just died. Talked nonsense. Grabbed my arm tight he did. Said we ruined this land. Said we ruined this land. Treated it like our whore. That's what he said. Like the land was our whore. Can you imagine, Mary? Said we ruined the land. I knew he was a different kind of man, but we was friends. Never talked like that to me before. Said the land was our whore."

The two women and Jesse stood silent, waiting to offer comfort but not knowing what to say. Robert continued.

"Who's Demeter? Spoke of Demeter. Said we stole her daughter and this drought, these dusters, was our punishment. Who in God's name is Demeter?"

Alice spoke softly. "Demeter is a goddess from ancient Greece. I think she was a harvest or hearth goddess. Her daughter was abducted, and the land died because of her grief. It's how the ancient Greeks understood the seasons. It's an old myth, Daddy."

"That so?" He was silent for a while, shaking his head. "Ol' Kurt knew more'n most men. Wonder where that all came from? Belle, glad to see you," he said to his daughter and gave her a warm embrace. "Mary, White Mare said she'd bury him with her sister and her sister's husband. Said she'd join 'em in time. She wants to see you tomorrow. I'll go with you."

As the Jennings and Hawkins arrived in scattered caravans and the children squealed with cousin fed joy, the day began as planned. Mary quietly told the grown children of Kurt's death, all of whom had met him. Even little Kendall had seen Kurt devour twenty of Mary's big flapjacks at breakfast a year ago. Some had thought he had died long ago so they didn't share in the sadness, but Jesse recalled the bull riding cowboy from Germany and thought he would never die. Jesse thought of the Sunday years ago when Robert had told him of his great horse and his journey to Texas and Oklahoma. He thought about the roads Kurt and Robert had taken and had met right here on the North Canadian, and how he too had met Kurt along the very same road. Jesse thought about Germany where his own grandmother was born and how it must be pretty different from here, and why would a young boy jump on a ship and come so far to drive cows and marry an Indian? Maybe it was what Kurt had to do, but of all the places to be, he'd ended up here. As he pondered these things, he realized he'd hardly spent a night beyond Canadian County.

The day was a great success; the kind of thing people talk about their whole life. Everyone was there and the count went to fifty, plus one on the way. The adult children and spouses broke into groups and engaged in spirited discussion over politics and the weather. They were all New Dealers so the talk remained friendly as far as local and domestic politics were concerned. On the world stage, Newt spoke of the new threat from Germany and saw only bad to come. Others said no way we were going to fight another war in Europe, but Newt just shook his head, aware that so many times events roil independent of want or reason.

"The rains gotta come regular again," added Jack, wanting to change the subject and attention away from Newt, "and when they do, we'll be ready, and if there's another war, well then that will mean higher prices." Jack was certainly correct and felt justified as the men present nodded and said how Jack was sure right.

The women inside talked of their families and how smart all their children were. Mary finally spoke up and declared that children were to be loved and encouraged but don't go confusing cute with smart. They all laughed so hard, the men outside looked towards the kitchen to see what was causing the commotion.

Everyone present knew of Jesse's drinking and some of Alice's troubles, but it was not a topic for general discussion that day. Alice and Edna had not seen each other for a few weeks and were able to spend a few minutes alone before the big meal.

"How are you getting along?" asked Edna.

"Oh fine," replied Alice, but the lack of response from Edna told Alice she needed to say more. "Things are okay right now, Sister. Jesse's been working hard and we're doing okay, but Jesse drinks two or three or more days a week. Drinks a lot. Comes home staggering. Children know it. Iris Jeanne yelled at him last week. Called him selfish. He tried to slap her but he was too drunk. She just moved away and he missed her. I told him he was never to hit our Iris Jeanne. I told him that, Edna. Don't know if he remembered it the next morning or not." Once she started she couldn't stop. "He won't listen. Won't try. I swear, Sister, I am full of woe. Got a letter from the bank saying we were behind two payments. I didn't know. I asked Jesse. Said it was mistake. Edna, it was no mistake. Jesse skipped two payments. How on earth? Two payments."

Alice stopped, out of breath and in tears. Edna put her arms around her little sister and gave her a motherly hug, as Edna's own tears fell onto her delicate cheeks. Alice was taller and leaned her head down onto Edna's shoulder and cried. Ina walked by, stopped and patted Alice's shoulder, said nothing and walked on leaving the two alone in the parlor.

"Alice, we must talk each day. I don't want you to go a day without talking with me. We've both got perfectly good telephones and we must talk each day. Don't know what those Mental Hygiene magazines say, but we must talk every day." They separated. Both tried to wipe the other's tears and giggled a little at the awkwardness. They rejoined the women in the kitchen and the day went on.

The tall grass, the bison and the Indian were mostly gone, given way to the swelling population of immigrants from all over the world. The children had married men and women who could trace their heritage to most of Europe, Canada, Mexico, and even the blood of Oklahoma's Indians traced the veins of some of the Jennings' and Hawkins' grandchildren. In the depth of the depression, just east of the Dust Bowl, this little patch of prairie feasted and celebrated family.

After the main meal was finished, served in the usual men, children, women rotation, Ina brought the gramophone out to the porch and played some Sousa marches. Everyone loved it. Edna snuck in a Louis Gottschalk record and was pleased with the rapt attention it received. They expected something like that from Edna. After the last record was played, Jesse, standing on the grass below the porch, pulled his harmonica out and began playing some lively little jigs. His best was "Skip To My Lou" which he played through three times, stopping to sing along with no accompaniment. He began playing again, and the children quickly caught on and began singing. They were swaying back and forth in a happy trance. Kendall jumped up and caught his father's outstretched left arm and hung from it as his father continued to play on with his right. He changed tunes to "Get Along Home, Cindy, Cindy" and offered his right arm to any willing child. Carl Estep, Little Carrie's son, jumped up and pulled his chin to the level of Jesse's bicep then swung off and rolled on the grass in laughter. The harmonica kept playing and Jesse's offer continued. Next, Kendall and Bud Elliott, Edna's son, together jumped up and grabbed the extended arms determined to bend them down. Finally, with each suspended from an arm, Jesse gave way and they all fell to the grass in great glee and uncontrolled laughter. A few feet away, Iris Jeanne smiled but as she looked at her father, the laughter wouldn't come.

The sun was still above the trees when a lone car drove into the lane and Pete Jackson, owner of the Jackson Photographic and Portrait Studio in El Reno, appeared with his large camera on a steady tripod. Ina and Edna had arranged for a family portrait, and with a paid professional already present, there was no way Robert or Newt could say no. Jackson decided to frame the family in front of an automobile and chose Ina and Edwin's Buick. Edna wanted the picture taken in front of the house but was overruled by the photographer. It only took two tries to have most of the grandchildren hold still long enough for the shutter to open and close.

The women told Mary to sit while they cleaned the kitchen and left it immaculate for her. They divided the abundant leftovers among themselves for tomorrow's meals. The families were ready to leave. Robert and Mary stood side by side below the porch like a couple receiving wedding or funeral wishes. Everyone hugged Mary, and the women and children also hugged Robert. He shook hands with the men. Jack glanced at the goodbye given to Newt and measured it against his. He seemed satisfied. Jack and Ethel were the last to leave.

As the sun dipped below the trees of the west draw, below the same trees Robert and Dee-Day had camped and where Station was tattooed, where the claim was made by Uncle John, and where Robert and Ida Emma built their soddy for that first winter; the cars' taillights grew fainter as they topped the gentle rise of the old section road and disappeared.

"Mary," Robert said, "this was good thing you did. I hope you were smiling for that picture."

"You know I was," she said. "You must be tired, Mr. Jennings. Can I bring you anything?"

"I'm not so tired, but my chest is a bit tight. Bring me a nitro glycerin pill and three fingers of whiskey. That'd be all I need Mary."

"Would you like your fiddle?"

"Got a broken string, so just the whiskey."

Robert slowly climbed the three concrete steps to the open porch and sat in the old green rocking chair. He was looking south when Mary brought the glass of whiskey and the small white pill. She made sure he took the pill before touching his shoulder. "I'll be a soft call away inside," she said, "if you need me."

"Thank you, Mary." He touched her hand resting on his shoulder.

Across the river, the lights of El Reno were breaking the moonless night. Robert could make out the large elevators by their silhouette of darkness topped by dim red lights. The cicadas were rhythmically calling to each other between the trees, and a gentle coolness had arrived carried by a soft breeze from the north. He remembered the farewell, a blessing he now understood, given him by Dee-Day, *"To-hi-du, U-we-tsi."* "Good peace, Son," a peace beyond understanding. He took a full drink of the whiskey and held it against his palate long enough for the bite to subside, then swallowed. He closed his eyes and silenced his words and for a time he simply sensed, as he had done so long ago on Station, as they'd journeyed from Missouri through this land. In silence, he let other things fill him. He became an open vessel for all that was memorable and good. Memories flooded his senses. He became a reflection of powerful things beyond language, like the small ripple on a still river pool unmasking the strong wind shaking the cottonwood leaves high above, or like the sound of Ida Emma's soft breath passing over his neck. Robert felt these as the Divine gifts they were, and he would not attempt to put them into words. He knew the first language of silence. But even with these great gifts, Robert felt sadness because their earthly source of knowing was growing further and further away, and he knew there would be no replenishing. He remained still. The evening was in full darkness, as his memory was pierced with a barely perceptible sound. Ida Emma's waltz grew louder and louder until he thought the whole county must hear it flowing over this prairie's timeless folds.

CHAPTER 26

THE CLOUD OF UNKNOWING

Jesse's fall was predictable, embarrassing, and painful for Alice, and she chose not to tell her sisters the minutia of Jesse's behavior. She would still confide, but she didn't feel the need to recreate Jesse's latest binge to Ina or Edna over a cup of coffee. Jesse's collapse spread through his family, friends, and job. He felt assaulted by family, especially Ina and Edna and even forbade Alice from seeing her sisters, a command ignored by Alice and laughed at by others. Jesse felt the laugh as a knife, and the wounded animal's anger grew. His friend, Roy, was no help. His alcoholism mirrored Jesse's, and when one couldn't count on the other to cover their drunken days, their farmer clients quickly found new drivers to get their milk to the processors in Oklahoma City.

The foreclosure notices were posted in the fall of 1937. The bank representative told Alice through the screen door that she would have to leave her house. She knew this day would come. She quietly closed the door and sat on a straight back kitchen chair. She cried, not for the loss of the fine home, but for the loss of the fine man. She held her face in her hands and reached deep inside. "Jesse is a failure," she said, then added, "for now." She dried her eyes. It was her charge to take over the family. Her relationship, her love for Jesse would be addressed, but the immediate needs of money, food, and shelter needed her energies now. This was no time for tears or any vestige of herself as a poor victim-wife.

The cottonwoods were turning yellow gold, and the tallest branches from the trees at river level were higher than the iron bridge. As Alice drove north over the river, the golden walls of leaves bent towards each other, enclosing the bridge in a sunlit tunnel. Two miles farther, the old buildings of the Darlington Agency sagging and needing paint, came into view. The grounds were bare of grass and a little rain would turn it into a quagmire of mud. She waved to a few old Arapahoe men as she turned onto Hefner Road. The old section road was good gravel but the little lane to the house was rutted and needed plowing and fresh gravel. The thin rows of cotton had been picked and sold for just a bit more than it had cost to plant. Jack was not around and before she entered the yard, a smiling Mary came down the steps of the shadowed porch.

"Hello Dear," she said walking towards Alice. "What a nice surprise to see you,"

"Oh Mother, I needed to see you and Daddy and just thought I'd drive on out."

"Well so glad you did. Come on inside."

Alice entered the porch and saw her daddy sitting in the dark shade of the porch. His old rocker creaked as he shifted his weight. She gave him a warm hug around his neck and a kiss on his cheek

"Hi Daddy. How're you feeling?"

"Belle, I'm feeling just fine. Rather be on Jack's new horse though. You gotta see him before you go. That Jack's got a good eye for horses."

"I will Daddy."

Mary left the porch but returned shortly with a pitcher of tea. She poured three glasses over the irregular cubes of ice then sat in the second rocker. Alice sat next to her father on a straight back wooden chair.

"We have to move in two weeks. The five acres, our home, Jesse's job, it's all gone. It's gone and I can't stop it," Alice said, unable to make it sound any less that the disaster it was. "I was served papers by the bank. There's no way around it. I cried about it at first, but the crying's stopped. That's why I'm here."

"Knew it was comin' to this. Shaw and Dickerson told me they was getting new haulers," Robert answered.

"How are the children?" asked Mary.

"They don't know yet about any of it, but I'll tell them tonight. Iris Jeanne is mad at her daddy. Seen him drunk too many times. She goes all quiet. Kendall is just Kendall. Don't know any child as happy as him. Still thinks his daddy hung the moon. Just like me once."

"They're good children, Alice," added Mary.

"You have a plan?" Robert asked.

"I think I do, Daddy. Mr. Harry Fowler at the Crystal Laundry needs help. If he'll hire me, it would be enough to pay rent on one of your houses in town. I'm sure Jesse can pick up work some days with his brother or some friend. I think we can get by."

"The house on El Reno Street is vacant. You move there and pay what your earnings can for the rent. It's a good house and you'll have plenty of room. Room for a garden too," Robert said calmly. He had known the foreclosure was coming and had not rented the house when it became vacant a month ago.

Alice slowed her breathing down and sipped the tea. She looked around this old house where she was born, and she felt the strength of her father would keep these walls up forever. "Thank you, Daddy, and thank you, Mother. I'll talk with Jesse tonight and maybe we can get it all worked out."

"His drinking won't let that happen," said Mary, with arrow straight frankness. "If he can't get straight, then you have to get it right for yourself and the children.

Alice repeated those words to herself and understood their truth. She stayed for a few more quiet minutes then rose and hugged her father and hugged and kissed Mary. She had to get home before Iris Jeanne and Kendall returned from school. "I'll look at Jack's horse next time," she said as she climbed into her car.

Alice drove back to El Reno, headed for North Choctaw Street, and stopped at the Crystal Laundry. She told Harry Fowler that she was good at math and a hard worker and she knew a lot of people. She would be good for his business, and he should hire her right then. He did. She would start the next day after the children were off to school. She thanked him and walked out the door, the sun silhouetting her figure beneath a blue cotton dress.

Alice prepared a nice meal of baked pork chops in mushroom sauce, a special meal for a weekday. Jesse returned on time and sober after a few hours work with Floyd, and knew he could not duck the inevitable. After a blessing, Alice proportioned the steaming chops and then announced a family meeting to commence immediately.

"Iris Jeanne, Kendall, we will be moving next week, and tomorrow I will begin working for Mr. Fowler at the Crystal Laundry. I will need your help, Iris Jeanne, with breakfast and with your school lunches so I can be on time. I'll return home just as you return from school." Alice was very matter of fact and the children seemed to feel her resolve by remaining silent.

Jesse finished chewing his first bite of the pork and swallowed. "See here, Alice, you're not working! You'll stay here and tend your family," Jesse protested with bravado.

Alice tried to slow her breathing down and calm her racing heart, but the accumulated anger and frustration, building for years, broke through with the ferocity of a she-bear. She grabbed her plate, full of the steaming pork chops, and slammed it down on Jesse's full plate, splattering Jesse with the hot food. Then she stormed across the kitchen and threw them in the sink with such force that they shattered, sending food scraps and shards of the plates all over the counter and walls. In a rage, she turned to Jesse.

"Goddamn you, Jesse! You lost your goddamn job, and you lost the goddamn house, and you're losing your goddamn family! And you tell me I'm not going to work?" She yelled so loud her voice was suddenly hoarse. She coughed and cleared her throat. Iris Jeanne and Kendall were frozen. She touched each one and said simply, "I'm sorry you had to see that. Don't know where that came from."

"Are you all right, Mother?" asked Iris Jeanne in a worried tone.

"Thank you, Iris Jeanne. I'm fine. Would you do me a favor and get two new plates for the table?"

Jesse spoke up. "Alice you shouldn't have done that."

Alice's replied quickly and to the point. "You've no right to tell me how to act in front of the children. Tomorrow I'll be fine and the children will forgive me, but tomorrow you'll still be a drunk." She wasn't through. "I'll stay here and tend my family when you have a job that can support this family and a job that you can keep. And do you have such a job?"

Jesse shifted his weight, picked up a fork, speared another serving of pork and dropped it on his clean plate. He cut a small piece and placed it in his mouth. After swallowing, he took a long drink of water. Alice had slowed her breathing and regained her composure.

"I'm working with Floyd and got an application with the Rock Island," Jesse said. "And don't ever call me a drunk."

His tone was calm, even meek. Alice knew she had wounded him, but sometimes a stubborn mule needs the whip. She had his attention.

"Well your day work with Floyd won't fulfill your obligation to the family, and I'll believe the Rock Island job when I see it." Then to the children, "Your father and I have things to talk about, but for now, we'll finish our supper. Kendall, I made an apple pie for dessert and you may cut your own piece when your plate is clean." Alice was firmly at the helm.

Jesse's pride and masculinity had been challenged and defeated. Alice had not wanted to wound Jesse, particularly in front of Iris Jeanne and Kendall, but this whirlpool had to stop. The next two weeks were business-like for Alice and Jesse. They moved themselves with Floyd's truck and his help. The day after they moved, all four returned to harvest the last of the fall vegetables from their garden. Their furniture and belongings fit well into the old rental house, and Alice decorated it warmly. She planned new paint for the spring. With his brother Edwin's help, Jesse found a buyer for his Chrysler, paid off the loan, and bought a much older Model A. If he needed the car, Alice agreed to walk to work. The plan and their shared work showed early promise. Alice was through with feeling sorry for herself and being blown by winds beyond her control.

The loss of the milk run and nice home was tough on Jesse too, but he took a different tact. Jesse slowed his drinking after Alice's anger had finally exploded, but his anger continued, and in time, the drinking would return with force. He refused to hold himself fully accountable. Jesse figured that times was tough and lots of people lost work. He was no different. Sure he drank, but so did lots of folks. He was no drunk. A drunk can't ever stop. And lots of men had wives didn't want 'em to be men. He was no pussy-whipped weakling. He could handle himself, his liquor, and Alice.

The job with the Rock Island came through and the joy in the Sheets home was palpable. It was a non-skilled job, but because his name was Sheets, not Martinez or Limping Dog, Jesse was made the boss of a nighttime cleaning crew with two Indians and three Mexicans. He was delighted and the regular paycheck was a great relief. They were able to paint the house and buy a few luxuries.

Oklahoma prayed that seven years of drought were all God could ask of any people to endure and looked for the spring rains to come again. But God's attention must have been elsewhere, and the rains stayed away. The summer grew hot, and the dusters came. More Okies traded their last hopes for dusty despair. Alice and Jesse were at a stasis with just enough hope to keep them going. One Saturday in 1938, a truck with a trailer stopped in front of the house. Jesse motioned for Kendall to come to the window and take a look.

"Wonder who that is so early?"

The seven year old took a look out the window and exploded out the front door.

"Morning, Kendall. Got a delivery for you," said Bill Moore, the manager of Watson's Seed and Feed Store.

"For me?" asked an excited Kendall.

"Take a look here and see if I got the right address?"

Alice and Iris Jeanne had come outside and were staring with curious amazement as Bill backed a pony out of the trailer.

"Is it really mine?" Kendall squealed.

Jesse took the lead rope from Bill. "See what you think, Son. Her name's Queen." She was twelve-year-old paint with big red splotches of color on a bright white coat. She was recently retired as a rodeo parade horse due to developing arthritis. Queen was a small mare, smaller than most Indian ponies and the perfect size for a child.

"Put me up on her, Dad," pleaded Kendall.

Jesse swung Kendall onto Queen's back and led her around the yard. While Kendall was riding Queen with unsuppressed joy, Bill unloaded an old saddle and bridle and two burlap bags of feed. "Looks like Jesse didn't tell nobody," he said.

"He likes surprises," smiled Alice.

Alice knew the family was damaged and needed healing. Jesse's response was to try and insure his son's love. A pony? What child doesn't want a pony?

In the spring of 1939, a strange and wonderful thing occurred. The rains returned. Those farmers who had planted winter wheat saw green in their fields, a lush and soft green not seen in eight years. Those farmers who had not planted for fear of no rain, raced to Watson's Seed and Feed Store with what little cash they had, sometimes coins saved in a canning jar, to buy their chance at a real harvest. Talk of war again in Europe pushed prices higher, and the palpable optimism of the twenties started to dust off its long forgotten smile.

On a hot July afternoon, Alice got a call from the manager of the Rock Island roundhouse telling her Jesse was in the hospital with injuries. She left the laundry immediately and rushed to the emergency room of the El Reno Hospital where a kindly nurse escorted her to a bed just inside the emergency entrance. Jesse was lying with his head propped up and his left side and arm extensively bandaged from above the shoulder to below the elbow. His eyes were open and a faint smile greeted Alice as she bent over and gave him a concerned embrace.

"What happened to you, Jesse?"

"Steam line broke. Got scalded pretty bad."

"How are you feeling? Are you hurting?"

"They give me a pain shot. I'm more sleepy than hurtin'. They say I can come home with you after they check me over one more time."

"That's good. The nurse can show me how to take of you."

The nurse that had first cleaned and dressed Jesse's burn came to the bedside and introduced herself to Alice. She told Alice she could take her husband home, but she must bring him back every second day to have his bandages changed. She helped Alice wheel Jesse to the car she had borrowed from Mr. Fowler. Their old Model A was still at the roundhouse.

"Nice of Mr. Fowler to loan you this ride," said Jesse as he crawled into the front seat.

Alice wasn't sure but she thought she smelled alcohol on Jesse's breath.

"Jesse do I smell alcohol? Were you drinking at work? Lord, tell me you weren't drinking."

"That's the dressing you smell. Swear I wasn't drinking. That's the honest truth." Jesse was sleepy.

She wanted to believe him, but when the Rock Island fired Jesse after only a week's absence, she figured they knew something she only suspected. Alice was frustrated that Jesse didn't protest his firing, but Jesse had taken a lesser role in his own life, and Alice saw Jesse's strength flow from him like a wound that refuses to heal.

Canadian County began to stand a little taller as the new moisture was wicked into the tallest trees, and they once again showed their towering green splendor. A few new businesses came to town, and Jesse was able to find work driving trucks. He was well known and still liked by many, so once he made himself available, he could count on a few days of work each week. Alice worked hard at the laundry, and with their combined income, they were able to do well enough to pay the rent and keep the household above water. They once again had the opportunity to reestablish themselves as a well-functioning family. The children were doing well in school. Iris Jeanne was beginning to develop her personality with a healthy bent of independence. She remained loyal and loving to her mother, but harbored resentment towards her father and would never allow herself to trust him again.

She would repeatedly ask her mother during quiet times across the kitchen table.

"What are you going to do, Mother?"

Alice would look at her at first like, "What do you mean?" then just shake her head. She still had no idea how to cure, cope, or escape.

Jesse just kept drinking and just getting angrier. He might maintain modest control while working but he began to endanger himself and others. Loud arguments, once rare, now increased in frequency and intensity and frightened both children. Iris Jeanne's question would be asked again, "What are you going to do, Mother?"

"I'm no Amelia Earhart. Can't just fly away, now can I?" Alice tried to smile.

"Last time Amelia flew away she never came back. Seriously, Mother, what can you do about Daddy?" she asked thoughtfully.

Alice looked at her daughter and realized she had been forced to grow up sooner than she should have. No child should have to see her parents like that. Alice knew that her daughter's sense of security had been broken. Alice took two cups and filled them with hot coffee.

"You should have seen your father when he was a young man. He was a fine man and so polite. I really thought love would be the bond to heal any problems." She paused. "Listen to me, going on about what's past."

"I'm not going to live in a small town ever, maybe not even in Oklahoma," said Iris Jeanne.

"Well that would be fine. Here we are with me talking about the past and you talking about the future. What do you say we both talk about the future from now on?" As Alice said these words, she recalled nighttime buggy rides with Jesse and the old cedar flat. Always the old cedar flat.

Jesse became a regular at three bars. They took their deduction and Jesse never brought a full paycheck home. One new favorite was Primo's Tavern near what the locals called Little Mexico. The prices were good there and he remained friends with two of his crew from the Rock Island, and one or two nights a week he would visit with them and down a few beers. Jesse could drink three or four beers, drive home, and still function, but when Jesse crossed the line to hard liquor he was a different man. Every day was a challenge for Alice and she exerted great emotional energy to adapt and counter whatever alcohol laced man showed up each evening. Sometimes the Jesse that showed up was a good one, and the four would enjoy the evening and maybe Kendall would ride Queen for his father to see and critique. On some weekends when Jesse was home and not drinking, the Sundays remained as a reminder of how good things had been and just maybe could still be.

Jesse's earlier command for Alice not to see her sisters had been forgotten, and the three sisters remained very close. The days Jesse spent riding and hunting sometimes gave Alice hope. Dove, duck, and quail were always a welcome addition to the table, and Jesse had given Kendall a single shot .410 shotgun. He quickly developed a good eye and was growing into a tall thin little boy with excellent athletic skills. Their neighbors, the Maines, had a little boy, Bob, a little younger than Kendall, and the Maines' dirt patch with a basketball hoop on a ten-foot pole became a good place to find Kendall after school when he wasn't tending to Queen. He didn't mind the dirt court, and along with his basketball skills, he found ways to make friends with just about all he met. He was taller than most kids his age but didn't press his physical advantage and was thought of as a fair and honest boy. He and Bob Maine became close friends and even long after Bob had grown up, Kendall saw him as his little brother.

Harry Fowler was a good employer and very generous with Alice's wages and time off when the children required it. It became apparent to Alice that his kindness and gentle touches signaled the introduction of sexual attraction. Alice did not admit it to her sisters, but she finally admitted it to herself. She liked it. She liked the way it made her feel as a desired woman and just as real, she liked the way it made her body respond. Jesse showed less interest in Alice as his drinking continued. The occasional union was brief and void of the tenderness Alice craved. Jesse saw it as something that he deserved and by God, that's what men do.

Alice stopped initiating any lovemaking and would oblige his rare advances as a duty fulfilled.

The thought of making love with Harry Fowler brought her fantasies close to reality. Could she again experience the joy of long ago, but with a different man? How would she respond, and how would she feel afterwards? These thoughts in the present mixed with the thoughts of the past, and she couldn't reconcile soft grass and the smell of green cedars with the undiscovered future, at least for now. Mr. Fowler was seven years older than Alice, not bad looking, a little shorter than Jesse but thinner. He was going bald on top and his closely shaved face revealed soft skin and shallow wrinkles that would deepen when he smiled. His jaw line was firm, and Alice thought his brown eyes were nice. He was any man. There was nothing about this man that set him apart from all the men she knew. There was no singular great attribute or talent or gift that he possessed that would make him stand out in a line. Why then, was she even thinking about these things? He had been married and his wife and son lived in Oklahoma City, she thought, and then realized she knew so little about him. She realized that what he represented appealed to Alice more than who he was. Still, she did like her blood to stir and the little flush to her face was difficult to control.

Alice was alone at the front desk on a cold day in February, when Father Edward Hoffmann, the pastor at Sacred Heart Catholic Church, walked in with an armload of black shirts and clerical collars. He introduced himself and asked prices then gave very specific cleaning and ironing instructions. Alice wrote this down and prepared his claim tab.

"Excuse me Father," she said, "but don't you have women at your church that clean and prepare your shirts and vestments and altar linens?"

"Why yes, Alice, we do, but Mrs. LaRue just passed, and I thought I would familiarize myself with your establishment."

She wondered how he knew her name. "I didn't mean to seem inappropriate, Father."

"Not at all, Alice." He walked to the door. "I'll see you in three days."

Father Edward Hoffmann was 65 but looked older. His once tall athletic frame was now bent, and his bad left hip caused him a noticeable limp that he refused to moderate with a cane. His diminished body only seemed to highlight his gentle soft-spoken demeanor and others listened to his quiet voice respectfully. He was a priest of the Benedictine order and had embraced the monastic vision of the order's founder, St. Benedict. At the nearby St. Gregory's Abbey in Shawnee, he was able to find the time and quiet to further his understanding of the mystical presence of God. He was well educated in Rome, and his priest brothers thought he would stay at the Vatican as a resident scholar. Instead he loved the quiet of the Abbey and began to further his study of the Divine Presence and delved into the writings of the Church Doctors, St. Teresa of Avila, St. John of the Cross, and medieval masterpieces of contemplation and mysticism such as *The Cloud of Unknowing*. He had recently begun to exchange lengthy letters with the Jesuit paleontologist and mystic, Pierre Teilhard de Chardin. The Abbot didn't encourage these diversions because it removed Father Hoffmann from his obligations at the Abbey. He was told to choose either the life of a contemplative monk with the religious community in the Abbey, or to leave the Abbey to serve in a parish community. The Abbot was sure Father Hoffmann would remain with the Abbey and was stunned to receive a letter from the Bishop in Oklahoma City, requesting Father Hoffmann's release from the Abbey to assume the duties of Pastor at Sacred Heart Church in El Reno. Father Hoffmann had arrived at this decision after a lifetime of prayer and of wonder and of frustration. He knew a life of study; his personal search for the mystical presence of the Divine must progress or wither. He would experience the Divine in the faces of His people.

He immersed himself into this small town of El Reno and its mix of Catholic parishioners. He was the most educated man in the county, yet no one knew. He would walk whenever time allowed, and he became a common sight downtown and at the hospital. He felt it was important to "show the collar" and was particularly concerned with recent Klan activity in Oklahoma. His parish had a significant Mexican presence and even at his church, they were sometimes scorned or ignored. He spoke out often and was given the opportunity to write an occasional article for the El Reno Daily Democrat.

Alice knew none of this at the time, but discovered much later why this kind priest had entered her life. Father Hoffmann had met Jesse at the home of two sisters, his parishioners, Carmen and Teresa. Teresa was Jesse's mistress. That was probably too kind a term since "mistress" implies some affection. Teresa was a sister of Pedro Gallegos, one of Jesse's former crew at the Rock Island. She was widowed without children and, long past forty, had given up hope for a family. She was plain and overweight and had lost her happiness years ago. She welcomed any attention a man would offer and she returned the attention for a fee. Jesse thought of her as his mistress; others called her a whore. She had stopped making Jesse pay, and he gave her just the little bit of attention she needed. Jesse could play out his role of the virile male and Teresa, the compliant concubine.

Father Hoffman returned as promised in three days.

"Good morning, Father. I have your shirts and collars all ready for you." Alice retrieved his order from the shelves behind her and placed the neatly tied bundle on the counter.

"This looks fine, Alice. What do I owe you?"

"A dollar twelve," she said flatly.

He took time finding the exact change and counted it out slowly. "Alice, you seem removed to a far off place today." He waited for an answer.

"I'm sorry, Father. Just not a good day."

"If you ever wish to talk, I'm a pretty good listener."

Alice took a slow breath then said as if to finish their conversation, "Well, you don't know my Jesse."

"I believe I met Jesse once," he said.

Alice didn't stop to ask under what circumstances her husband would have met a Catholic priest. Her words flowed.

"My husband drinks. Won't stop. Don't know what to do. I couldn't have loved him any more than I did." Alice didn't realize she had shifted to the past tense. "I've read. I've talked to my pastor. I've prayed. I've loved him and loved him some more, but he gets worse. Why is that?"

Father Hoffmann took a slow thoughtful breath before speaking. "You must feel the wound deeply, Alice, to love someone so tenderly and not to have that love returned."

Alice thought about that for a moment and knew it was true.

"Alice, we experience the Divine when we love, and when we are loved in return the great Breath of the Divine may be experienced."

"But why can't he just take the love, Father? Why can't he say, 'Yes,' to being loved? I think it could heal him."

"Dear child, you have asked a question I cannot answer. Years ago I thought I could. I thought that receiving love was so natural, a part of our humanity. What I found is that receiving love can be most difficult." He stopped and an expression of pain and uncertainty came over him. He continued with the impossible, trying to explain the unknowable. "I know this, my dear child. Without receiving this love, whether from someone like you or from God, we are unable to give it freely in return. Alice, it's a great cloud of unknowing that starts with the Divine and sweeps earthly to embrace His children and to gather them back to Him, the Ultimate Source." He felt inadequate. He felt he was failing this searching woman. "The ability, the willingness to accept love must, I suppose, be a gift. Not all receive the gift." He shook his head side from side to side then he sighed audibly.

"I can't fix him, Father. I can't fix him."

"When the husband fails to protect the family, then the mother must protect the children. That is what you must do, Alice." He closed the door and walked slowly away, his limp pronounced.

Alice watched him depart and walk down the sidewalk. "What a wise and lovely man." She smiled.

CHAPTER 27
BROKEN HEART'S RESOLVE

Jesse drank, then he didn't. He raged, then he didn't. He apologized, then he didn't. He brought a paycheck home, then he didn't. Alice struggled daily, but as each crisis quieted, a new one appeared and she began to see a life without Jesse. His weakness had made her stronger.

While this Sheets family was unhappy in their own way, there were good moments still for Alice and the children. Jesse's father, Charles, had died, so after a lifetime on the farm, Anna had moved into town. She bought a house on K Street, only a few blocks away, and her house was always open for Alice and the children. Kendall was treated like a little prince. Alice and Anna drew closer and both took comfort in the happy memories when they had shared a roof.

"Alice," Anna would say, "you've got your hands full with Jesse."

"What happened to Jesse, Anna? Alice asked one day. "Can you tell me anything that could help me?"

"That Jesse was the sweetest boy I ever knew. It's nothing you don't know, but I loved that boy somethin' special. I always thought that'd be enough. Alice, I'll make no allowance for Jesse, and I'll not side with him just because he's my son. I want you to know that."

"Thank you, Anna," said Alice. "I'll be calling on you."

On a Saturday in late February of 1941, Alice's heart was broken. Jesse had not returned by eleven that night. In earlier times, Alice would have called Jesse's friends and even the hospital, but she knew the rumors filtered from Floyd to Edwin then to Ina were most likely true. He had a girlfriend and was probably with her. The shock of a phone call confirming the affair was more than Alice could take, so she was alone and miserable thinking it all must be true. After midnight, exhausted, she fell on her bed asleep. She was awakened by the noise of the kitchen chairs being knocked over. For a moment she lay there gathering her thoughts. Would he come to bed drunk and carrying the aroma of alcohol and perfume or just sleep on the parlor sofa? She rose and put on her robe and just then noticed the first whiff of smoke. She quickened her pace and saw the orange flames before she turned on the light. Jesse had fallen into the kitchen table, dropped his cigarette, and was passed out on his stomach between the table and the window. The cotton gauze curtains were in flames and the orange fingers were almost to the curtain rod. If the ceiling and walls took the flame, the kitchen and house would be enveloped in only moments.

She shrieked, but Jesse didn't move. She ran to the window and with her arms outstretched, she pulled the two curtains down with one bold sweep. She clutched the flaming curtains in her arms, but she felt no burn. Quickly, she crossed to the door left open by Jesse, pushed through the screen door and threw the flaming curtains on the ground safely outside. She dusted herself and found her nightclothes hot and dirty, but she was not hurt. She stood silent catching her breath.

Back inside, she filled a large pan with water, doused the smoking curtains, and sprinkled water along the wall, making sure no live embers had imbedded. She poured the rest over Jesse's head, but after making a few odd noises, he settled back into unconsciousness. Alice did a powerful thing. She crossed the room to the large cupboard by the door and took all of Jesse's ammunition for his rifles and shotguns. She placed everything in the trunk of their car to take to Ina's. When these tasks were completed, she once again tried to rouse Jesse, but he was fast to the floor.

"I can't fix you Jesse," she said softly, then returned to bed leaving her husband on the floor.

Early the next morning, Iris Jeanne found her father asleep on the wet kitchen floor and saw the burned curtains and ashes outside the door. She figured it out quickly and ran to her parents' room to find her mother still asleep. She lay beside her and put an arm around her. "What are we going to do, Mother?"

Alice said nothing at first but returned her embrace. She thought of Father Hoffman's last words. "I'm going to protect you."

Later that morning, Alice heard Jesse in the bathroom cleaning up. She gathered the children for a cold cereal breakfast and exited the door for church. Kendall saw the curtain-less window and the ashes in the yard and asked his mother what happened.

"Your father fell last night."

After church, the three went to Ina and Edwin's for Sunday dinner. Alice told Ina everything and Edwin, sitting in his old Mission chair, just shook his head. "Sorry, Alice. I'll keep the ammo for you. Jesse probly won't even notice. Hasn't been huntin' in months."

Alice wasn't about to go down the "poor me" road so there was little talk, only the comforting presence of her big sister. The quiet was broken by Ina as she poured a second cup of coffee.

"Helen is taking the civil service test. The deadline to sign up in Oklahoma City is Wednesday. I think you should take it with Helen." Ina and Edwin's oldest child was only nine years younger that Alice and was the first Jennings or Sheets to graduate from college. "She says she could take a job in Oklahoma City or even in Washington D.C. She's not sure if she wants to be a schoolteacher anymore. World's changing Alice. Maybe Helen's right. Maybe you should think differently."

"Maybe I should."

The next morning, she told Jesse she needed the car and drove to the Federal Building in Oklahoma City and registered for the exam.

She returned home after noon. Jesse met her at the kitchen door and told her Mary had called, and she should go there at once. Alice, alerted by Jesse's tone, was overcome by dread and drove hurriedly to the farm. She noticed Ina's car and a few she didn't recognize. She walked slowly up the old steps crossed the porch and entered the kitchen. Ina and Doty Dickerson were seated at the table. Robert was dead. Mary had found him in the barn that morning. His heart had given way. Alice went to the bedroom to the old wood framed bed that held her father's body in a last embrace. Sitting at his side in a simple chair, was Mary. Her wailing had slowed for now, but she was still crying. Alice sat on the bed beside her father, then bent over and hugged him to her heart one last time. His Belle's great sobs of grief and tears were heard throughout the house, and Mary, once again, began to weep uncontrollably. Alice stayed with her father and Mary for a time as she recalled memories warm and true, of a man she adored and loved, of a creator and protector. Mary stood, walked to Alice, and put her arm on her shoulder.

"He was the best man I ever knew," said Mary.

Robert was buried to the right of his Ida Emmy in the Oakland Cemetery. His mother, Martha was to Ida Emma's left. There were now three Jennings sharing the cedar canopy.

After the graveside service, the mourners returned to the farm to be with Mary and the family. They were milling around in small groups, talking softly and all making their way in time to offer their sympathies and prayers to Mary.

Ina, Edna, Helen, and Alice found a place to be alone for a few minutes. Edna began. "Alice, you'll do fine with that exam. I know you will," she said strongly, bypassing any debate of whether Alice should or should not proceed.

"Thank you, Edna. Helen and I will do just fine," she said, indicating she would indeed take this leap.

"What are you going to tell Jesse?" asked Ina.

"Not sure. Not sure yet."

Three weeks later, she told Jesse that she was taking a test in Oklahoma City for a government job. If he took that to mean the state government, then that was just fine with her. On the first page of the exam, below the lines for personal information, address and such was a small box. "Do you wish to have your examination scores sent to the Government Service Employment Agency in Washington D.C. in consideration for employment?" Alice checked the box. Alice received notice of her scores ten days later and spent the next few weeks in anticipation of a letter from Washington.

The waiting calm was disrupted by a new crisis. Robert's will was simple. His property and all belongings were to be given one half to Mary and one half divided equally among the eight children, and Mary was to live on the farm as long as she wished. Robert owned three rental houses in El Reno and with the farm being held by Mary for the foreseeable future, there was pressure from some of the children and Newt's wife, Bertha, to sell the three houses in town. With only Alice's modest income, she could not pay higher rent to a new owner and support the children by herself. Even with a small inheritance from the sale of the houses, the money wouldn't last long. The letter from Washington came.

She was offered an entry-level GS position at the Bureau of Engraving and Printing. She had two weeks to respond and to report July first for work. The salary was only eighty dollars a month. Her determination and drive had brought her to this moment. She realized, holding the envelope, she had made the decision to leave. Now she had to tell her husband.

Jesse had not had a drink since the kitchen fire. Superficially, Alice knew that was good, but she also knew Jesse well, and she recognized his sullenness and anger as a compression of his alcoholism, and in a day or week or month it would all blow again. The pattern had been set. She was determined to proceed.

After sharing her decision with Ina and Edna and swearing them to silence, she knew that she must talk with Anna. The next afternoon, she stopped at Anna's home after leaving the laundry. Anna welcomed her with a hug and an offer of coffee as they sat across from each other at the kitchen table.

"Jesse told me about the fire, Alice. Seems regretful."

"I'm sure he is, but I don't know what the future holds for Jesse. He can't stop."

"He says he hasn't touched a drop since the fire, Alice," Anna said.

"He will and we know it to be true, Anna." Anna nodded silently and Alice continued. "Anna, I've made some decisions and I have to bring you abreast. I took a civil service exam and I'm taking the children and moving to Washington D.C. in two months. I won't be able to pay the rent to the new owner. Well, maybe I could for a while, but Daddy's money is only going to last so long. Where will I be? Anyway, Anna, I can't trust Jesse. Can't trust him to not drink, to not protect our children. I can't trust him to lead me out of this constant misery."

"Misery?" asked Anna.

"I don't know what else to call it. As long as I had hope, I could maybe see a new better day coming. But once that hope is gone, it's misery that's left. I don't know who I'm waking up with each morning or who I go to bed with. Don't know if his anger's gonna spill over and explode. I worry about our safety." She slowed her speech and composed herself. She began again calmly. "You know what I'm saying, Anna. I'm not doing it anymore. I've got to stop the slide and if Jesse can't stop, well then I'm not going with him. There I've said it." She straightened her back and looked squarely into Anna's eyes for a reply.

"Figured you were headed there. I love my son but I'm not blind. You got to do what's right." Anna offered no defense of her son and in these few words, told Alice she would support her in these difficult times.

"Anna, would you do me a great kindness?"

"Of course, Dear."

"Will you be with me when I tell Jesse I'm leaving?"

Anna knew the Sheets men well and knew that blood relation doesn't mean blind acquiescence. "If it helps you, Alice, you can count on me being there and supporting you and the children."

That Sunday, Alice and the children picked up Anna for church then all returned to Alice's where she and Anna and Iris Jeanne prepared the Sunday dinner. While they were in the kitchen, Jesse and Kendall were outside with Queen. Kendall was riding up and down the street, staying close for the dinner call. They were brushing Queen when they were called inside. The dinner was kept lively by the chatter of Iris Jeanne and Kendall. Alice was noticeably nervous but Jesse didn't notice. Dessert was chocolate cake. Jesse wiped his face and looked ready to leave the table. Alice spoke quickly once she reached for a little more courage.

"Iris Jeanne, just leave the dishes on the counter. Take Kendall outside. We adults have to talk." In a short minute, the three were alone in the kitchen.

Jesse looked curiously at Alice, then at his mother. He seemed genuinely perplexed. "So what do you want to talk about?" There was an edge to his tone.

"You know I took that government exam. Well I passed it, and I've been offered a job."

"That's good news, Alice. I got an interview at Tinker Field in Oklahoma City next week. Could be a good thing. We'll see about getting another car. We can figure it all out after we get a few pay checks."

"Stop, Jesse," she interrupted, "there's more. It isn't a state job. It's a federal job, and it's in Washington D.C."

Jesse's attention was finally focused on the shocking statement, but he didn't fully understand all its repercussions. "Washington D.C.?"

"I'm leaving and I'm taking the children," Alice said matter-of-factly, finally stating the inevitable. She felt a sudden unexpected release. The course was set and she knew it was irreversible. She repeated it as Jesse sat stunned and silent. "We're leaving in June."

Alice had prepared for this moment but Jesse was caught completely by surprise. "No, you ain't!" Jesse roared as he stood up angrily, knocking the kitchen chair over.

"You pick up that chair and sit down, young man," Anna said sternly. Jesse looked at his mother, righted the chair and sat down. "Jesse, if you love your children you must see to their safety. A drunk can't do that." Her words cut deeply. She had never called her son a drunk and that one word hung in Jesse's mind.

"I ain't no drunk, and I love Arse Jeanne and Kendall. Alice, I know I've not been the best husband to you these past few years." His tone was contrite at first. "Times've been tough here. Lots of men take the drink. But no woman would take her children and go clear to Washington D.C. You can't do that. I'll work harder. Try to make up for the bad times I've given you. Things'll get better. You got to give me more time to show you."

For one brief moment, Alice weakened, then her final resolve returned.

"We'll be leaving in June, toward the end of June. I can't afford the rent, and you haven't brought a regular paycheck in Lord knows how long."

"You ain't taking my kids."

"They're our kids and I'm taking them with me, like it or not." Alice felt stronger with every word she spoke. Any grey of indecision was forever past.

Everyone was quiet for a moment. Jesse's initial anger had faded. He was broken.

"Well how much money you'd be making?" Jesse asked.

"I start at eighty a month."

"You can't pay for rent and take care of two kids, one in high school, on eighty a month."

"I can if you send money."

"Well I can't. Besides, Kendall won't want to come."

The truth of these two statements was unassailable. She could not afford to be alone with two children in an expensive and strange city. She held back the tears and maintained her resolve.

Anna broke the silence. "Alice, Jesse will have to move in with me when you leave. If you decide, and I'm telling you it's yours to decide, but if you find you can't afford it all, well then you know I'd take care of Kendall."

Alice let these thoughts find a place in her mind. She really hadn't figured a budget and the needs of a family of three in a big city. She felt sure she would work it out. She just needed to think. "I'm going out," she announced and firmly pushed the screen door open and went to the garden and stared at the hollyhocks beginning to shoot their bud laden stalks high. Jesse left with his mother a few minutes later and drove her home.

The following days shared by Alice and Jesse were surprisingly polite. They spoke very little and didn't talk of the separation for another week. Alice brought Iris Jeanne into her confidence and predicted emotions raced through this budding young woman. Relief and then fear of the unknown came first and then she settled on the excitement of a great adventure. She and her mother would meet the big city.

The Carnegie Library had Sunday papers from around the country so Alice made regular visits to read the classified ads in the Washington Post for apartments to rent. She also found maps of the city and the bus routes. She was shocked at the cost of apartments and shifted her focus to simple rooms to rent and sent multiple correspondences to potential landlords. She secured a large room in a house on Biltmore Street with a full bathroom off the hall. She would have use of the kitchen and parlor. It was near a bus route to the Bureau of Engraving and Printing but it was not large enough for two children. It was all she could afford. The tightening in her chest and the sleepless nights would not subside, as she faced the possibility that she might not be able to bring Kendall.

She sought the advice of Ina and Edna. They looked at the simple math and saw the dilemma. Alice pleaded for an answer but the sisters knew the time of giving comfort was past. Alice needed to face the hard edges of her decision and to back it up with the law.

Sidney Baker II was the son of the attorney who had helped Robert and Ida Emma obtain the deed for their quarter section back in 1889. He was a prosperous and respected attorney. He was proud of his mixed Cherokee heritage and his law office displayed the art of his ancestors. He had been the best athlete in El Reno as a young man and had seen Kendall play basketball a few times. He was aware of the problem in the Sheets family even though his social circle did not overlap with the Sheets. His advice was straightforward and devastating. Alice could file for divorce, but if Jesse contested, the delay and cost would prove a great barrier and unless there was an agreement, there would be no promise of resolution. For Jesse to agree, she knew the price.

Alice loved Anna as her third mother. It was only Anna who could provide the comfort Alice needed at this difficult time. Anna was not the typical mother defending a wayward son as innocent or misunderstood or with stupid platitudes like, "He's really such a good boy." She instead spoke honestly of Jesse's problems and his failure to correct them. She acknowledged Alice's decision as reasonable and told her she would have done the same if Charles had been so inclined. It was not her obligation to coddle her son, but it was her gift to still love him.

"A mother will always love her son, Alice. If I can love Jesse in all his ways then, for now, that's all I can do. And no matter what comes, a son will always love his mother. It's the natural thing, Alice." This wise woman looked deeply into Alice's eyes. "And Kendall will not hold this against you. You must know that. If you don't, then you'll not be able to give a good life to Iris Jeanne. Sometimes you're faced with a decision that isn't perfect, but you can't let that stop you from making a good one. He's only ten, but Kendall is known by half of this town. Anything happens, any strayin' goes on, I'll know that same day. You get settled in, then when you can afford a bigger place, let Kendall decide. He'll be man enough to think it out."

Alice had to have her heart and her mind come together. She heard Anna's words as true, and knew perfect was not to be.

CHAPTER 28
HALFTONES

The job at Tinker Field came through for the first of June. Jesse moved into his mother's home and used her car to commute to Oklahoma City. He hadn't had a drink, but he was a broken and meek man. His posture and tone allowed his inner defeat to show through. He was at a point where the hole kept getting larger, and Jesse didn't know how it would be filled. He begged off meeting with friends and limited his social contacts to Floyd and George. Ina, Edwin, and Helen, and Edna and Hill became non-persons, and he shunned them like a cottonmouth moccasin. He constructed a web of blame that did not place him at its core. He could control his drinking, but not his wife and those two sisters and Helen. They were the reason he'd lost Alice. Hell, his kids were doing great, and Kendall was always there to give his father that dimpled smile. He'd show Alice and Iris Jeanne, and Helen and those damned sisters. He'd begin with a good job at Tinker Field, and he didn't need no civil service exam for that.

Alice tried to keep those weeks of late spring structured for Iris Jeanne and Kendall. The rains had come again, and Canadian County was bursting with more green than Alice could remember. She packed their personal items and kitchen fare in boxes to be shipped later, if she could afford it. She moved Kendall's nice bedroom set over to his new room at his grandmother's.

The evening before she and Iris Jeanne were to depart for Washington, she and the children had supper with Ina and Edwin. Ina said she would pick them up tomorrow at seven, and she and Edna would drive them to the station in Oklahoma City, then take Kendall to his grandmother's. Alice and the children said their good-byes and thanked them for the meal. They drove home. Near sunset, Jesse knocked on the kitchen door. He spoke quietly with Iris Jeanne for a few minutes, and then gave her a long silent hug. They parted, and Jesse and Alice stood facing each other through the open kitchen door.

"I'll try to send some money," Jesse began.

"I'm not expecting things, but Iris Jeanne will be a junior in a new school. I'm sure she'd appreciate a few things, maybe a new dress and a pair of shoes. She says she's going to take a job after school if she can find one."

"You'll take care of her now, I know."

"That's not in question is it, Jesse? What about our son?"

"Aw, you don't have to worry 'bout Kendall. Me and everybody loves him."

"Love isn't enough sometimes," Alice interrupted. She wasn't going to let this last meeting dissolve into platitudes. She needed hard assurances. "Most of this town knows you and your family and me and my family. That plus the teachers and coaches at school and your mother and the church. Well, there're a lot of people who know what's going on and," she paused. "Kendall better be safe. And in time, if Kendall chooses to move north, you just have to let him."

Jesse didn't answer, but after a moment he raised his eyes to hers. "Sure you don't want me to take you to the station tomorrow?"

"Ina and Edna are taking us. They'll bring Kendall to your mother's house afterwards."

Jesse and Alice stood apart, not touching, and their eyes had dropped their connection. Alice felt the anger of a dozen years drain from her limp body, leaving only the hurt. She once again found his blue eyes. "Jesse Sheets, I gave you everything I knew to give. I gave it to you. My love and the children and my faithfulness and my trust, then again my belief that we could make things good again. You had it given to you and you couldn't take it. I know now that not every man's got that part that lets him take that gift, and I know now it's not something I could have changed. It's not forgiveness that I can offer right now, time come I will, but for the now, I can offer you my understanding. After seventeen years, I think I understand the darkness you can't escape."

Jesse said nothing but would ponder those words the rest of his life. He turned and walked down the steps into the halftones of light and broken shadows he had created.

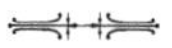

The next morning, Alice prepared a simple breakfast, emptying her kitchen of its last food. Iris Jeanne was talkative, and her energy helped lift the three. She and her mother sipped coffee as Kendall waited patiently. Alice asked Iris Jeanne to clean the dishes and she took Kendall for his bath. She spoke softly as she scrubbed his hair and ears then cleaned his fingers and toes. Kendall enjoyed the attention and tried to comfort his mother.

"I'll be fine, Mom."

"Promise you'll write every Sunday and obey your grandmother?" she asked.

"I've told you a hundred times, Mom. I promise."

"I'll write you too, Sweetheart, and I'll call you when I can."

Alice wrapped her son in a clean towel and rubbed him dry. She then took a lotion that had a faint scent of lavender and rubbed his chest and back then his arms and legs. He didn't mind the hint of flowers. She bent down and kissed each toe then put his hands together at their palms and kissed each finger so sweetly. She handed him his best Sunday trousers and his leather shoes she had polished the night before. She removed a shirt from the counter, folded and wrapped in tissue paper. She carefully unwrapped the new shirt and removed the pins that were holding the crisp folds together. It was a white shirt of finest Egyptian cotton from Youngheim's Department Store. It was bleached white and so fine you could almost see through it. She buttoned the collarless shirt full to the neck then fastened the two buttons at the cuffs of the long sleeves. It was a fine shirt.

"This is for you, Kendall. I'm hoping you remember me kindly when you wear this at special times."

"I promise." They held each other.

Alice heard Ina's car crunching the gravel outside the kitchen, and soon the four suitcases were in the trunk, and Alice and her children were in the back seat. The drive to the train station in Oklahoma City was given to small talk. It had all been said. Alice thanked her sisters. Ina had shared her strength and Edna had shared her shoulder. The three knew each other's thoughts so simple good-byes and God bless were said.

Iris Jeanne and Kendall hugged each other. Iris Jeanne's tears were met with an "Aw, Sis," from Kendall and his dimpled smile. She bounded onto the train.

Alice bent down to Kendall's level and faced him straight. All she could say was, "I love you, Son."

"I love you too, Mom." His smile was gone and tears lined his cheeks.

The train ride to Washington was exciting for Iris Jeanne. She spent most of the daylight looking out the windows at the new world unfolding, and her youth and exuberance gave her mother the lift to her spirit that she desperately needed.

The train slowed as it approached Union Station in Washington D.C. The large buildings and broad avenues dwarfed anything they had ever seen in Oklahoma. It was dusk. The streetlights were beginning to brighten, and the lights of the cars stopped at the crossings gave the train a path illuminated and clear. The station was overwhelming to Alice, and for a moment, she started to lose her composure.

The porter's words brought her back. "Shall I take your luggage to the bus stop or to the taxi stand, Ma'am?"

She spoke clearly, "To the bus stop. Thank you. I believe the number seventeen departs from there in twenty minutes." She took Iris Jeanne's hand, and together they walked outside to the lights and sounds of their new country.

CHAPTER 29
TO HEAR IT ALL AGAIN

The coolness was taking over, and I slipped my hands into my pockets for a little warmth. Jesse had stopped talking, and I wasn't sure if I should remain silent or prompt him to continue. Jesse was still sitting on the old concrete steps of the Jennings' home. After a long pause, he slowly rolled onto his right elbow and shifted his hips to the same side, pulled his left leg over and stood upright facing the opposite direction. He wanted no help, and with a few short steps, turned back towards me. His gaze was across the river where the lights of El Reno tried to delay the coming darkness. The sky was a deep amethyst. The scattered tufts of cumulus caught the last rays from the west, burst momentarily into brilliant swaths of color, then were gone, leaving grey in their place.

"You feel all right, Granddad?" I asked.

"Yeah. Just tired."

"You hungry? Where can I take you for supper?"

"I'm not hungry. Could have one of those beers you bought me."

I wasn't happy to hear that and wanted to keep Jesse talking. "Can I ask you a question, Granddad?"

"Go ahead."

"Did you try to stop drinking so maybe Grandmother would come back?" It was a tough question.

Jesse looked deeply into my eyes and spoke words that had never left him. "Losing Alice was the saddest thing ever happened." He began to speak more fluidly. "I knew soon enough that was never gonna happen, but she sent me a silk tie for Valentine's the next year. I tell you, Cavin, she carried that heavy. That leavin' Kendall. Still carries it today. But by God, I did good by Kendall. D'you know he lived with her in Washington for his eighth grade, but came back here?"

"I never knew that, Granddad. Tell me about it."

"He just had to come back here. He and the Maine boy wanted to play basketball and he just, well he belonged here. I guess Alice understood. Our kids did good, Cavin. Your mother stayed in Washington and married your daddy during the war when he was a Navy pilot. She did fine, and look at you and your sisters and brother. You all went to college and made somethin'. You know Kendall done fine, too. The El Reno Indians won state and then he played for Coach Iba at Stillwater. D'you know the Aggies went to Milwaukee and almost won the national title? They was good. Floyd and me'd drive to Stillwater and watch Kendall play. The pro team in Syracuse offered him a contract, but Caterpillar offered a real job and a chance to play on their amateur team. Hell, they won the world championship in Brazil. Coach Iba said he was the best kid he ever coached."

"You and El Reno must have been plenty proud, Granddad."

"I liked watchin' him play. If you'd growed up here, I'd watched you too."

"I never got off the bench, Granddad. I'd rather hunt with you. Say, where was the bottomland we hunted quail years ago with your dog, ol' Sport?'

Jesse pointed downstream to the east. "Two miles thataway."

"Where'd you work after Tinker Field?"

"Well, I told you 'bout drivin' those German POWs out to farms that'd hire 'em. Then after the war I ran the Kerfoot Hotel. Torn down now. Cared for Floyd when he took cancer. He died there."

"Is that where you met Buena?"

"She ran the Ritz Café alongside the hotel. Took a shine to me. Didn't marry her till Alice married her boss, the widower Oberndoerfer. Ended up marryin' and divorcing' Buena twice. I made two women rich." Jesse laughed with that last comment.

"You sure that's how it was?"

"Guess they'd say not. Ain't gonna argue it."

"Buena's son was a cop here in El Reno, wasn't he?"

"Yeah," Jesse nodded and kept talking. "Did you know Aubra arrested me once? Got into a fight at the Kerfoot and the sonofabitch put the cuffs on me. Floyd bailed me out."

"Really?"

"Might've had a drink or two. Cavin, I wasn't no drunk. Just enjoyed the time."

I wondered if that was one of the binges that would bring my mother from Dallas or Kendall from Peoria. Jesse outwardly resented their care and claimed he didn't need no mothering. Doc Johnson, a fellow alcoholic, would give him a few vitamin shots and after a night in the hospital, send him home to dry up. It was more of a two-step program.

I took my grandfather's arm and walked him to the car. Jesse was breathing with shallow movements then a big catch up breath would bring him back. His eyes were closed. "Need to go home. Take me there first," he said.

The old Chrysler's four barrel roared to life and I pulled back on the dirt road then west onto Hefner Road, the old section line. At the highway we turned south. I kept well below the speed limit. I crossed the bridge and looked into the channel to see the North Canadian again. To my right, the old trestle bridge was over the spot where the ferry had brought the men and women for the Run of '89. Once in town, I found grandfather's little house. Jesse had fallen asleep.

"Come on, Granddad. Let's go in and wash up for supper."

Jesse slowly climbed the steps and entered the kitchen heading straight to the refrigerator. He pulled out the four beers. I sat on the sofa and watched helplessly as Jesse finished two beers and opened the third. There was enough Hiram Walker left to put any man down.

"Let's go eat, Granddad."

"I ain't hungry. You go on ahead."

"How are you going to drive me to the airport tomorrow?" I asked. The answer was clear. "Guess I need to find another way, huh, Granddad?"

"You go on and eat. I got some cheese here in the icebox."

Jesse was finishing the fourth beer when the low rumble of the Buick made its way to the back of the house. Jim Bob had returned unexpectedly. I opened the screen door and shook his hand.

"What on earth are you doing here, and how did you find this place again?"

"Wasn't I supposed to bring you back?" asked Jim.

"Hello there," said Jesse, forgetting Jim's name, but still glad to welcome a visitor.

"Hi, Mr. Sheets. How're doing and so forth like that?"

"You boys fix yourself a drink there," commanded Jesse, as he turned to find the bathroom.

"He's pretty drunk, huh?" asked Jim.

"He'll be fall down drunk soon. Can't stop him. Do you think I could spend tonight with you and get a ride to the airport tomorrow? I'll buy you dinner in the city."

"Sure thing, Kevin. It'll be fun."

I gathered my few things and carefully folded my great-grandmother's yellow quilt. Jim took the suitcase outside and waited by the car.

"Granddad, Jim's taking me to Oklahoma City tonight. You won't have to drive me."

"It's best," Jesse said as he walked past me towards the kitchen. He took the old yellow cheese out of the refrigerator and cut a thick slice then took a dirty glass out of the sink and poured three fingers of whiskey. "Sure glad you came, Cavin. Maybe next time we'll go huntin' some quail." I nodded. "I said a lot of things today. All of it true. You ask your grandma. It's all the truth. Not forever did I say all that before. I got six grandkids, but you're the one who comes. Don't know why I tell you all this. Don't nobody care now but maybe--"

"I care, Granddad."

Jesse finished his thought, "Maybe I just wanted to hear it again. Just me and Alice left of those people. Just me and Alice, and I just wanted to hear it all again." Jesse placed his hands on my shoulders and squeezed them tightly. "Cavin, you and your Linda, you take care of them two boys."

CHAPTER 30

EPILOGUE

Jesse died the following spring. Linda and I and our two boys, Matthew and Luke, made the long drive the day before the funeral. My mother Iris Jeanne, my little sister Kimberly, and Alice had driven up from McKinney two days earlier to complete the arrangements. Grandmother Alice's beloved husband George had died after ten happy years of marriage, and Alice had moved to Dallas to be near her daughter Iris Jeanne, and our family. Kendall and his second wife Sue had flown down from Peoria to help his sister. Iris Jeanne and Alice arranged for the service at the Wilson Funeral Home and found a local minister to say a few words. He didn't know Jesse, but neither did any other minister in El Reno.

The oak planked floors of the old funeral home creaked with every step. Scattered among the pews were Jesse's friends from the Elk's Club, the club he never joined, fellow retirees from his Canadian County truck driving days, and a number of old El Reno men and women. Buena and her son Aubra sat alone. The organist played a few old standards. The minister's words were simple and predictable, and I remembered none of it. Matthew and Luke squirmed but were mostly silent.

We trailed the hearse and the few cars across the river then east to the Oakland Cemetery. Jesse's grave was next to his mother and father. I watched my grandmother's face as the last words were said. Her eyes were heavy with sadness but no tears ran down her cheeks. Alice led us all to the crest of the old cemetery near her mother's and father's graves and pointed to the space next to her father.

"That will by my rest there," she said with a little smile. The three cedars behind the site were a cooling green, and high in these trees, two magpies began a raucous chatter.

We had our boys give their grandmother and great-grandmother good-bye hugs. I wanted to get as far as Amarillo that night. We waved one last time and climbed into the car. Kendall and Sue and Iris Jeanne and Kimberly remained under the cedars with Alice.

Back on Hefner Road, I turned down the lane and opened the gate of the old homestead. I drove onto the pasture and parked beneath the large hackberry tree. We walked across the pasture, and I found the site of the house. The old windmill tower and the steps to the porch remained.

I wanted Matthew and Luke to remember this place. The sun was high overhead and the sapphire blue sky was crystalline. The new green of the trees and the Bermuda grass was brilliant and clean and bursting with new growth. The boys couldn't be stilled and ran down the hill to where the barn had stood. I held Linda's hand then pulled her closer with my arm around her waist. And here, where heaven and earth touched, we watched our sons dance, floating on grass.

READING GROUP GUIDE

1. Jesse rarely left Canadian County, yet the outside world visited him in Kurt and the three visitors. He also heard Newt's story of a forbidden romance and he experienced the Jennings' homestead. Did Jesse have a mature worldview?
2. Kurt is a fascinating character, an obvious homage to Joseph Conrad's *Heart of Darkness*. Discuss Kurt's youthful idealistic vision of the American Indian and his journey to a mature reality.
3. Edna's play, the *Captive Maiden*, foretold Jesse's future. At what age could Jesse or any child write their own lines and set their future?
4. Jesse and Robert each celebrated a ritualistic meal with older wiser men. Discuss the symbolism of these two meals and its lasting effect on Jesse and Robert.
5. The Trail of Tears, the Oklahoma Land Runs, and even the migration of the Comanche onto the plains displacing existing tribes, suggest that ownership of the land is not absolute. Discuss.
6. The Jennings' and the Myers' Oklahoma homesteads can be viewed as an attempt to return to the Garden. Discuss Mankind's search for such a place, remembering that Dee-Day and his people were expelled from their Garden.

7. Jesse and Robert can be seen as archetypal characters in Grail mythology, specifically the myth of the *Fisher King*. Discuss their very different journeys in search of the Holy Grail and its great question, "Who does the Grail serve?"
8. Why did Kurt say that the land had been treated like a whore? Was this a dying rant or an expression of his wisdom?
9. Robert's decision to lease five acres to Fredrick James placed both families at risk from the Klan. Why did he make such a decision?
10. Alice becomes the prevalent protagonist in the final chapters. Her decision to leave her son in El Reno haunted her for the rest of her life. What alternatives were available for Alice?
11. Father Hoffmann's last words to Alice were an admonition to protect her children. Did she?
12. In Grail mythology, Perceval is male but can be viewed today as male or female. Discuss Alice's Grail Quest.
13. Was Jesse a failure?

ACKNOWLEDGMENTS

I am indebted to many for their assistance and support. *El Reno,* though a work of fiction, is laced with the recollections, writings, and interviews of Newton and Carrie Myers, Ida Emma Myers Jennings, Sara Anna Stafford Sheets, Edna Jennings Elliott, Alice Jennings Sheets Oberndoerfer, Jesse Sheets, Iris Jeanne Sheets Evans, William Elliott, Carl Estep, Helen Sheets Hawkins, and Kendall J. Sheets. The many hours my wife and I spent with Kendall and his wife Sue, remain a loving memory.

My thanks to the good people of the Canadian County Historical Museum in El Reno, and to the long ago Indian-Pioneer History Project for Oklahoma by the Work Progress Administration in 1937.

My deepest gratitude to our monk friend, Father Edward Hoffmann of the Cistercian Monastery outside Snowmass Colorado, for allowing his name to be given to an earlier priest, his kind words of encouragement and his tweeking of my toe dipping foray into mystical theology.

I give my love and admiration to ours sons: Matthew, the best writer in the family, and Luke, the brilliant geneticist who gave many valuable hours as my IT man.

My wife, Linda, must receive more than my thanks. Beginning many years ago, she became my guide and companion on our discovery of the Collective Unconsciousness, the contemplative way of Father Thomas Merton and Father Thomas Keating, and of the Golden Threads of the Divine within us all. Her intellect, beauty, and love remain my inspiration.

To the patient reader, I offer my own faults, omissions, and clumsiness as a writer for any failure to sense the historical significance of those times, or of the profound depth of love found and lost, paradise. It is my hope that the reader will have an emotional and a cognitive response to the multiple themes I have explored. Accountability rests solely with me.

77653325R00163

Made in the USA
Columbia, SC
02 October 2017